EVOS

EVOs are a diverse group of humans, flora, and fauna that possess unique and extraordinary abilities from birth. These abilities, often referred to as 'gifted traits,' can range from mind control to superhuman strength, the ability to manipulate elements, accelerated healing, telekinesis, to plant regeneration and animal metamorphosis. The origin of these abilities is a closely guarded mystery, often linked to environmental anomalies, genetic mutations, or ancient mystical sources. EVOs exist in every corner of the world, blending in with regular beings or living in secluded communities where they are free to harness and develop their powers. The existence of EVOs gifts humanity with hopes of evolution beyond its natural limitations, while also posing threats due to the unpredictable and sometimes dangerous nature of some abilities.

Altered Human

Altered Humans are individuals who have undergone experimental procedures or taken experimental serums, leading to significant changes in their physiological or cognitive capabilities. This might include heightened senses, superhuman strength, accelerated healing, or other extraordinary abilities. Some might also have cybernetic enhancements, integrating advanced technology into their bodies to augment their natural abilities. These alterations often come with unforeseen consequences, prompting questions about the nature of humanity and the ethical implications of such modifications.

code name= Stalker
Real Name= Charles Colten
Base Of Operation =New York City
Age= 70

powers
_____

Enhanced Strength
Healing Factor
Enhanced Senses
Photographic Reflexes/ Memory / learning
Physic Screen
berserker rage

Danger sense

Equipment
Kevlar body suit with polymer plate armor over top of it
Katana
Varity of firearms
Assorted Grenades
Assorted Bladed weapons

Origin Story
Charles Colten, dubbed 'Stalker,' is a formidable figure born from secrecy and desperation. Once a soldier serving in Vietnam, he struggled with PTSD before being confined within a mental institution. His life took an extraordinary turn when he was subjected to Project Spartan, a clandestine military endeavor aimed at engineering the ultimate super soldier. The procedure not only rejuvenated his body from a weathered 65-year-old veteran to a robust 25-year-old with immense physical prowess, but it also amplified his natural abilities to superhuman levels. He gained enhanced strength, agility, extraordinary senses, regeneration capabilities, and the ability to mimic physical actions perfectly - photographic reflexes. However, the cost of this power surge was high, stripping Charles of his memories. After causing a catastrophic explosion while fleeing the laboratory housed on an off-shore oil platform, he found solace and purpose among the homeless community of New York City. As their silent guardian, he patrols the night cloaked in a protective ensemble: a Kevlar body suit layered with ballistic polymer plates, topped with a nondescript trench coat. Concealing his identity, he dons a polymer face mask beneath a broad-brimmed hat. Charles's combat repertoire includes a customized utility belt packed with grenades, flashbangs, and

an array of weapons. His tactical gear is completed with a katana fastened on his back, dual sidearms, and an array of throwing blades, with his weapon of choice being a riot 12-gauge shotgun. Mysterious and formidable, Charles 'Stalker' Colten has become not just a protector for the forgotten, but an urban legend whispered about in the dark corners of the city.

Known Allies

Global Defense Administration
Dark Knight
Weasel
Father Alex
Detective Rogers

Known Enemies

Jimmy O'Rourke and the Irish mob
Blade
Reiver
The Outlaw
Kill Spawn
New York Police Department

Skills =
Hand to Hand combat
Firearms
Marksmanship
guerilla warfare

Code Name= Night Ranger
Real Name = Hunter Averys
Base of Operation = L. A. California
Age = 23
Powers = None

Equipment

Exo- Power armor =Enhanced strength
Kevlar body armor with polymer plate armor over top of it
Ekrama sticks= Electro stun Effect
Collapsible Compound Bow
Assorted trick arrows=Stun, Explosive, Gas, Sonic, Cable.
Gravity discs
Anti- gravity boots
Stealth camouflage
Motorcycle= Auto pilot, Stealth camo. Turbo boost for fast get a ways
Kinetic energy Absorbing technology

Origin Story

Hunter is the son of a wealth billionaire inventor by the name of William Averys. his father was the head of Averys International. a multinational tech company. When his parents died from a mysterious disease. Hunter began his own investigation into their deaths. after uncovering evidence that an EVO calling himself Plague was responsible for his parents' death. he found his father's secret lab on the mansion's property. there he found several inventions his father had been working on. there along with his best friend Skyler Slater the two of them built the Night Ranger battle armor from his father's inventions. During his investigations he met Agent Naomi Sato. An agent of the Global Defense Administration. Together with the resources of the G.D.A. he tracked down Plague and got his revenge. but during his crusade to find Plague he discovered a shady and brutal under belly of L.A. and once he had his revenge on Plague he began to serve as a protector of L.A TAKING ON THE GANGS AND ORGANISED CRIME.

Known Allies

Naomi Sato
Skylar Slater
Global Defense Administration
Dark Knight

Known Enemies

Plague
The Irish Man
Train Wreck
Crossbolt
L.A.P.D.

Known skills

Karata
Chemistry/ Electronics
Hand to hand combat, Archery
Throwing,   Kung fu
Hand to hand combat

Throwing   Marksmanship
Bladed Weapons/Ninjutsu / Blunt Weapons
Bladed Weapons/Ninjitsu / Blunt Weapons

Real Name = Naomi Sato
Code Name = Lotis
Age = 28
Base of operations = L.A. California

Powers

None

Equipment

Lotis Armor
* Body Armor
* Enhanced Strength
* Electo Field
* High Tech Visual and Audio Sensors
* Filtration System
Utility Belt
* Smoke Bombs
* Throwing Blades
* Sonic Discs
Two Katanas
Two Kamas

Origin Story

Naomi Sato Avery, known by her codename Lotis, is a vigilant protector of Los Angeles alongside her husband, Hunter AKA Night Ranger. After their marriage, Naomi joined Hunter in his mission to safeguard the city. Coming from a lineage of skilled martial artists, she has mastered an ancient Japanese martial art passed down through her family for nearly 10 centuries. This formidable legacy makes her a force to be reckoned with on the streets. Naomi's combat outfit is a marvel of modern engineering and traditional craftsmanship. She wears a full Kevlar bodysuit enhanced with futuristic polymer plate armor for maximum protection. Her helmet, also made from the same advanced polymer, resembles a futuristic ninja uniform, offering both anonymity and a terrifying presence. Lotis is armed with an array of weapons including two Kempo sticks, a razor-sharp katana sword, and a highly specialized utility belt loaded with high-tech gadgets designed by Skylar and Hunter. Whether by sword, sticks, or her advanced gear, Lotis utilizes her skills and technology to bring justice to the streets of Los Angeles.

Known Allies

Night Ranger
Global Defense Administration
Skylar Slater

Known Enemies

Plague
The Irish Man
Train Wreck
Crossbolt

L.A.P.D.

Known Skills

Ninjitsu   Throwing
Swordsmanship   Kung fu
Acrobatics   Advanced W
Par core
Law Enforcment

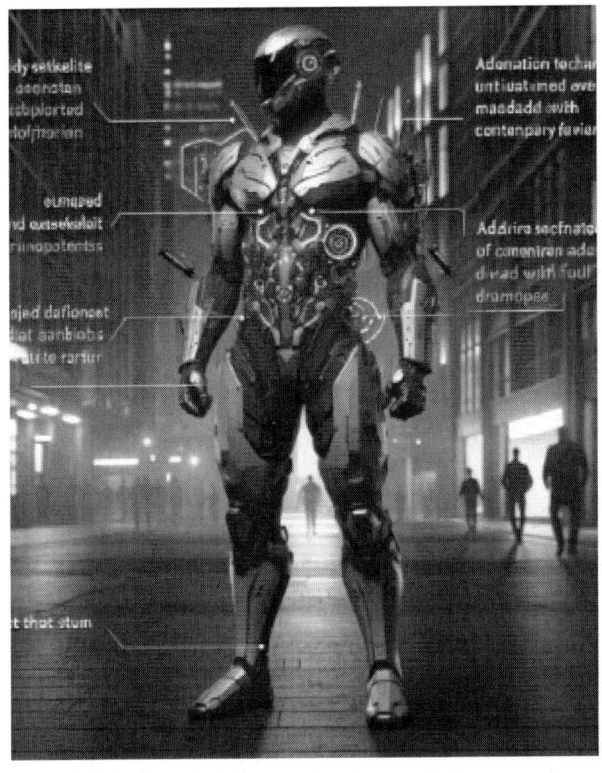

Code Name = Dark Knight
Real Name = Hunter White
Base of Operations = L.A. California
Age= 30
Powers =None

Equipment

Battle Armor = Flight, Stun darts, Blasters, Force Field. High tech visual and audio sensors. Enhanced Strength. Cloaking Device.
Detachable Drone= Camra's Microphones, Stun Darts, Flight, Cloaking device.
Battle Staff= Retractable blades, stun charge,

Origin Story

Within the turbulent world of technological marvels and archaic brutality lies Hunter White—the Dark Knight of the modern era. Vigilantism courses through his veins as a former acclaimed pugilist whose fists once spoke the language of sheer force in the shadowy domains of the criminal underworld. Retiring as a fighter, he metamorphosed into a hitman, a profession he pursued with alarming detachment and chilling efficiency, all while fueled by an unquenchable thirst for retribution. The tragic demise of his parents at the hands of organized crime was the ignominious birthplace of his vengeful saga. With a shrewd financial intellect, Hunter invested his earnings into founding White Industries, which quickly rose to the pinnacle of scientific progression, developing bleeding-edge tech that captivated the world's gaze. Among Hunter's most groundbreaking innovation was the creation of his personal arsenal—a high-tech micro exoskeleton body suit, interwoven with a visually intimidating medieval armor. This suit conferred upon him superhuman endurance and potency, the capacity for flight, and a formidable force field, while his helmet was outfitted with advanced sensory trackers to ensure situational dominance. Carrying an eclectic array of armaments suitable for any manner of confrontation, Hunter White has transcended his former existence to embody the relentless crusader, dedicating his life to dismantling the corrupt tapestry of crime—a lone knight waging an unwavering war against the vile puppeteers of society's darkest corners.

Known Allies

Night Ranger
Stalker
Global Defense Administration

Known Enemies

Black Spider
Melee
Microwave
Wipe out
Jack-O-Lantern
Nathanal Toll

Known Skills

Martial Arts
Electronics
Mechanical Engineering
Genius level intelligence

Computer Coding
Business
Aerial Combat

Code Name = Spartan
Real Name = Sargent Chad Barlow
Base of Operations= U.S.S. Monitor
Age= 28

Powers

Enhanced Strength
Enhanced Reflexes
Metal Coated Bones
Healing Factor
Danger Sence

Equipment

Kevlar Body Suite with polymer plate armor over top of it.
Multi sensor array in helmet
Diuranium Sheild

Multiple firearms
Access to any and all military weaponry including experimental weapons.

Origin Story

Sargent Chad Barlow, known by his code name Spartan, is a commendable figure of valor and fortitude. As a seasoned military officer, he stood out amongst his peers for his dedication and skill in combat. His unwavering commitment to service led him to volunteer for a groundbreaking endeavor, Project Spartan Designation Weapon Two. Directed by the astute Dr. Sarah Sloan, the project promised to transcend human limitations, and Sargent Barlow emerged as its triumphant testament. The procedure imbued him with extraordinary attributes; his musculature was fortified, amplifying his strength and speed to remarkable levels. His resilience soared, granting him durability comparable to the toughest materials. His senses sharpened, becoming akin to those of a primordial hunter, and his healing factor enabled rapid recovery from injuries. Perhaps the most intriguing enhancement was his danger sense—an intuitive premonition of forthcoming peril, acting as an early warning system to evade threats. Donning his mantle as Spartan, he's clad in a tactical ensemble. His attire consists of a Kevlar bodysuit melded with advanced polymer plates, offering a balance of flexibility and defense. Concealing his identity and augmenting his strategic capabilities, his futuristic helmet is kitted out with cutting-edge visual and audio sensors. At his command is a singular shield, crafted from an enigmatic material harvested from the heart of a meteor's crater—a testament to Spartan's unique synergy with the cosmos. This circular shield, as dark as the void but emblazoned with a luminescent white star, can be hurled with precision, only to be summoned back to his gauntlets, which are equipped with a magnetic recall mechanism. The gauntlets further boast a stun blaster, adding electrical might to his arsenal. Spartan embodies the spearhead of human advancement, a sentinel in the night donning the heraldry of the stars.

Known Allies

Global Defense Administration
United States Military
Doctor Sarah Sloan

Known Enemies

Freedom Liberation Front
The Brotherhood
The Arian Brotherhood
Hamos
Isis
T.N.T
Nathanial Toll
Kill Spawn

Known Skills

Hand to Hand Combat.
Jungle Warfare
Urbin Warfare
Driving
Pilot
Firearms
Bladed Weapons

Counter terrorism
Espionage

Team_____

Task Force One

Real Name = Sargent Major Allen Adams
Code Name = Patriot
Base Of Operations = Global Defense Administration's orbital space Station (The Lighthouse)
Age = 40

Powers

Enhanced strength
Enhanced reflexes
Enhanced senses
Healing Factor
Natural Body Armor

Equipment

Polymer Battle suit
Taser Gauntlets
Sheild
Variety of high-tech weapons
High Tech visual and audio sensors in helmet

Origin Story

Sargent Major Allen Adams, also known as 'Patriot', is the epitome of strength, resilience, and unyielding loyalty. As the leading super soldier of Project Patriot, he was meticulously engineered to possess enhanced physical abilities, superior tactical acumen, and a resilient psyche, all honed for the defense of his country. With a body fortified to withstand the rigors of battle and a mind sharpened for strategic warfare, Allen's prowess in combat is virtually unrivaled. His unwavering devotion to his nation and its ideals made him the prime candidate for recruitment by the enigmatic Agent Smith into the elite assembly known as Task FORCE ONE. Gridiron in spirit and chiseled in form, Patriot carries the weight of his namesake with both honor and a sense of profound duty. His presence on the battlefield is both an inspiration to allies and an omen to adversaries, signifying the imminent arrival of justice delivered with surgical precision. Patriot's story is one of sacrifice, valor, and the ceaseless pursuit of peace through superior firepower and unbending will.

Known Allies

Global Defense Administration
Task Force One
United States Military
United States Government

Known Enemies

Nathanial Toll
Kill Spawn
Scourge Armada

Known Skills

Hand to Hand Combat
Jungle Warfare
Urbine Warfare
 military Strategy
Counter Terrorism
Leadership.

Team

Task Force One

Real Name = Yuri Romanov
Code Name = Red Scorpion
Age = 35
Base of Operation = Global Defense Administration's orbital space Station (The Lighthouse)

Powers

psychic link with the techno-organic substance

Equipment

Alien Techno-organic Battle Suit
Create Advance tech from his Techno-Organic fluid Armor

Origin Story

Yuri Romanov, known by his codename Red Scorpion, is a formidable special forces officer in the Russian military. His transformation began when the Russian government, stumbling upon alien technology from the Soviet era, resurrected their super soldier program. This alien tech was a techno-organic fluid that bonded with Yuri, covering his entire body in a red, armor-like substance. This fusion not only enhanced his physical attributes—strength, agility, and endurance—but also provided impenetrable body armor. Yuri formed a psychic link with the techno-organic substance, merging them into a single entity. With this bond, Yuri gained the extraordinary ability to form complex weapons and technology at will, utilizing the red techno-organic substance that envelops him. His appearance, entirely coated in red from head to toe, strikes fear into his enemies and portrays him as an unstoppable force on the battlefield.

Known Allies

Global Defense Administration
Task Force One
Russian Military
Russian Government

Known Enemies

Nathanal Toll
Scourge Armada

Known Skills

Hand to Hand Combat
Jungle Warfare
Urbine Warfare
military Strategy
Counter Terrorism

Team

Task Force One

Real Name - David Masters
Code Name = Divide
Age = 20
Base of Operation = Global Defense Administration's orbital space Station (The Lighthouse)

Powers

Duplication. Self and Whatever he is touching or is touching him.
psychic link with his duplicates.
Higher than average Strength, speed, and Endurance.

Equipment

Kevlar Body Suit with Polymer plate armor over top of it.
Helmet with a verity of visual and audio sensors
Swords
A verity of firearms.

Origin Story

David Masters, also known as Divide, is an extraordinary individual with a rare mutation granting him the astounding ability to clone himself without limit. These duplicates are not mere illusions or mirages; they are flesh and blood, fully autonomous extensions of David himself, each possessing his memories, skills, and intellect up to the moment of replication. Born into the turmoil of a world fraught with superhuman conflict, David's unique talent quickly gained the attention of governmental agencies specializing in the recruitment of those with special abilities. He was subsequently inducted into Task Force One by a stoic and enigmatic operative known only as Agent Smith. The dynamics of this squad, teeming with a panoply of powered individuals, offered David a chance to hone his abilities for the greater good, often deploying his proliferating personas on reconnaissance, infiltration, or the sheer overwhelming force required for the missions at hand. One vital aspect of David's power is the lifeline it offers; as long as a single clone endures, David continues to exist, making him an invaluable asset in battles where the stakes are nothing short of life or death. Meticulous coordination among his selves and an unbreakable will to protect innocents make David Masters a name whispered with both respect and awe in the circles of heroes and villains alike.

Known Allies

Global Defense Administration
Task Force One

Known Enemies

Nathanal Toll

Scourge Armada

Known Skills
_____

Hand to Hand Combat
Weapon Expert
Martial Arts.
Hacking
Computer Programming
team
_____

Task Force One

Real Name = Atlan
Code Name = Atlan
Age = Unknown
Base of Operation = Global Defense Administration's orbital space Station (The Lighthouse)

Powers

Atlantean physiology
Enhanced Strength
Water Breathing
Atlantean Magic
Telepathy
 aqua kinetic powers

Equipment

Sword
Atlantean Battle Armor
A verity of Atlantean tech

Origin Story

Atlan stands as a formidable figure among the Atlantean Royal Guard, embodying the peak physical and mystical traits of his ancient underwater lineage. His indomitable strength, swift agility, and impressive durability are matched only by his remarkable ability to breathe both on land and beneath the tumultuous waves of the sea. A master of the storied Atlantean mystic arts, Atlan wields his aqua kinetic powers with the finesse of a seasoned sorcerer, manipulating water with an ease that belies the immense power at his command. Clad in armor crafted from mystically enhanced materials, his protective gear is as much a work of arcane art as it is a symbol of his status. The blueish-green scales that envelop his skin shimmer in the light, tracing the contours of his naturally muscular physique and lending an aquatic grace to his already striking appearance. His visage, reflecting his oceanic heritage, bears features that hint at the depth of his abilities. In battle, Atlan is a dance of lethal precision, his twin Kamas slicing through the water with the same fluidity as the currents that obey his summons.

Known Allies

Global Defense Administration
Task Force One
kingdom of Atlantis

Known Enemies

Nathanal Toll
Scourge Armada
Governments of the surface world.

Known Skills

Atlantis Martial Arts.
Atlantean Weapons Expert
Swimming
Knowlogy Of the Atlantean mystic arts.
 Team

Task Force One

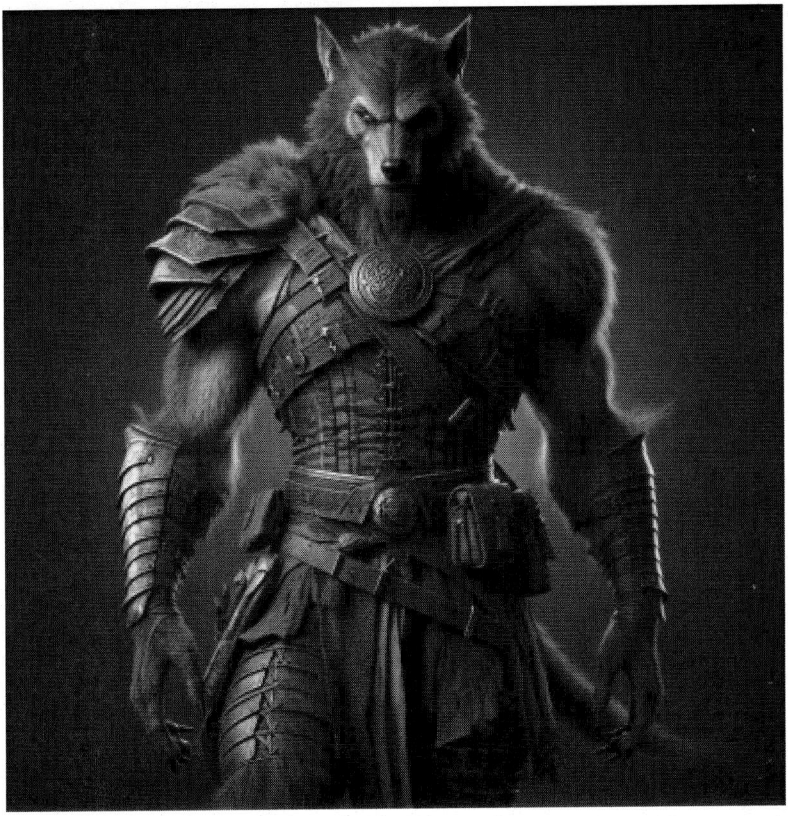

Real Name = Sebastin Cole
Code Name = Fenris
Age = 200
Base of Operation = Global Defense Administration's orbital space Station (The Lighthouse)

Powers

Lycanthropy
Enhanced Strength
Enhanced Reflexes
Healing Factor
Claws
Teeth
Enhanced senses
Infectious bite.

Equipment

Mystical Armor
A verity of high-tech weapons.
Amulet of the moon.

Origin Story

Fenris emerges from the legacy of Kainaan, a realm where the blood of humans and werewolves is intertwined with honor and mysticism. As the living embodiment of werewolf legends, he personifies the dichotomy inherent in his kind—the feral power and the dignified restraint. Bound by his Oath, Fenris represents the werewolf's commitment to their nation's protection, symbolizing their valor and unity. In the eyes of the world, he is a figure that inspires both awe and trepidation; his impressive stature and intense gaze betray his ancient lineage, while his calm countenance reflects a strategic mind that rivals his physical prowess. Endowed with wisdom that flows from the ancient teachings of werewolf sages, Fenris upholds his ancestors' legacy by demonstrating that werewolves are more than their dreaded curse; they are capable of camaraderie and coexistence with humankind. Despite the weight of history and the challenge of bridging two worlds, Fenris's optimism never falters. At every turn, he endeavors to cultivate a mutual respect between his kind and humanity, proving that even a creature of the night can hold the torch of hope for a united future. Towering at seven feet with a mantle of thick brown fur over his muscular frame, Fenris is both revered and feared—a being whose very existence is a testament to the enduring spirit of his people.

Known Allies

Global Defense Administration
Task Force One
European Werewolf Clans

Known Enemies

Nathanal Toll
Scourge Armada
Transylvanian Vampire Clans

Known Skills

Martial Arts
Bladed Weapons
High Tech Weapons.
Tracking
Team

Task Force One

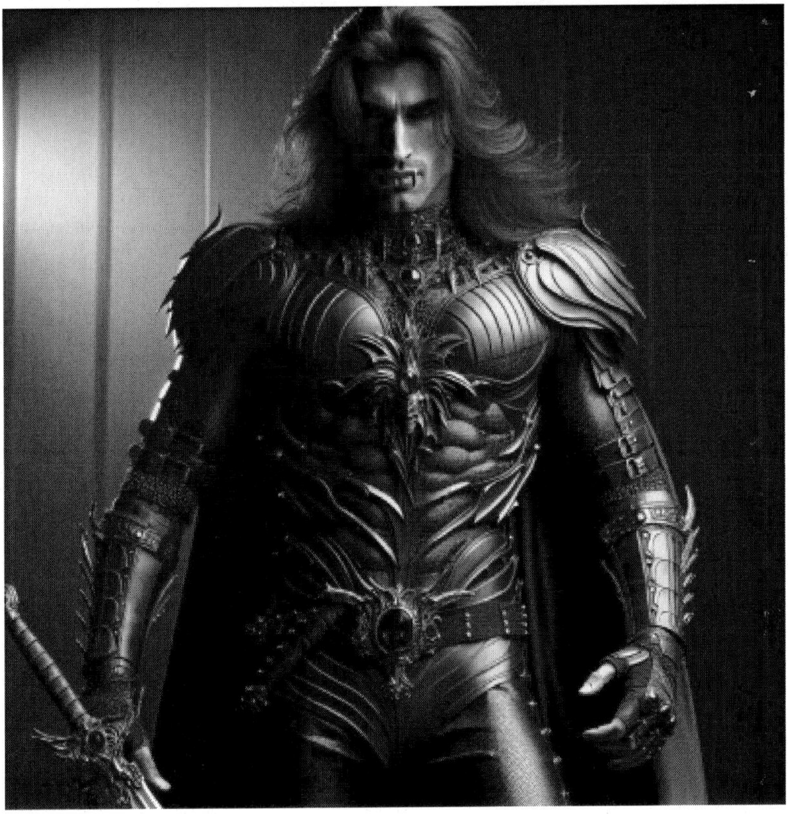

Real Name = Marious Dracula
Code Name = Marious
Age = 700
Base of Operation = Global Defense Administration's orbital space Station (The Lighthouse)

Powers

Enhanced Strength
Enhanced Speed
Immortality
Levitation
Shape Shifting = Man Bat From
Flight
Claws
Teeth
Telepathy
Vampiric Bite

Equipment

Mystical Armor
Sword
Access to High tech Weapons

Origin Story

Marious serves as a formidable member of Taskforce One, personally recruited by the legendary Count Dracula to serve in the Vampire kingdom's elite unit. With his roots tracing back to the 13th century, Marious possesses centuries of battle experience, making him one of the most adept warriors among his kind. A master swordsman, Marious wields his blade with a precision that's almost poetic, while his proficiency in multiple martial arts makes him versatile in hand-to-hand combat. As a vampire, Marious is endowed with supernatural abilities such as flight, exceptional strength, remarkable speed, and a regenerative healing factor, all of which make him an asset to his team and a terror to his foes. However, his vampiric nature comes with a weakness to sunlight, a vulnerability he counteracts with a magical amulet which shields him from the sun's deleterious effects. Clad in a modern Kevlar body suit integrated with advanced polymer plate armor, Marious strikes a balance between ancient warrior and futuristic soldier. Despite the many centuries he has walked the earth, Marious maintains the youthful appearance and vigor of a 30-year-old man, boasting an average build and long black hair that frames his enigmatic presence.

Known Allies

Global Defense Administration
Task Force One
Vampire Nation of Transylvania

Known Enemies

Nathanal Toll
Scourge Armada
European Werewolf Clans

Known Skills

Swordsmanship
Strategy
Arcane Magic
Hand to Hand combat

Team

Task Force One

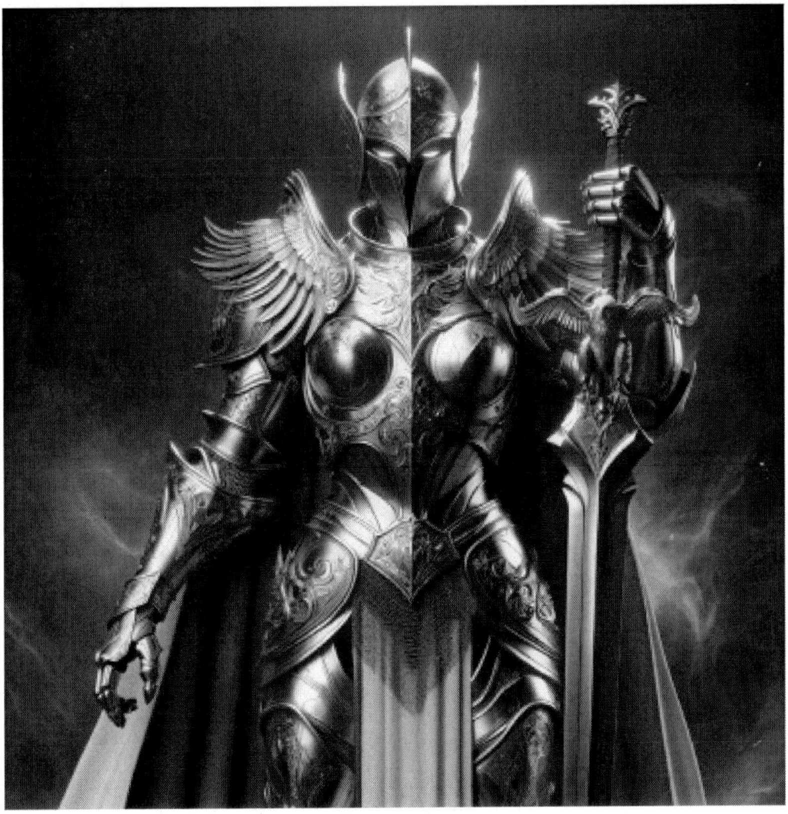

Real Name **Elizabeth Cromwell**
Code Name = Brittania
Age = 35
Base of Operation = Global Defense Administration's orbital space Station (The Lighthouse)

Powers

None

Equipment

Magical Sword Excalibur = Can do damage to magical beings
Magical suit of plate armor = enhanced Strength, Speed, endurance, mental shield, Self-sustenance, Body Armor.

Origin Story

Elizabeth Cromwell, known as Brittania, is the modern embodiment of the Arthurian legend, the rightful heir to the mystical powers of her ancestor, King Arthur. She alone was found worthy to draw forth the mythical blade from its stone sheath, a feat which cemented her lineage and destiny. Her extraordinary abilities do not end at the threshold of physical prowess; her sword crackles with arcane energy, allowing her to channel destructive mystical bolts against her adversaries and invoke protective measures beyond mortal capabilities. Elizabeth wields her power with a grace born of nobility, encased in spectral armor that conjures images of medieval knights, yet fitted for future conflicts. This armor, shining with the luster of the Arthurian age, bears the insignia of an eagle, symbolizing her strength and sovereignty. In a time when shadows grow long and threats loom large, Elizabeth Cromwell stands as a sentinel against the dark, a modern-day custodian of an ancient trust. Brought into the fold of Task Force One by Agent Smith, she has pledged her inherited might to the preservation of justice, assuming her place as the team's stalwart defender and the hope for an era in need of legends.

Known Allie

Global Defense Administration
Task Force One
United Kingdom Military
United Kingdom Government

Known Enemies

Nathanal Toll
Scourge Armada

Known Skills

Hand to Hand Combat
Swordsmanship

Martial Arts	
Archeology	
Anthropology	
Linguistics	
Team	

Task Force One

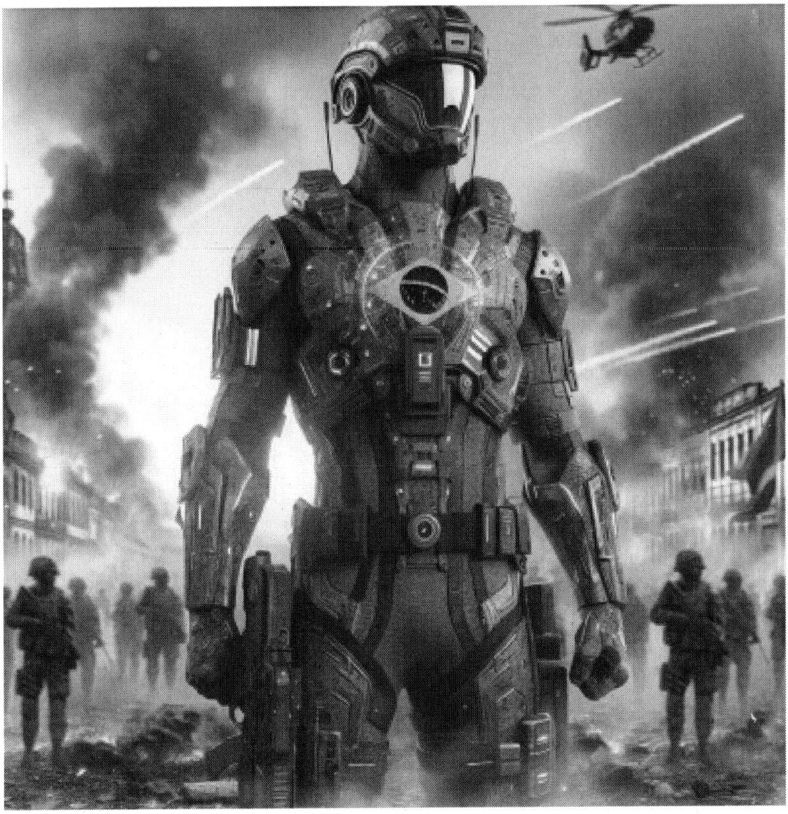

Real Name = Miguel Santos
Code Name = Brazilian Guardsman
Age = 35
Base of Operation = Global Defense Administration's orbital space Station (The Lighthouse)

Powers

None

Equipment

High tech Battle suit
Blasters
Anti- gravity belt
Energy shield
Life support
High tech visual and audio sensors
Enhanced strength exoskeleton
Cutting Lasar
Electromagnetic pulse generator

Origin Story

Miguel Santos, also known as the Brazilian Guardsman, is a character who epitomizes the fusion of intellect, innovation, and ironclad patriotism. A billionaire by fortune and an inventor by vocation, Miguel used his wealth and acumen to create the 'Guardian Suit' amidst the chaos of a Brazilian civil war. This advanced piece of technology features a revolutionary propulsion system, granting the power of flight to its operator. It also incorporates an energy matrix, which not only creates a nearly invincible force field but also allows the emission of powerful energy blasts, drawing from Miguel's own vital energy. The suit is self-sustaining with a state-of-the-art life support system, capable of weathering hostile terrains and sustaining the wearer in life-threatening zones through its complete environmental seal. Adorned with the Brazilian flag proudly placed on the upper left breast, the suit acts as a symbol of national pride. It is complemented with a Kevlar body suit layered with futuristic polymer plate armor and is accessorized with a utility belt equipped with tools that enhance his strength and grant him additional combat capabilities. As 'Brazilian Guardsman', Miguel stands as a towering figure of resilience and hope, particularly after being recruited by Agent Smith into the illustrious Task Force One, where he fights to reestablish peace and protect the values of his homeland.

Known Allies
___

Global Defense Administration
Task Force One
Brazilian military
Brazilian government

Known Enemies

Nathanal Toll
Scourge Armada

Known Skills

Genius level intellect
Areil Combat
Engineering
Computer programing
Hand to Hand Combat
Electronics

Team

Task Force One

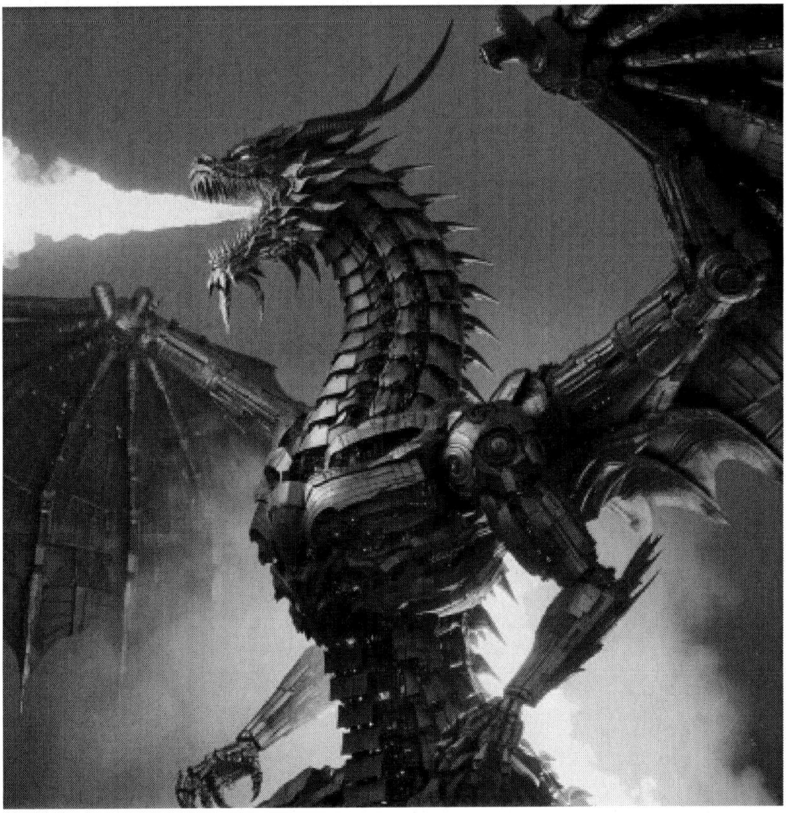

Real Name = Senzo tanoka
Code Name = Kaiju
Age = 20
Base of Operation = Global Defense Administration's orbital space Station (The Lighthouse)

Powers

Shape Shifting into a giant Dragon
Fire Breath
Claws
Body Armor
Tail
Flight
Teeth

Equipment

Adapting Body suit.

Origin Story

Senzo Tanoka, known by the codename 'Kaiju', is a former Japanese soldier who underwent a mysterious mutation, allowing him to transform into a colossal beast akin to the mythic Kaiju. Before this life-altering event, Senzo embodied the virtues of discipline and loyalty, being deeply rooted in military service. His life trajectory diverted upon meeting Agent Smith, a secretive operative intent on recruiting uniquely gifted individuals for Task Force One—a team facing extraordinary threats. As Kaiju, Senzo wields enormous strength and resilience, soaring above the Earth as a gargantuan dragon with the power to breathe fire and the majesty of flight. Despite his 200 feet tall monstrous form, Kaiju is a character caught between his intrinsic honor as a soldier and the chaotic might he possesses. His internal battle, juxtaposed with his role as both protector and potential destroyer, adds layers of depth to his narrative, making him an intriguing addition to any story.

Known Allies

Global Defense Administration
Task Force One
Japanese Government
Japanese Military

Known Enemies

Nathanal Toll
Scourge Armada

Known Skills

Martial Arts
Firearms
Bladed weapons
Pilot
Areil Combat.

Team

Task Force One

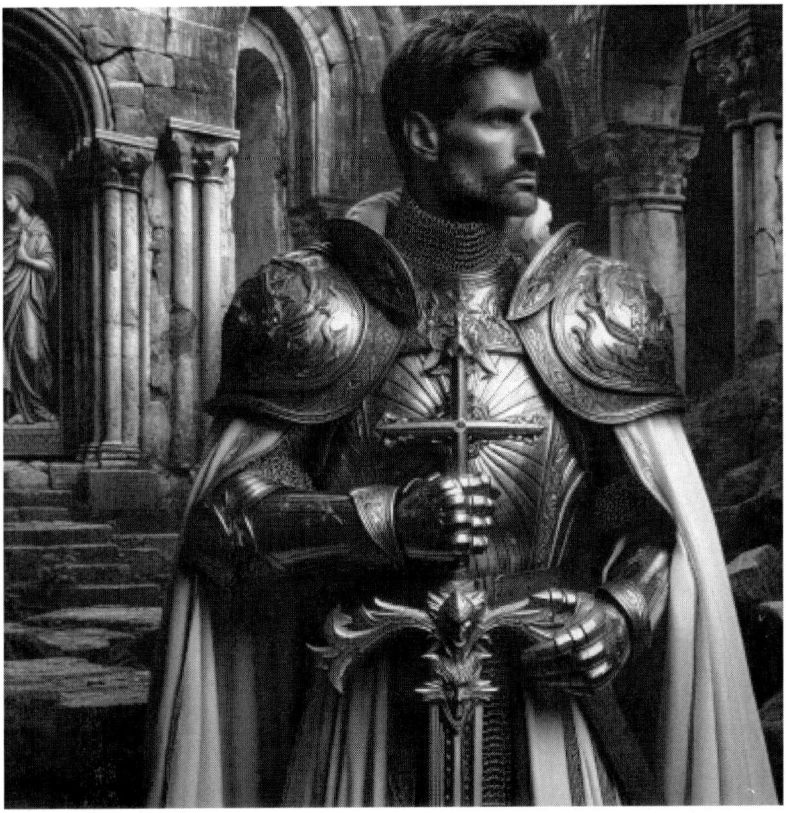

Real Name = Sir Thomas Westborn
Code Name = Caviler
Age = 1000
Base of Operation = Colorado Military base

Powers

Faith
* Healing Factor
* Enhanced Strength
* Enhanced Speed
* Smite = only affects those with a corrupt soul
* Bless = Spiritual Protection
* Long Life

Equipment

Holy Sword = Able to deal damage to the corrupted
Holy Armor = Protection from normal attacks and Magical attacks
Holy Shield = Protection from normal attacks and Magical attacks

Origin Story

Sir Thomas of Westborn, revered as the Caviler, is a character immortalized in the annals of history, a valiant knight who distinguished himself during the tumultuous period of the first crusades. Renowned for his indomitable spirit and martial prowess, he joined forces with six steadfast companions in search of the Holy Grail. Their undertaking carried them to the furthest reaches and into the heart of darkness, where among the dust and shadows of an archaic temple, they stumbled upon the legendary chalice. Veiled in malevolence, the grail's curse shattered the brotherhood, leaving Sir Thomas standing - a hollow victor amidst the chaos of betrayal. His subsequent communion with the Holy Grail bestowed upon him remarkable abilities and eternal life but at the cost of a perpetual reminiscence of his brethren's demise. Clad in Arthurian armor that is the embodiment of spiritual resilience, and brandishing a divinely-forged sword, Sir Thomas has transcended mortal fragility. The emblem of the Christian cross is emblazoned boldly upon his impervious armor, echoing his unyielding faith. Now, he walks through the epochs as both protector and penitent, his existence a testament to the quintessential battle between sacrilege and sanctity.

Known Allies

General Howell
Home guard
United States Military
Gad rill the angel

Known Enemies

Doctor Marrow

Nathanial Toll
Project CyberCron

Known Skills

Medieval Warfare
Modern Warfare
Historian
Biblical Scholar
Demonology
Swordsmanship

Team

Home guard

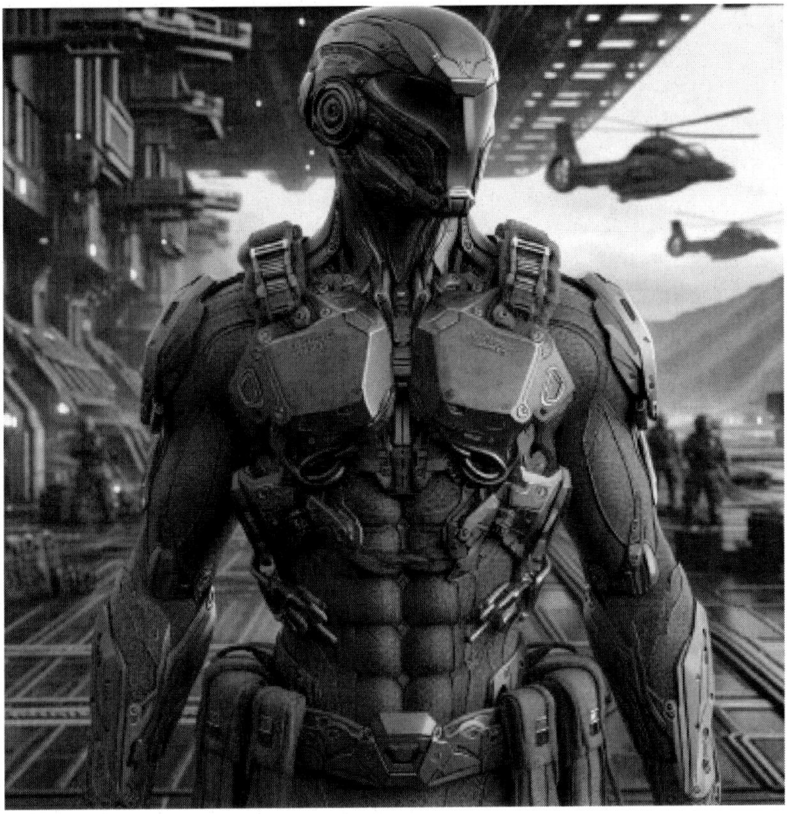

Real Name = Johnathan Green
Code Name = The Marine
Age = 30
Base of Operation = Colorado Military base

Powers

Enhanced Strength
Enhanced Speed
Enhanced Endurance
Healing Factor
Environmental adaptation = His body will automatically adapt to whatever environment he is in.

Equipment

Kevlar and polymer plate Battle Armor
Helmet with A verity of visual and audio sensors.
Blaster Rifle
Retractable Gauntlet Blades
Energy Shield
Cloaking system

Origin Story

Johnathan Green, once a mere soldier, emerged from Project Backlash as the epitome of military innovation and human potential. Selected for his valor within the Marine Corps, he was transformed into a super-soldier whose capabilities defied the conceivable limits of conventional warfare. He boasted Herculean strength, enabling him to deform metal with his bare hands, and possessed agility so extreme that he could chase down the fleeing dusk. His durability was such that he remained unscathed where others would succumb, borne of a flesh that rendered conventional weaponry obsolete. Johnathan's acute senses conferred upon him an almost precognitive awareness, elevating his tactical acumen to heights unmatched. Among his astonishing abilities was a unique respiratory system, akin to gills, allowing him to breathe underwater by filtering and replenishing his oxygen supply—a testament to both his inhuman endurance and his deep connection to the aquatic world. He was at ease under the waves as he was on land, a warrior redefined for an age where the laws of warfare were rewritten. Clad in a tailored Kevlar suit festooned with advanced polymer plates, he was a sight to behold—a human in form, unchanged in appearance by the DNA alterations that remade him internally.

Johnathan's narrative is one of inner conflict and exploration, a life tethered to the merciless nature of duty, and an ongoing search for his place in a society that had transitioned beyond its archaic notions of soldiery. Amid the echoes of battle cries and the silence of the deep sea, his is a story of humanity within the husk of a living armament.

Known Allies

General Howell
Home guard
United States Military

Known Enemies

Doctor Marrow
Nathanial Toll
Project CyberCron

Known Skills

Hand to Hand Combat
Jungle Warfare
Urban Warfare
Weapons Expert

Team

Home guard

TACTICAL SUPERHERO

MIDDLE EASTERN NINJA SUITA, POLYMER
NECK LATEX

COMMBOW + EXPERENTIVAL PLATEES

Real Name = Wesley Baker
Code Name = Long Bow
Age = 26
Base of Operation = Colorado Military base

Powers

Probability manipulation
Hyper Reflexes
Enhanced Strength
Enhanced eyesight
Healing Factor

Equipment

Kevlar and Polymer plate Body Armor
Bow
Quiver
A verity of Trick Arrows
* Ice Arrows
* Explosive Arrows
* Stun Arrows
* Flash Bang Arrows
* Grapple Arrows

* Sonic Arrows
Katana

Origin Story

Wesley Baker, known by his code name 'Longbow', is an ex-scout/sniper from the U.S. military, whose life took a dramatic turn when his latent mutant gene was discovered following a combat injury. His exceptional talent with firearms became evident in childhood, a precursor to his later specialized abilities. Recruited by General Howel for a specialized command unit, Wesley's mutation granted him superhuman agility, strength, and a remarkable power named 'Dead Eye'. This allows him to create an invisible energy field around objects, directing them with perfect accuracy towards any target. His uncanny ability to never miss makes him an invaluable military asset, capable of making any projectile his weapon of choice. Wesley's preferred arsenal includes a compound bow equipped with a diverse array of trick arrows for various tactical situations. For close-quarter combat, he relies on a katana forged from experimental material. His attire is a fusion of protection and stealth, featuring a Kevlar body suit amplified with futuristic polymer plate armor, providing a balance between mobility and defense.

Known Allies

General Howell
Home guard
United States Military
Navaho Nation

Known Enemies

Doctor Marrow
Nathanial Toll
Project CyberCron

Known Skills

Archery
Chemistry
Explosives
Swordsmanship
Martial Arts
Marksmanship

Team

Home guard

Waase Sutsut — fahtimed megentale

Nanite Plates — Infused an flating

Boddly Suit

Nymerr Pl

wdted of etervee mnology

Advon sehymp

Real Name = Curtis Jackson
Code Name = Wasp
Age = 29
Base of Operation = Colorado Military base

Powers

None

Equipment

Wasp Battle Armor
* Flight
* Blasters
* Body Armor
* Mini Drones
* Visual and audio Sensors
* Enhanced Strength
* Enhanced Speed

Origin Story

Doctor Curtis Jackson, branded as 'Wasp' in the field, represents the pinnacle of human ingenuity fused with the marvel of insect biomechanics. His intellect, which burgeons at the genius level, has led him on a path of innovative pursuits deeply influenced by the captivating world of insects. It's this very curiosity that has catapulted him into becoming a formidable presence amidst those who suit up to protect or to battle. His creation, the high-tech battle suit, is his magnum opus, amalgamating his knowledge with his passion and materializing as an embodiment of a wasp's fierce anatomy. This anthropomorphic armor, engineered with overlapping Kevlar layers interwoven with reactive nanotechnology, grants Curtis Jackson superhuman strength while minimizing vulnerability. The suit's outermost shield is composed of advanced polymer plates, articulated to mirror the segmented exoskeleton of a wasp, stark in aesthetic and impressive in defense. Integrated within this chassis of the future are bio-mimetic wings, allowing Wasp to soar with agility and precision across the heavens. His helmet, a homage to the creature that he emulates, is not simply a protective gear but a sophisticated nexus of sensory extensions providing amplified sight and sound. The gauntlets, potent in their simplicity, are termed 'Wasp Stings'; blasters capable of discharging energy pulses with devastating impact. His prowess did not go unnoticed, leading to an invitation by General Howel to join the 'Home Guard', an elite assemblage sponsored by the government, their mission: to harbor safety for their nation as enhanced soldiers. With the heart of a hero beneath the exoskeletal armor, Curtis Jackson stands vigilant, a testament to human innovation and a guardian by choice. his armor contains hundreds of micro drones shaped like tiny wasps. he can use them for surveillance. or program them to swarm detonate on a target.

Known Allies

General Howell
Home guard
United States Military

Known Enemies

Doctor Marrow
Nathanial Toll
Project CyberCron

Known Skills

Ariel Combat
Hand to Hand Combat
Mechanical engineering
Computer Programming
Electronics

Team

Home guard

- Foictionl air body pillot not tied a a rea persor
- Polyetldaple mar with polce-age armur
- etxpable wings fit truled with darge lateres
- tatcas tage py platter / system
- Enerice plat egintaltes sai
- Adtunicte al nalort tecred ua pul aryna
- Enery shielding sidstem fight
- Entergy shiedding with a pic – gal
- Enerrity belt fuilet minctall spters

Real Name = **Captain Malcolm Davis**
Code Name = Raven
Age = 27
Base of Operation = Colorado Military base

Powers

None

Equipment

Raven Flight Armor
* Flight
* Wrist Basters
* Mini Missiles
* Energy Field
* Advanced Visual and audio sensors
* Life Support
* Body Armor

Origin Story

Introducing Captain Malcolm Davis, call sign 'Raven,' the United States Air Force's most elite test and fight pilot, renowned for his unrivaled skills in aerial combat and aviation prowess. Captain Davis has been selected for the prestigious Project Raven, an Airforce classified initiative aimed at revolutionizing modern aerial warfare. Davis dons an extraordinary state-of-the-art flight suit, the culmination of advanced military research and secret technology, enabling him to dominate the skies like never before. The suit boasts a full-body Kevlar layer complemented by an outer shell of cutting-edge polymer plate armor, integrating both protection and flexibility. At the heart of this innovation is the jet pack, powered by an avant-garde propulsion system, along with deployable wings crafted from an alien material discovered in a meteor impact site. These wings are not just for flight; they are razor-shaped, offering strategic offensive capabilities as well as exceptional maneuverability. Captain Davis's gauntlets are no mere gloves; they are armed with potent energy blasters for ranged confrontation. An advanced energy shielding system weaves around the suit, providing a near-impenetrable defense against incoming attacks. Incorporated within the engine's architecture are miniaturized missile arrays, ready to strike with precision at any designated target. His helmet, a marvel of design and technology, houses an array of sophisticated visual and auditory sensors, granting him unparalleled battlefield awareness. Lastly, the utility belt is an arsenal unto itself, featuring an assortment of pouches holding varied grenades and tactical gear, ensuring Captain Davis, or 'Raven,' is prepared for any scenario. With Project Raven, Captain Davis transcends the role of a pilot, transforming into an airborne sentinel, the embodiment of next-generation warfare.

Known Allies

General Howell
Home guard
United States Military

Known Enemies

Doctor Marrow
Nathanial Toll
Project CyberCron

Known Skills

———
Hand to hand combat
Ariel Combat
Acrobatics
Ariel Acrobatics
Survival

Team

Home guard

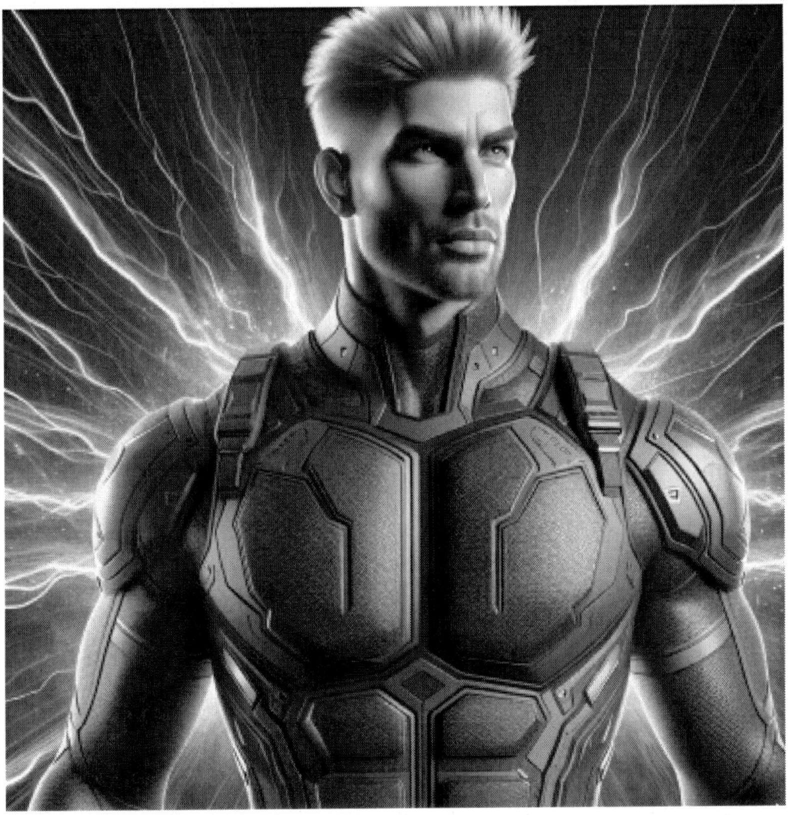

Real Name = Dwayne Peterson
Code Name = Power Man
Age = 21
Base of Operation = Colorado Military base

Powers

Damage Absorption and Conversion
* Body Armor
* Superhuman Strength
* Superhuman Agility
* Healing Factor
* Kinetic Blaster
* Kinetic Energy Projection

Equipment

Kevlar with polymer plate Armor
Blaster Rifle

Origin Story

Dwayne Peterson, known as Powerman, possesses a rare and astonishing ability. Born with the inherent power to absorb any form of damage and redirect that energy for multiple uses, Powerman has become a figure both enigmatic and charismatic. From the absorbed energy, Dwayne can accelerate his natural healing processes, exponentially increase his muscle density for superior strength, and even project concussive blasts capable of neutralizing threats. His formative years were spent in modesty, joining the military at the tender age of 18. With 15 years of dedicated service to his country, Dwayne's extraordinary abilities eventually surfaced, catching the attention of the military top brass. He was swiftly reassigned to General Howell's elite unit, where his skills could be honed and put to strategic use. Powerman's physical features are typical of a disciplined military man: sharp blonde hair cut to regulation standards, and a stature that, while average at rest, holds the promise of immense power. His attire merges function with protection, donning a tailored Kevlar body suit for agility, overlayed with cutting-edge polymer plate armor designed to reinforce his resilience on the battlefield. Characterized by unwavering bravery and a commitment to his unit, Dwayne 'Powerman' Peterson stands as a stalwart guardian, an unyielding force against those who would threaten his nation.

Known Allies

General Howell
Home guard

United States Military

Known Enemies

Doctor Marrow
Nathanial Toll
Project CyberCron

Known Skills

Hand to Hand Combat
Wilderness Survival
Firearms

Team

Home guard

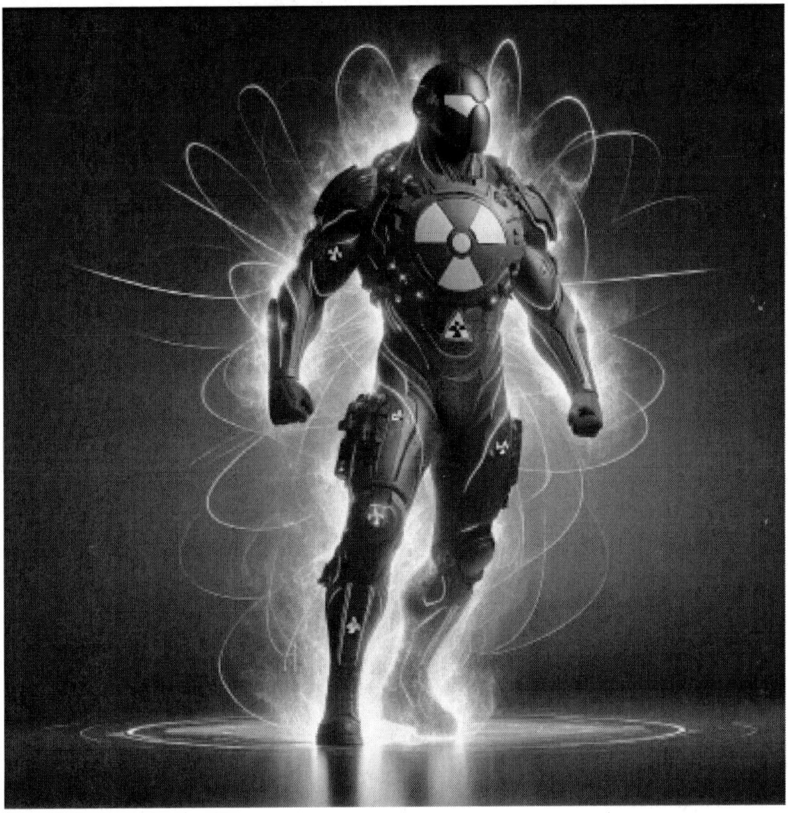

Real Name = Doctor Adam Dill
Code Name = Gamma
Age = 44
Base of Operation = Colorado Military base

Powers

Gamma Energy Body
* Flight
* Gamma Energy Projection

Equipment

Containment Suit
* Body Armor
* Radiation Shielding
* Channeling Gauntlets

Origin Story

Doctor Adam Dill, a paragon in the field of alternative energy, is an esteemed scientist specializing in Gamma radiation. His conviction in Gamma energy as the remedy to the global energy crisis was unmatched, prompting him to dedicate his entire career to its exploration and utility. The apex of his achievements was the construction of an innovative Gamma energy generator, which promised to redefine the paradigms of power generation. However, during the generator's trial run, a devastating mishap caused a massive release of Gamma radiation, remarkably sparing only Dr. Dill in its wake. The event inexplicably altered his physiology, rendering him a human Gamma reactor, possessing extraordinary capabilities derived from the Gamma energy coursing within him. Among his new powers were the emission of intense Gamma blasts and the creation of resilient force fields. Dr. Dill, in a bid to protect others from his harmful radiation, ingeniously designed a bespoke suit to contain his formidable energy. Transformed into a beacon of endurance and adaptability, Dr. Dill now navigates the duality of his existence: using his powers in a crusade for the greater good, while wrestling with his own volatile essence.

Known Allies

General Howell
Home guard
United States Military

Known Enemies

Doctor Marrow
Nathanial Toll
Project CyberCron

Known Skill

Physics
Engineering
Chemistry
Gamma Energy Expert
Ariel Combat
Hand to Hand Combat
Team

Home guard

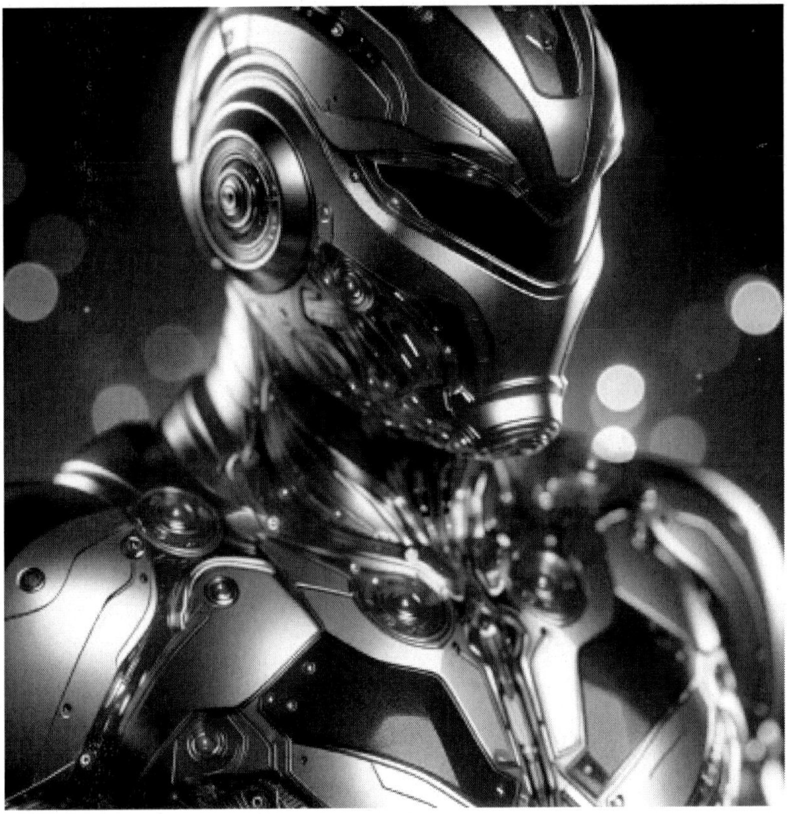

Real Name = Professor Jeffery Allen
Code Name = Crimson Cyber Cron
Age = 45
Base Of Operations = Secret Labotory In North Carolina

Powers

Techno-Path
* Communicate with any electronic device
* Genius level Intelligence
* Techno- Understanding
* Resistance to Telepathy

Equipment

Battle Armor
* Flight
* Blasters
* High tech visual and audio sensors
* Body Armor
* Life support
* Photographic Memory
* Cloaking Devise
* Mini missiles

Combat Droids
* Flight
* Blasters
* High tech visual and audio sensors
* Body Armor
* Cloaking Devise
* Mini missiles
* High tech visual and audio sensors

Origin Story

Within the hallowed halls of Yale University, Professor Jeffery Allen imparts knowledge on evolutionary theory, yet his presence among academic peers harbors a wondrous anomaly. Classified as an EVO, Allen belongs to a unique subset of humanity graced with extraordinary capabilities. From birth, Allen's veins coursed with bio-mechanical nanites. These microscopic architects forged his brain into a computational marvel akin to the most sophisticated processor, far surpassing the bounds of conventional human intellectual capacity. His resistance to telepathy, a wireless communion with technology, and an unparalleled ability to process data a thousand-fold faster than an average person are testaments to his evolved state. His mental prowess is complemented by an eidetic memory and the exceptional talent to actualize complex inventions spawned from his imagination. Armed with a bespoke device to identify fellow EVOs, Allen has become their mentor and guide, helping them integrate within society and harness their abilities constructively. Despite his noble intentions, his journey unveiled EVOs who veered from the path - some unable to govern their powers, others wielding them for nefarious ends. Thus, Allen engineered the Crimson Cyber cron armor, a bastion of futuristic technology tailor-made for confrontation. Operable through his innate Wi-Fi capability, the armor is a synergy of offensive and defensive systems, crowned with a helmet containing an elaborate suite of sensory equipment. As Professor Allen continues his dual life of educator and sentinel, he stands as a beacon for EVOs and humanity alike.

Known Allies

EVO Underground
Power X

Known Enemies

The Brotherhood
United States Government
Project CyberCron

Known Skills

Engineering
Electronics
Computer Programming
Invention
Accounting
Hand to Hand Combat
Leadership
Teaching

Team

Power X

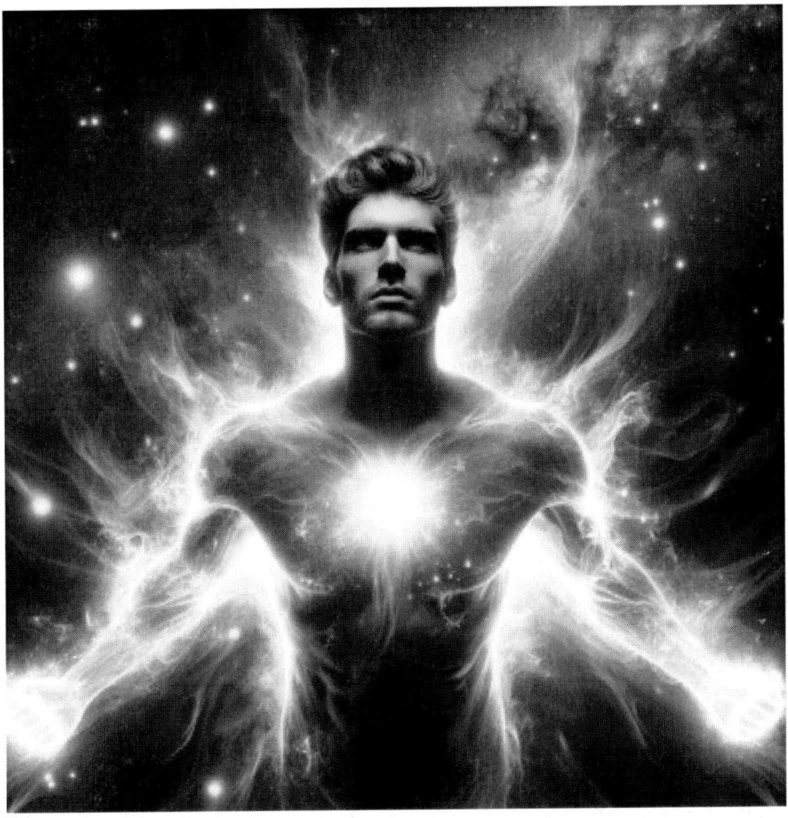

Real Name = Marcus Thompson
Code Name = Fire
Age = 35
Base Of Operations = Secret Labotory In North Carolina

Powers

Heat Generation
* Laser Projection
* Body Armor
* Flight

* Super Nova Blast
* Fire Body
Cold immunity

Origin Story

Marcus Thompson's life before his EVO powers erupted into existence could be considered unremarkable. Living under the radar, he had no inkling of the inferno he carried within him until a surge of untamed energy led to tragedy. The flames that claimed his family home also consumed any remnants of his normal life, setting him on a nomadic journey through the care system. Despite his grief and guilt, Marcus learned to cloak the fiery secret that burned inside him, carrying it unseen until adulthood. On the verge of being discovered, it was Professor Allen who stepped in to become the mentor Marcus desperately needed. Under Allen's tutelage, Marcus grasped the reins on his abilities, discovering his potential to channel and wield heat. His mastery of temperature manipulation allowed him to transform into a conduit of combustion, a human furnace able to soar unbound by gravity, discharge scorching heat blasts, and cocoon himself within barriers of blistering energy. In times of dire need, he could push himself to the brink, radiating a destructive brilliance that rivaled the sun. This ultimate expression of his power, his supernova, could lay waste to all it encompassed, mirroring the devastating might of a nuclear detonation. Yet, with such a cataclysm comes a price—complete depletion of his powers, leaving him vulnerable. Marcus stands as a being of paradox, his very essence a fusion of creation and ruin, warmth and woe.

known Allies

EVO Underground
Power X

Known Enemies

The Brotherhood
United States Government
Project CyberCron

Known Skills

Ariel Combat
Martial Arts
Leadership
Team

Power X

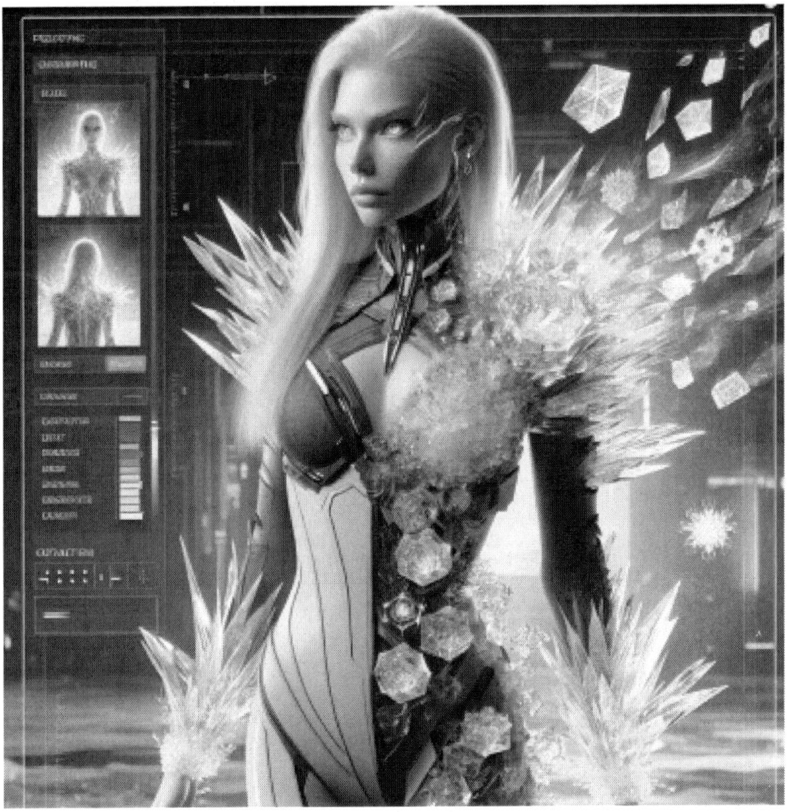

Real Name = Kelly Winters
Code Name = Solstice
Age = 30
Base Of Operations = Secret Labotory In North Carolina

Powers

Cold Manipulation
* Ice Constructs
* Temperature Control
* Ice Body Armor
* Self Substance
Heat Resistance

Equipment

Kevlar with polymer plate Armor

Origin Story

Hailing from a universe where exceptional individuals known as EVOs exhibit remarkable abilities, Kelly Winters stands as a testament to the power of elemental mastery. Endowed with the ability to generate and manipulate extreme cold, she transcends her human limitations, transforming at will into a living sculpture of ice. Her mastery over cold enables her to craft intricate ice constructs ranging from razor-sharp weapons to impregnable domes of frost, making her a formidable being in both offense and defense. Discovered by the benevolent Professor Allen, Kelly was bestowed with guidance to harness her chilling talents. Her bonds with the professor and fellow EVO Marcus deepened beyond mentorship—the latter evolving into a partnership that blossomed into marriage. Their union is one of love and shared strength, fortified by their unique abilities. With piercing blue eyes reminiscent of winter skies and fair hair that vanishes in her ice form, Kelly's transformation is a spectacle of frozen beauty. Yet, it's not just her powers that demand attention; her physically striking presence is equally captivating. In her ice form, she becomes a crystalline vision, her hair replaced by the sheer radiance of her glacial guise.

Known Allies

EVO Underground
Power X

Known Enemies

The Brotherhood
United States Government
Project CyberCron

Known Skills

Martial Arts
Bladed Weapons
Acrobatics
Melee Weapons
Team

Power X

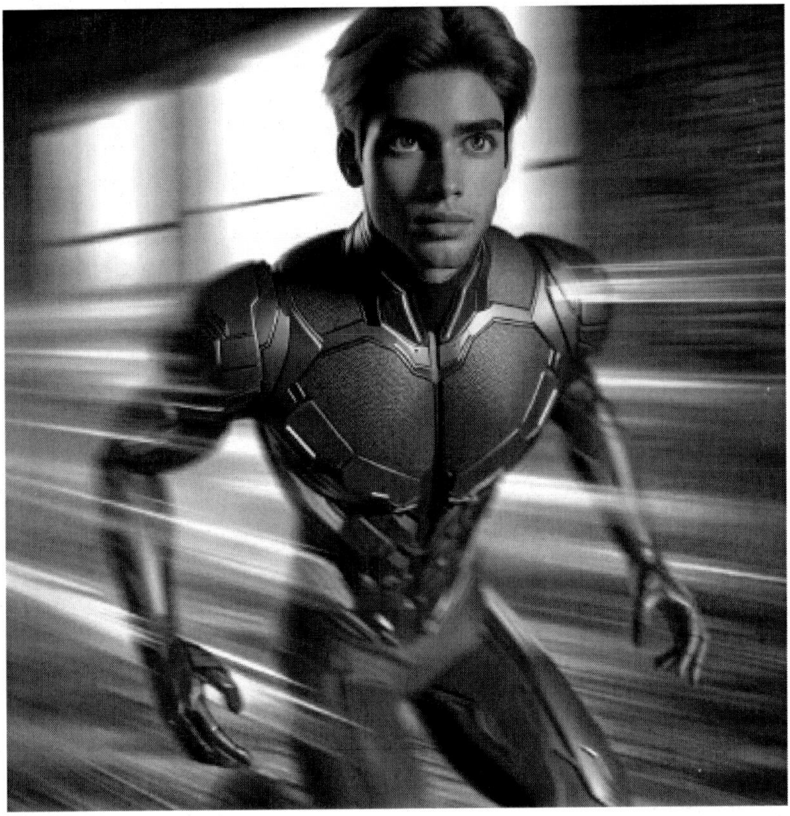

Real Name = Jason Adams
Code Name = Mach One
Age = 18
Base Of Operations = Secret Labotory In North Carolina

Powers

Super Sonic Speed
* Body Armor
* Kinetic Charge
* Phasing
* Sonic Boom
* Hyper Vision
* Hyper thinking

Equipment

Kevlar with polymer plate armor suit

Origin Story

Jason Adams, known as 'March one,' is a remarkable character who stands at the nexus of superhero prowess and youthful ambition. An EVO with the extraordinary ability to propel himself at staggering speeds nearing 1000 mph, Jason possesses a kinetic mastery that extends beyond mere locomotion. His reflexes allow him to perform actions with his limbs at a rate defying the limits of the naked eye, while his ability to vibrate his molecules provides him the phenomenal power to phase through solid objects, an ability often associated with ghostly apparitions rather than a young man. At 18, he is the protégé of the venerable Professor Allen, though he grapples with the full potential of his own abilities. Despite the extreme velocities he subjects his body to, a natural resistance to the friction results from his rapid movement, rendering him impervious to the wear both the air and material world would otherwise inflict upon him. His attire is a unique blend of form and function; a sleek full-body suit envelopes him up to his neck, with a striking blue coloring dominating the chest area, and sections of futuristic polymer plate armor adorning his arms and legs to offer protection without sacrificing mobility. Topped with short brown hair and piercing green eyes, Jason is the paragon of a new age of heroes-in-training - ambitious, powerful, and on the precipice of becoming something greater than he is.

Known Allies

EVO Underground
Power X

Known Enemies

The Brotherhood
United States Government
Project CyberCron

Known Skills

Marial Arts
Geometry
Acrobatics
Team

Power X

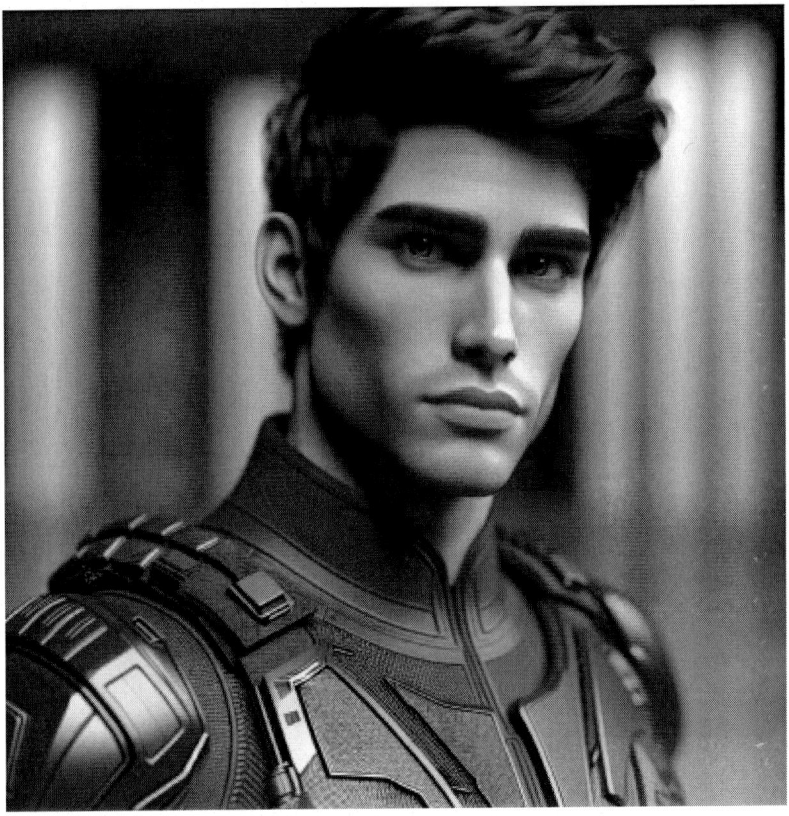

Real Name = Simon Worthington
Code Name = Soul Jumper
Age = 21
Base Of Operations = Secret Labotory In North Carolina

Powers

Phasing
* Power / Skills Duplication
Genetic Memory
* Genetically store any power / Skill he has duplicated
Genetic Recall
* Can recall any power / Skill he has genetically stored at half its original power rank
Telepathic Link with his twin Brother Alex

Equipment

Kevlar Body suite with polymer plate armor over top of it

Origin Story

Simon Worthington, also known as 'Soul Jumper', is a unique EVO— a human with evolved supernatural abilities. His primary power is phasing, which allows him to move seamlessly through solid matter as if it were air. However, his abilities extend beyond mere physical translocation. Whenever Simon phases through an ordinary human being, he experiences a form of psychic osmosis, absorbing their memories, experiences, and knowledge, granting him an ever-expanding mental library that could prove as much a burden as a gift. His powers escalate to new heights when phasing through another EVO, assimilating not only their psyche but their special abilities as well. This rare talent positions Simon in the crosshairs of both benevolent researchers and nefarious entities eager to exploit his powers. Adopted as a ward by the enigmatic Professor Allen, Simon is provided with a mentor figure and protector, guiding him on how best to harness and refine his potent gifts. Equipped for combat and defense, his attire is a cutting-edge Kevlar body suit, augmented with lightweight futuristic polymer plates for heightened protection. Simon is a complex youth, manifesting an outward appearance that masks the turmoil within: he is described as having an intense gaze, dark hair, and deep brown eyes that seem to hint at the depths of souls he's encountered. As he strides through the battlefield of good and evil, Simon is a figure both desired and feared — an EVO on the brink of either greatness or destruction, depending on the paths he chooses and the allegiances he forges.

Known Allies

EVO Underground
Power X

Known Enemies

The Brotherhood
United States Government
Project CyberCron

Known Skills
_____

Martial Arts
Surfing
Par Core
Acrobatics
Team
_____

Power X

Dramestic
emomatier
Polymer plate armo
domaide moder comarr

Real Name = Alex Worthington
Code Name = Wind Rider
Age = 21
Base Of Operations = Secret Labotory In North Carolina

Powers

Weather Manipulation
* Flight
* Lightening
* Wind Control
Enhanced Strength
Telepathic Link with his twin Brother Simon
Empathy for the planet

Equipment

Kevlar Body Suit with futuristic polymer plate Armor

Origin Story

Alex Worthington, also known as Wind Rider, is the embodiment of the storm's fury with the serene control of a seasoned sailor navigating the breeze. As the older sibling of the enigmatic soul jumper, Simon Worthington, Alex's genetic makeup places him in the ranks of EVOS, beings with extraordinary abilities. His particular gift lies in his mastery over the elements, granting him the phenomenal power to manipulate the weather to his whims. Under the guardianship of the astute Professor Allen, Alex hones these formidable abilities, ensuring that his tempestuous nature does not lead to inadvertent destruction. Striking in appearance, Alex boasts a head of fiery red hair that cascades down to his shoulders, a visual testament to his volatile powers. He is outfitted in a cutting-edge Kevlar bodysuit, which provides a flexible defense against forces that would seek to harm him. This is overlaid with sleek polymer plate armor that offers additional protection without sacrificing mobility. Despite his impressive capabilities, Alex maintains an average physique, a reminder that it is not brute strength, but the mastery of his elemental control that makes him a force to be reckoned with. With the skies as his domain, Alex Worthington strides forth as Wind Rider, a guardian whose watchful eyes are set to the horizon, ready to command the wrath of the heavens.

Known Allies

EVO Underground
Power X

Known Enemies

The Brotherhood
United States Government
Project CyberCron

Known Skills

Martial Arts
Computer Programming
Meteorology
Team

Power X

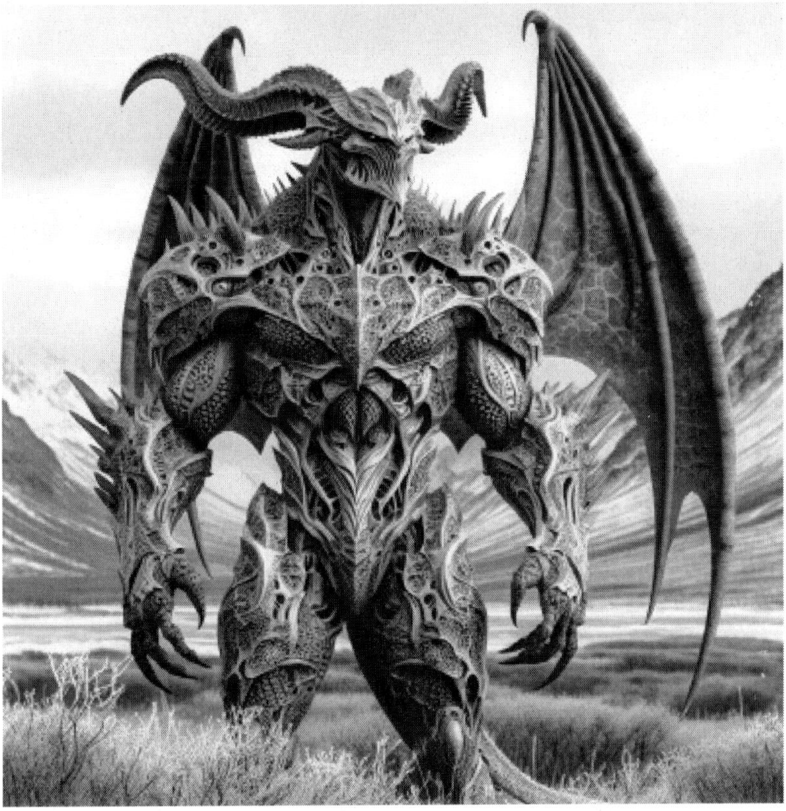

Real Name = Jake Gillyard
Code Name = Demon
Age = Unknown
Base Of Operations = Secret Labotory In North Carolina

Powers

Demonic Body
* Super Strength
* Flight
* Claws
* Teeth
* Prehinsial Tail
* Body Armor
* Dark Energy Generation
* Long Life
* Healing Factor

Equipment

None

Origin Story

In the realm where evolutionary outliers known as EVOs emerge, Jake Gillyard stands as a formidable beacon of power and otherworldly presence. Once an ordinary human, Jake's latent EVO abilities triggered a profound transformation, morphing his physique into a leviathan of monstrous proportions. Towering at an intimidating eight feet, Jake's body is now encased in thick, scale-like dermal armor, impervious to high-caliber ammunition. His muscular build exudes raw strength capable of superhuman feats. From the sides of his cranium, two robust horns curve outward, a testament to his beastly alter-ego. A pair of vast, bat-like wings fold against his back, suggesting potential for flight. Originally human fingers have been replaced by formidable claws, both in structure and toughness, and his mouth boasts an array of razor-sharp fangs, adding a predatory edge to his visage. Isolated and fearing for his existence amidst the harsh, unforgiving wilds of Alaska's tundra, it was there that the compassionate Professor Allen discovered him. Recognizing Jake's inherent humanity beneath the beast, Allen offered sanctuary, a place among his other extraordinary wards, and ultimately, a family. Struggling with the dichotomy of his nature, Jake endeavors to reconcile his newfound monstrous form with his undying human soul.

Known Allies

EVO Underground
Power X

Known Enemies

The Brotherhood
United States Government

Project CyberCron

Known Skills
_____

Hand to Hand Combat
Demonology
Theology
Areil Combat
Team
_____

Power X

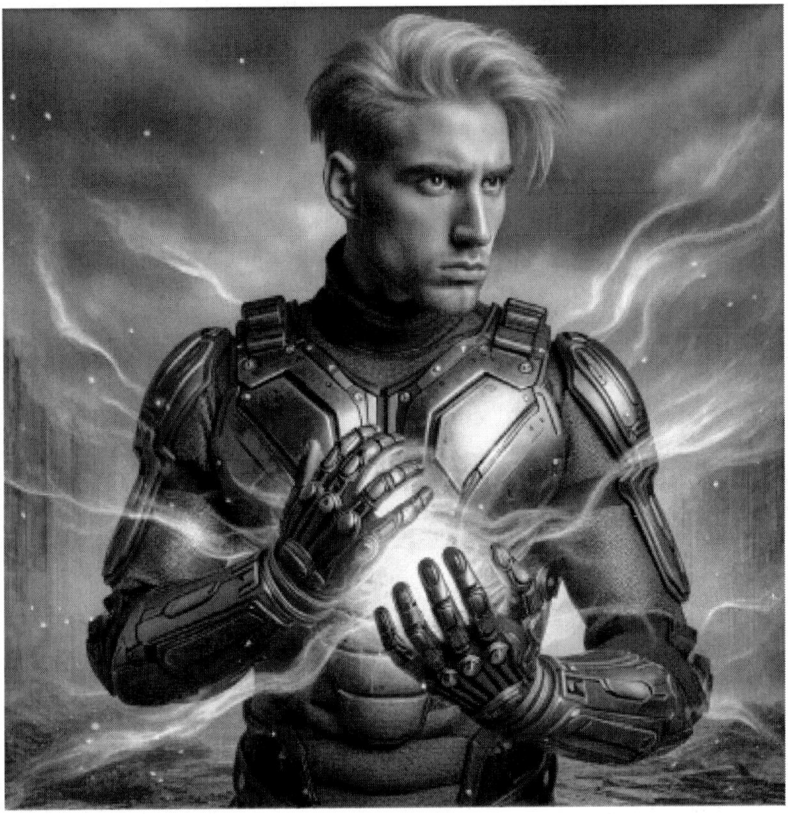

Real Name = Micheal Nova
Code Name = Shield Cutter
Age = 35
Base Of Operations = Secret Labotory In North Carolina

Powers

Omni - Energy Manipulation = All forms of Energy in his surrounding Area
* Energy Spheres
* Force Field
* Flight
* Energy Blasts.

Equipment

Kevlar Body Suit with polymer plate armor

Origin Story

Micheal Nova, also known as 'Shield Cutter,' is a remarkable EVO with the unique ability to manipulate all forms energy. His exceptional control over these energy's grants him the power to create varying types of force fields, each with their own special characteristics tailored to different defensive scenarios. These force fields serve as his primary mode of defense, capable of absorbing and deflecting a multitude of attacks from diverse adversaries. Alongside his defensive capabilities, Micheal can craft specialized containment fields, which are force fields meticulously designed to imprison even the most formidable opponents, tailored to neutralize their particular abilities. Offensively, Micheal has mastered the skill to form concentrated force projectiles, referred to as 'force bubbles,' which he can launch or hurl at his adversaries, causing significant damage upon impact. As for his appearance, Micheal is a striking figure with blonde hair and deep brown eyes that hint at a past filled with intricate stories. His attire consists of a cutting-edge Kevlar bodysuit, tailored for flexibility and impact resistance, over which he dons futuristic plate armor, providing an additional layer of protection while symbolizing his moniker. The ensemble not only serves as his battle gear but also as a representation of his dual role as a protector and a warrior.

Known Allies

EVO Underground
Power X

Known Enemies

The Brotherhood
United States Government
Project CyberCron

Known Skills

Martial Arts

Firearms
Areil Combat
Bladed weapons
Team

Power X

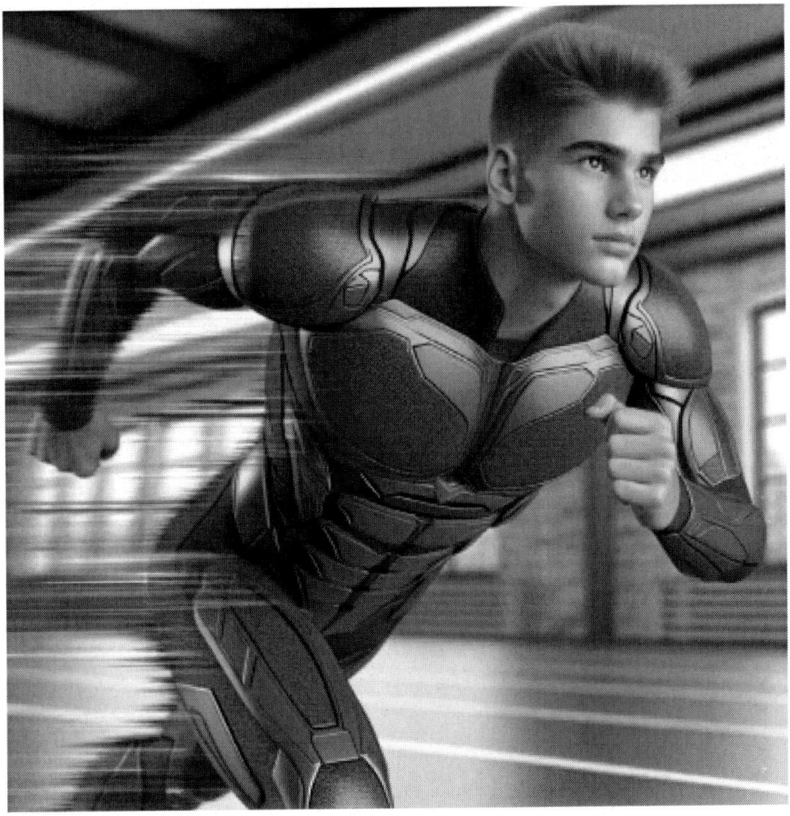

Real Name = Bryson Clark
Code Name = Speedy
Age = 19
Base of Operations = U.S.S. Monitor

Powers

Super Sonic Speed
* Body Armor
* Kinetic Charge
* Phasing
* Sonic Boom
* Hyper Vision
* Hyper thinking

Equipment

Kevlar Body Suit with polymer plate armor

Origin Story

Bryson Clark, known by his code name 'Speedy,' is a dynamic and formidable EVO with the extraordinary ability of super-speed, making him one of the most elusive entities in his world. As a teenager discovering the vast potential and the upper limits of his powers, Bryson was enrolled in an exclusive academy designed for individuals like him, where he not only hones his abilities but also learns how to harness them responsibly. With an average build that belies his exceptional agility and endurance, Bryson has short, tousled blonde hair that seems perpetually windswept, a testament to his swift movement. His suit is a marvel of modern science, combining the resilience of Kevlar with a sophisticated overlay of futuristic plate armor, crafted to minimize resistance and maximize protection. The suit's sleek design complements his rapid motions, making him look like a blur even to the sharpest eyes. An intriguing aspect of Bryson's super-speed is the collateral hyperactive healing factor, allowing him to recover from injuries at an accelerated rate, a boon in his high-risk confrontations. Furthermore, his extreme velocity endows him with a natural resistance to high temperatures, a necessary adaptation to the intense friction he encounters. Despite the spectacular nature of his abilities, Bryson remains grounded, focused on mastering his gifts and understanding the responsibility that comes with such power.

Known Allies

Global Defense Administration
United States Military
Doctor Sarah Sloan

Known Enemies

Freedom Liberation Front
The Brotherhood
The Arian Brotherhood
Hamos

Isis
T.N.T
Nathanial Toll

Known Skills

Martial Arts
Acrobatics
Melee Weapons
Firearms

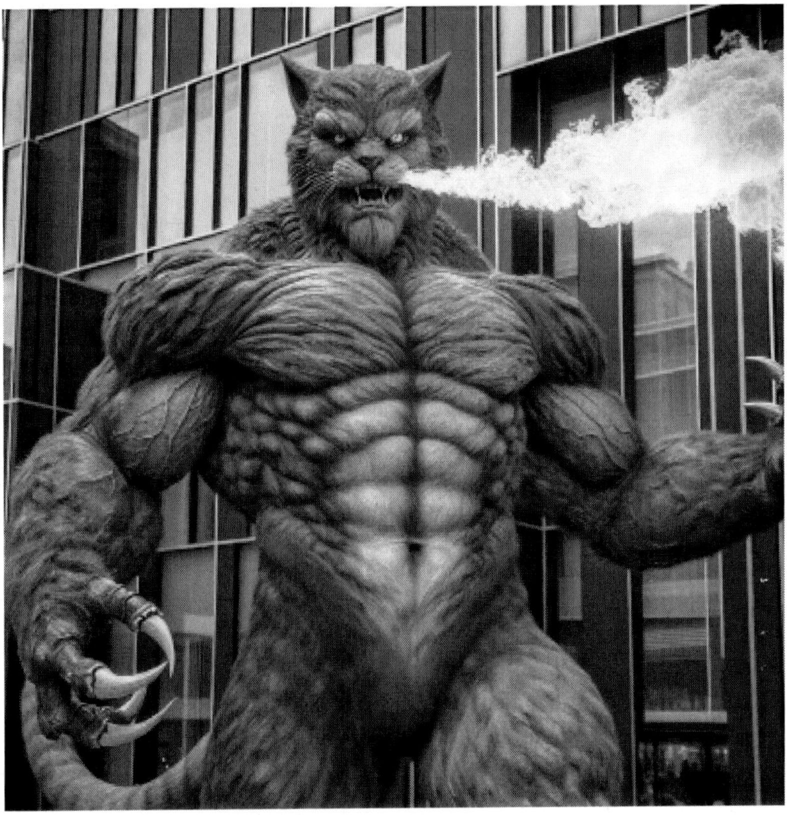

Real Name = Lenix Andrews
Code Name = GORO
Age = 35
Base of Operations = U.S.S. Monitor

Powers

Beast Body
* Super Strength
* Agility
* Fire Breath
* Healing Factor
* Claws
* Teeth
* Body Armor
* Rage = Increases base abilities by five while in a mindless blind rage attacking everyone around him.

Equipment

Kevlar Body suit With Polymer Plate Armor

Origin Story

Lenix Andrews, known as Goro to those who witness his fearsome form, is an evolved being or 'Evo' who has undergone a rare and radical transformation. Unlike his counterparts whose enhancements remain within human norms, Lenix's body has undergone a dramatic mutation, symptomatic of his unique genotype. Standing at a formidable height, he is the embodiment of raw power with a large, muscular build akin to ancient legends of half-beasts. His frame is layered with dark brown fur, each strand thick and coarse, providing him with a primal armor against adversaries and the elements. Notably, Lenix sports four robust arms, each ending in hands equipped with sharp talons capable of rending metal asunder, portraying an almost mythological creature in the vein of a multi-limbed warrior. His evolutionary gifts are not merely superficial; his senses are extraordinarily keen, akin to a predatory feline, allowing him to track and engage with uncanny precision. Despite his monstrous appearance, one of Lenix's most astonishing abilities is his superhuman strength, far surpassing that of an average Evo, capturing the essence of a titanic force of nature. Coupled with this might is a rapid healing factor, enabling him to recover from wounds that would be fatal to ordinary beings with astonishing swiftness. His visage bears feline features; broad nose, sharp cheekbones, and piercing eyes, creating an intense and beastlike countenance. Completing his fearsome presence is his ability to breathe fire, a trait that invokes the awe and dread of dragons from lore, making Lenix a formidable adversary or a powerful ally. He exists at the crossroads of man, beast, and something altogether mythic, forging his legend with every use of his incredible powers.

Known Allies

Global Defense Administration
United States Military
Doctor Sarah Sloan

Known Enemies

Freedom Liberation Front
The Brotherhood
The Arian Brotherhood
Hamos
Isis
T.N.T
Nathanial Toll

Known Skills

Brawling
Martial Arts
Painting

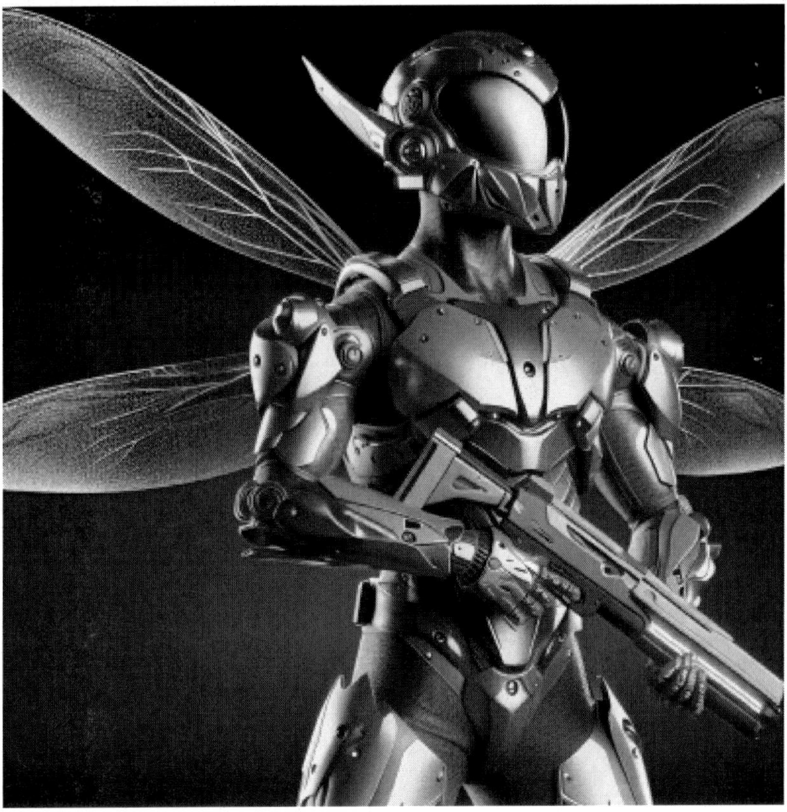

Real Name = Jordan Allen
Code Name = Dragonfly
Age = 40
Base of Operations = Colorado Military base

Powers

None

Equipment

Battle Armor
* Flight
* Body Armor
* Energy Shield
* Advanced visual and audio sensors
* Stinger Blasts
* Blaster Rifle
* Cloaking Device
* Remote Drones
* Enhanced Strength

Origin Story

Jordan Allen is a brilliant inventor, highly skilled in advanced technology and robotics. After years of research and countless sleepless nights, Jordan designed and built a cutting-edge battle armor that boasts the latest in high-tech features. This armor, sleek and agile, was designed not only for combat but for versatility in various challenging environments. The suit, which he named 'Dragonfly' due to its unique, multi-jointed wings that allow for rapid, darting flight similar to the insect, became his greatest achievement. Just weeks after completing the Dragonfly armor, tragedy struck when his wife was mysteriously kidnapped. Fueled by a mixture of fear, love, and determination, Jordan donned his revolutionary armor and took on the moniker 'Dragonfly' to embark on a perilous mission to rescue her. With enhanced strength, speed, and a plethora of advanced gadgetry at his disposal, the Dragonfly becomes a beacon of hope and a force to be reckoned with in his quest to bring his wife back safely.

Known Allies

General Howell
Home guard
United States Military

Known Enemies

Doctor Marrow
Nathanial Toll
Project CyberCron

Known Skills

Robotics
advanced technology
Engineering
Ariel Combat
Firearms

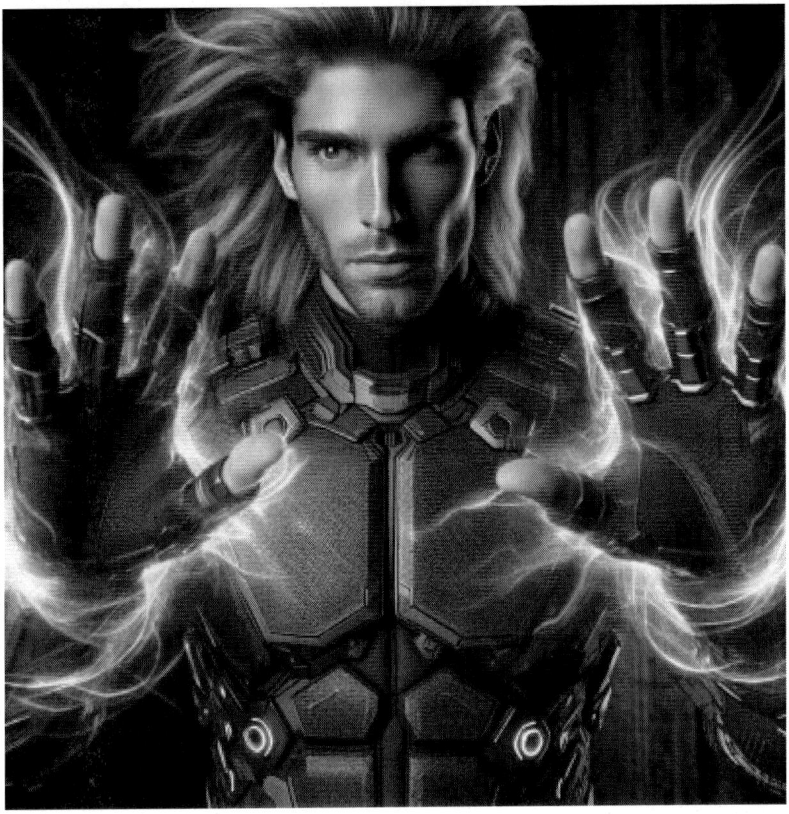

Real Name = Cody Church
Code Name = Blaster
Age 27
Base of Operations = Colorado Military base

Powers

Energy Generation
* Flight
* Energy Blasts
* Force Field

Equipment

Kevlar body suit reinforced with futuristic polymer plate armor

Origin Story

Cody Church, known by his code name Blaster, is an EVO with the extraordinary ability to project powerful energy blasts. Known for his striking appearance, Cody dons a Kevlar body suit reinforced with futuristic polymer plate armor, giving him both a sleek and imposing look. His long sandy blonde hair frames a face with piercing brown eyes that can charm almost any woman. Despite his rugged and formidable exterior, Cody has a charismatic personality that easily draws people to him. His armor is designed to withstand significant impacts, and his energy blasts make him a formidable opponent in any battle.

Known Allies

General Howell
Home guard
United States Military

Known Enemies

Doctor Marrow
Nathanial Toll
Project CyberCron

Skills

Martial Arts
Jungle Warfare
Urban Warfare
Firearms Expert

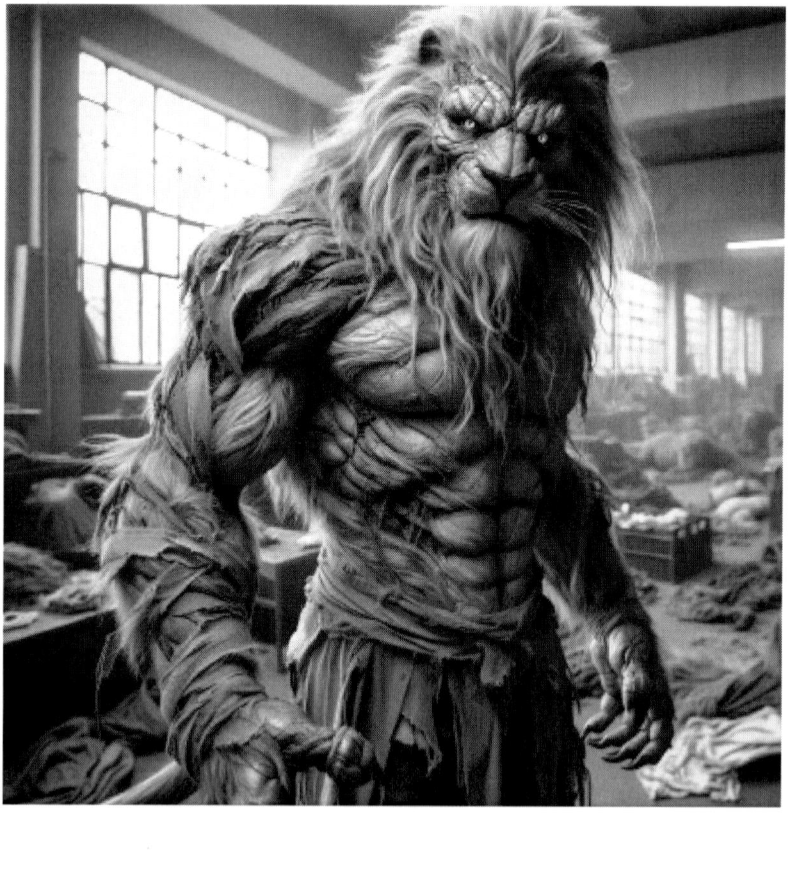

Real Name = Unknown
Code Name = Lionheart
Age = Unknown
Base of operations = Beast Island

Powers

Enhanced Strength
Enhanced Speed
Enhanced Senses
Healing Factor
Claws
Teeth
Probability Manipulation = on himself giving him a good luck aura around himself

Body Armor

Equipment

Sword
Shield

Origin Story

Lion Heart is a human who has had his DNA spliced with that of a lion, mutating him into a half-man, half-lion being. This transformation bestowed upon him the combined physical abilities of both species—a lion's strength, agility, and heightened senses, alongside human intelligence and emotions. Despite his beastly appearance, he retains his human mind and moral compass. The transformation was conducted by the mad scientist Doctor Marrow, who sought to create a new race of super-beings for his own sinister purposes. However, Lion Heart rebelled against Doctor Marrow, using his formidable abilities to free himself and lead his mutated brothers and sisters to freedom. Now, Lion Heart is a symbol of resistance and hope for an oppressed people, striving to protect his newfound family and ensure their liberation from those who seek to exploit them.

Known Allies

Anti- men

Known Enemies

Children Of Marrow
Humans

Known Skills

Brawling
Swordsmanship
History
Chemistry
Leadership
Poetry
Team

Anti- men

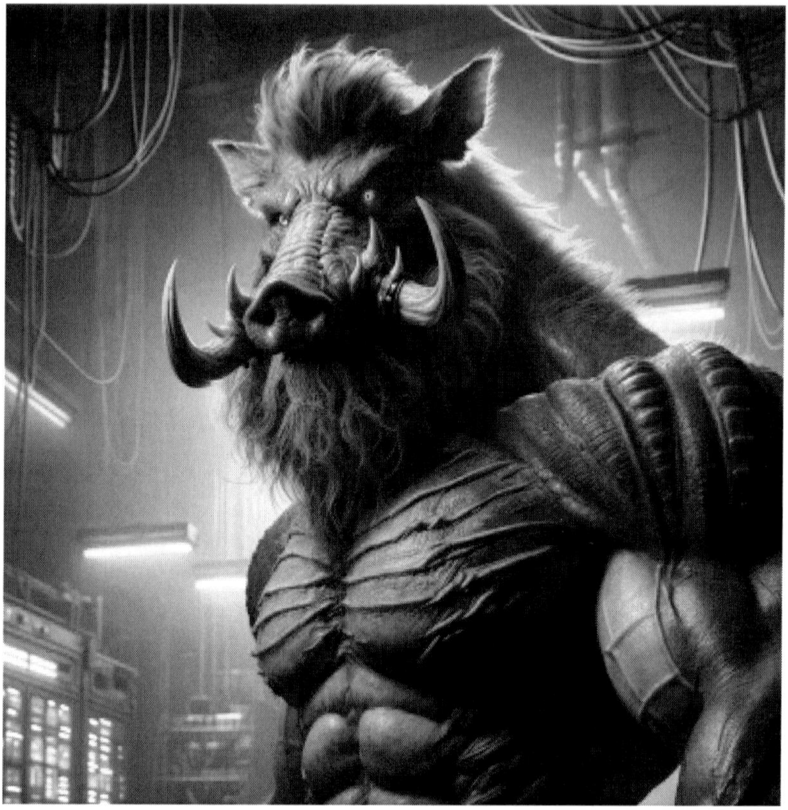

Real Name = Unknown
Code Name = Razorback
Age = Unknown
Base of operations = Beast Island

Powers

Enhanced Senses
Enhanced Strength
Enhanced Agility
Tusks
Healing Factor
Body Armor
Vibration Generation

Equipment

Mace
Sheild

Origin Story

Razorback is one of Doctor Marrow's most notorious experiments. His DNA was spliced with that of a wild boar, mutating him into a half-man, half-wild boar being. Razorback possesses the physical strength and fierce instincts of a wild boar, complemented by his retained human intellect. With tusks protruding from his lower jaw and a robust, bristled hide, Razorback is both formidable and terrifying in appearance. Despite his monstrous transformation, Razorback has a sharp mind and a strong sense of justice. He joined forces with Lion Heart and the rebels to oppose Doctor Marrow, becoming one of the key figures in their fight for freedom.

Known Allies

Anti- men

Known Enemies

Children Of Marrow
Humans

Known Skills

Brawling
Blunt Weapons

Team

Anti- men

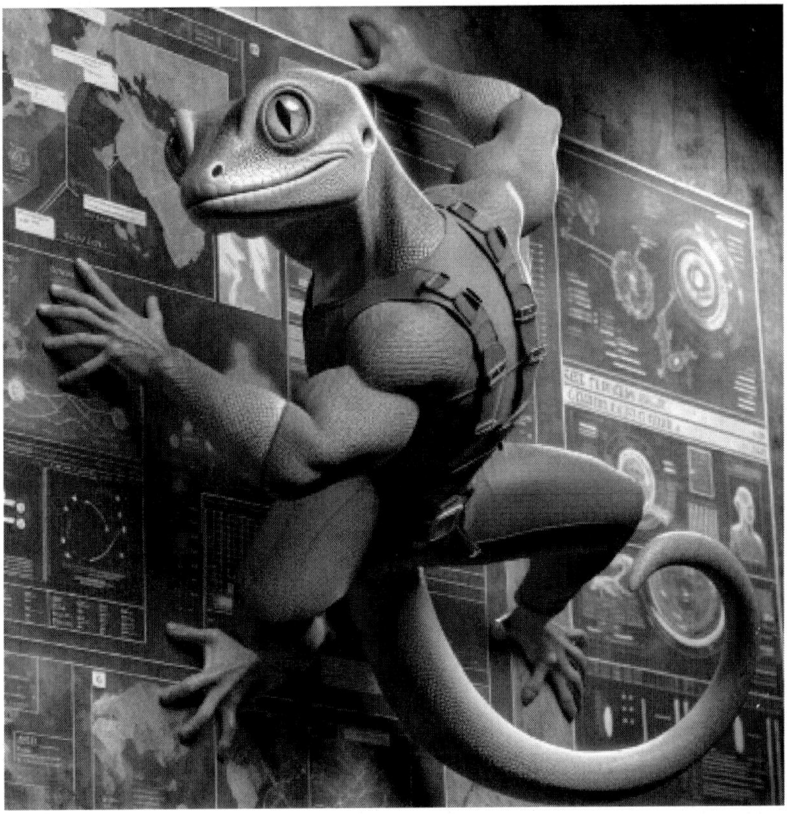

Real Name = Unknown
Code Name = Gecko
Age = Unknown
Base of operations = Beast Island

Powers

Wall Crawling
Camouflage
Regeneration
Exstendable sticky tongue
Enhanced eyesight
Danger sense
Body Armor
Prehensile tail

Equipment

Kevlar Body Suit

Utility Harness
* Lock picks
* Electronic Scrambling Device
* Minicomputer
* Smoke bombs
* hand gun

Origin Story

Gecko is a unique figure within the world marked by Doctor Marrow's grim experiments. Once an ordinary human, Gecko was transformed through the sinister melding of human DNA with that of a gecko by the notorious Doctor Marrow. The transformation left him as a half-man, half-gecko hybrid, boasting the remarkable abilities of both creatures. This intriguing combination bestowed Gecko with exceptional climbing skills, the ability to regenerate lost limbs, and a near-camouflage ability that allows him to blend seamlessly into his surroundings. Despite his altered appearance, Gecko retained his human intellect and emotions. Motivated by a strong sense of justice and a burning desire for revenge against the man who mutated him, Gecko allied himself with Lion Heart, a group dedicated to toppling Doctor Marrow's reign of terror.

Known Allies

Anti- men

Known Enemies

Children Of Marrow
Humans

Known Skills

Lock Picking
Hacking
Computer Programming
Martial Arts

Team

Anti- men

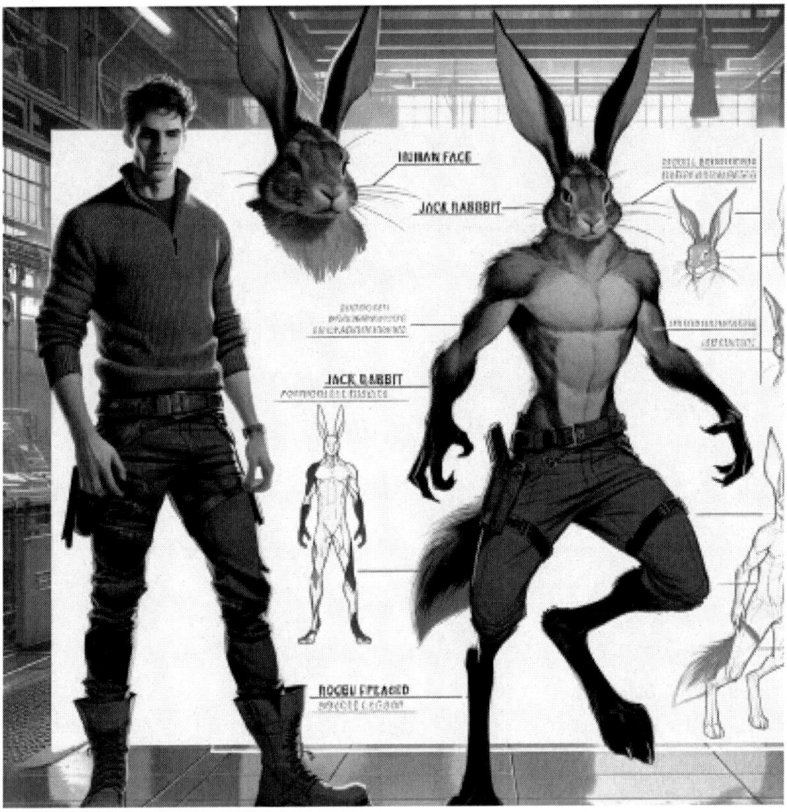
JACK RABBIT
JACK RABBIT

Real Name = Unknown
Code Name = Jack Rabbit
Age = Unknown
Base of operations = Beast Island

Powers

Enhanced Agility
Enhanced Strength
Healing Factor
Enhanced Senses
Danger Sense
Photographic Reflexes

Equipment

Kevlar body suit with polymer plate armor
Katana
Handguns
Throwing Stars

Origin Story

Jack Rabbit is a unique character who embodies a blend of human intelligence and the agile instincts of a jack rabbit.

Once an ordinary man, his fate took an extraordinary twist when Doctor Marrow, a scientist with questionable ethics, spliced his DNA with that of a jack rabbit. This mutation granted him unparalleled speed and agility, enabling feats such as leaping extraordinary heights, rapid reflexes, and heightened senses. Despite his transformed physical appearance, which includes long ears, powerful legs, and a lean, muscled frame, Jack Rabbit retains his human mind and soul. Choosing to harness his newfound abilities for a greater cause, he joined Lion Heart, a coalition of rebels fighting against Doctor Marrow's tyrannical experiments and oppressive regime. Jack Rabbit's dual nature serves as both a literal and symbolic reflection of his struggle to retain his humanity in an altered body.

Known Allies

Anti- men

Known Enemies

Children Of Marrow
Humans

Known Skills

Martial Arts
Throwing
Acrobatics
Marksmanship
Swordsmanship
Team

Anti- men

Real Name = Talen Warclaw
Code Name = Talen Warclaw
Age = 40
Base of Operations = Nomadic

Powers

Superhuman Strength
Invulnerability

Equipment

Sword

* Unbreakable
* Macic Damage
* Can damage Magical Beings
* Teleportation

Origin Story

Talen Warclaw is a towering barbarian warrior who was unexpectedly transported from an ancient realm into the modern world after a climactic battle with a malevolent wizard. During the intense combat, Talen absorbed a colossal surge of magical energy that transformed him into a superhuman being. His newfound strength surpasses all known limits, and his body has become entirely invulnerable to damage. This magical alteration also rendered his mighty sword indestructible. Standing at an impressive height with a large, muscular build and long, flowing black hair, Talen embodies both ferocity and resilience. As he navigates the complexities of the modern world, his primal instincts and extraordinary powers make him both a formidable ally and a daunting adversary.

Known Allies

None

Known Enemies

All Magic Users

Known Skills

Brawling

Swordsmanship
Wrestling
Blunt Weapons

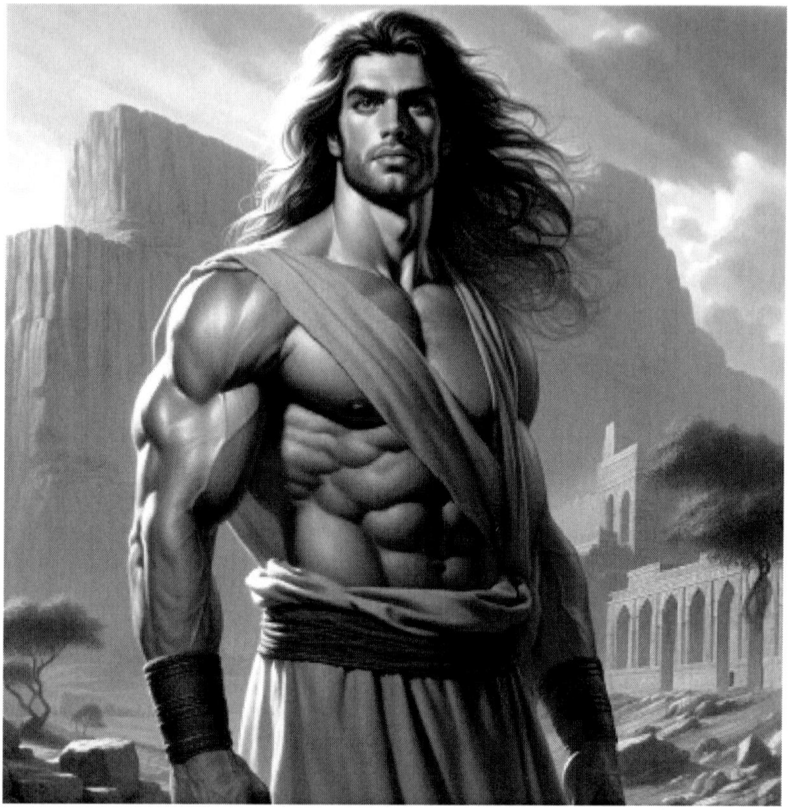

Real Name = Samson
Code Name = Samson
Age = 2000
Base of operations = Mobile

Powers

Faith
* Superhuman Strength
* Invulnerability

Equipment

Club

Origin Story

Samson is known as the Biblical hero endowed with unmatched physical strength. He is a towering figure, often depicted with long, flowing hair which is the source of his strength according to legend. Despite his formidable power, Samson's story is also one of vulnerability and tragedy, as his strength is linked to his hair and his downfall comes at the hands of those who betray him. He represents both the height of human potential and the depths of human weakness. In physical appearance, Samson is typically portrayed with muscular build, fierce yet compassionate eyes, and a mane of thick hair. His attire is often simple, reflecting his humble origins.

Known Allies

Unknown

Known Enemies

Philistines
Demons

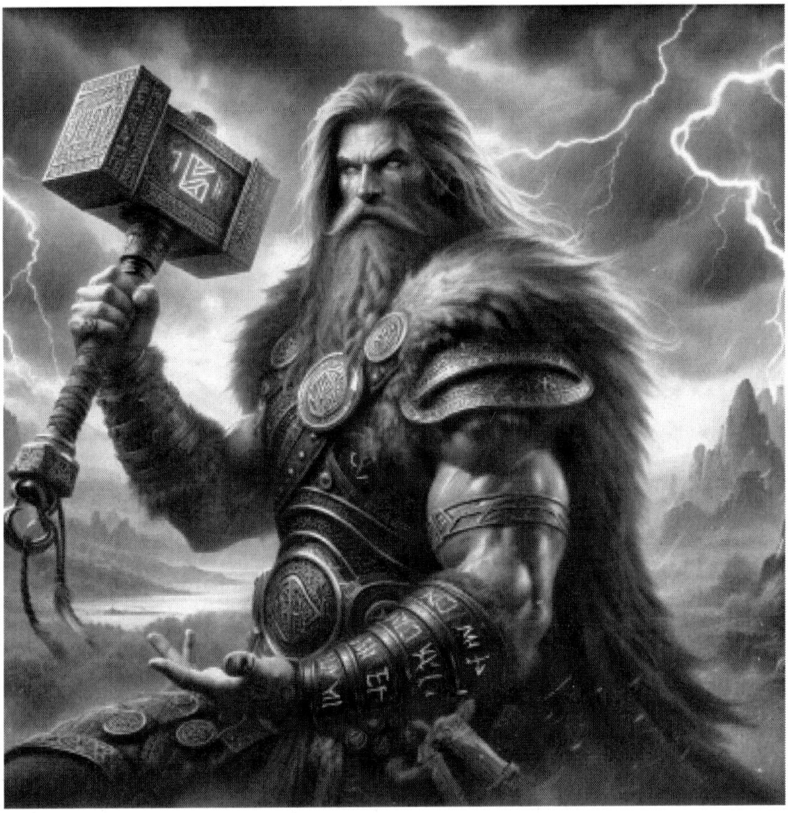

Real Name = Thor Odinson
Code Name = Thor God of Thunder
Age = 2500
Base of operations = Mid guard

Powers

Superhuman Strength
Superhuman Endurance
Invulnerability
Flight
Lightening Generation

Equipment

Asgardian Armor
Mjölnir = Magic Hammar

Origin Story

Thor, the mighty Norse God of Thunder, is known for his immense strength, bravery, and fierce loyalty. Wielding the enchanted hammer Mjölnir, Thor commands lightning and storms, capable of summoning thunder and devastating foes with a single strike. His physical presence is imposing—a towering figure with a muscular build, adorned in traditional Asgardian armor etched with ancient runes. Long, flowing blonde hair and a thick beard frame his noble face, while his piercing blue eyes radiate both kindness and a warrior's fury. Though often seen battling giants and mythical creatures, Thor is also a protector of mankind, revered not just for his power, but for his compassionate heart and indomitable spirit.

Known Allies

Norse Pantheon

Known Enemies

Frost Giants
Dark Elves
All other Pantheons

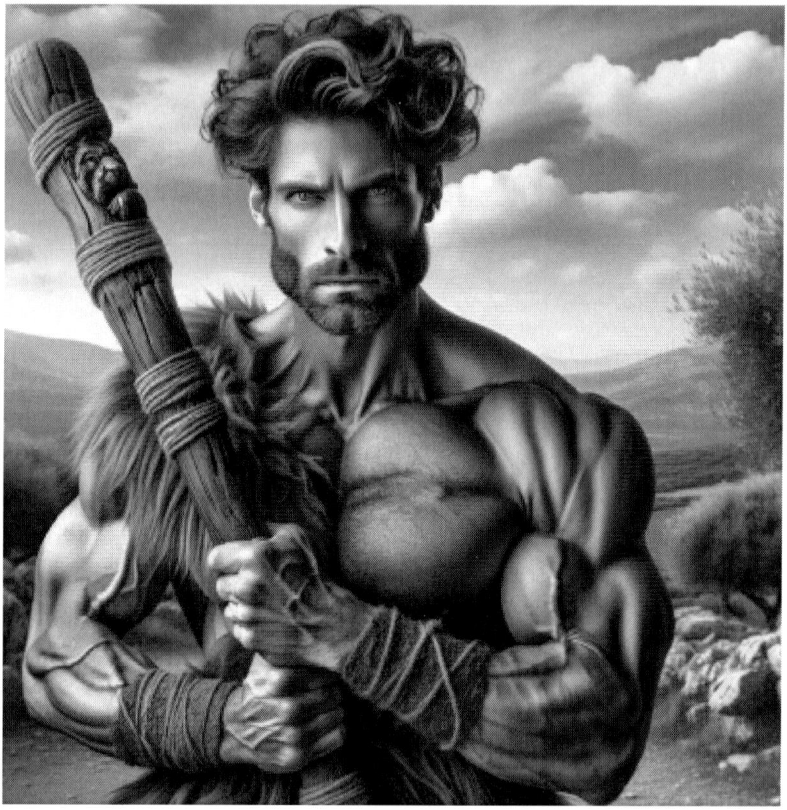

Real Name = Hercules Son of Zeus
Code Name = Hercules Son of Zeus
Age = 1500
Base of operations = Mobile

Powers

Superhuman Strength
Invulnerability
Superhuman Endurance

Equipment

Magical Mace
Magical Lion Skin Armor

Origin Story

Hercules, also known as Heracles, is one of the most renowned heroes in Greek mythology. The son of Zeus and the mortal woman Alcmene, Hercules is famed for his incredible strength, bravery, and numerous far-reaching adventures. Favored by the gods, he is often depicted wielding a club and wearing a lion's skin. Hercules' legend is marked by his completion of the Twelve Labors, a series of extremely difficult tasks assigned to him as a form of penance. Throughout his life, Hercules epitomizes the virtues of courage, endurance, and resilience. Despite facing numerous trials and tribulations, including acts of betrayal and divine spite, he achieves a heroic status that makes him immortal in myth. Often portrayed as a tall, muscular man with a rugged appearance, Hercules embodies the archetypal warrior whose story is filled with themes of redemption, the triumph of good over evil, and the complexities of divine-mortal relationships.

Known Allies

Greek Pantheon

Known Enemies

All other Pantheons

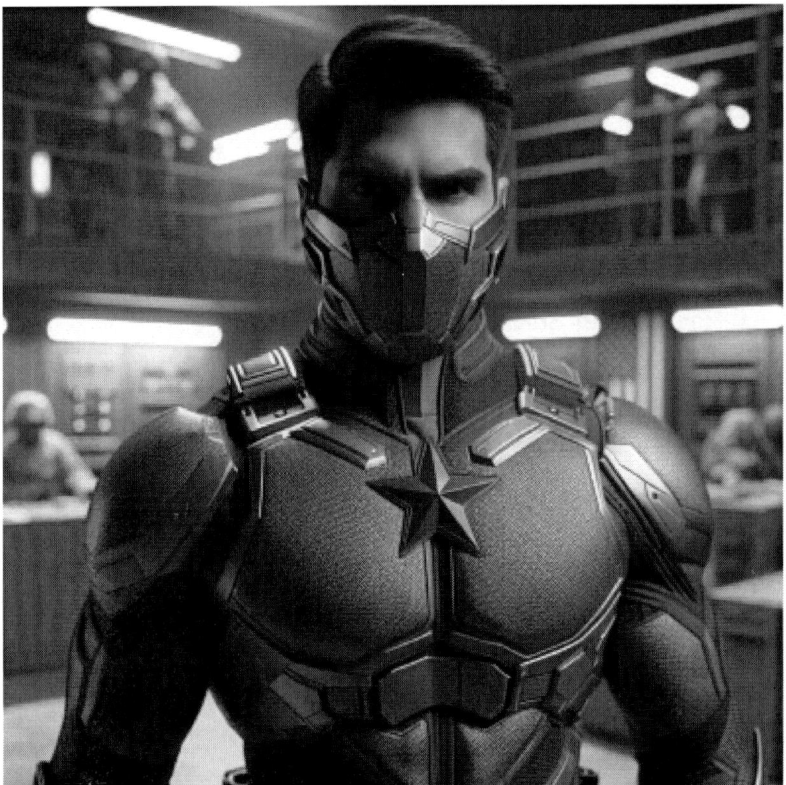

Real Name = Ivan Steranko
Code Name = Mind Swipe
Age = 35
Base of operation = Mobile Base

Powers

Telepathy
* Read the minds of others
* Psychic Attack

Telekinesis
* Lift or Move Objects with mind

* **Force Field**
* **Flight**

Origin Story

Ivan Steranko is a formidable character in the pantheon of Russian superheroes. Born in Russia, he is an EVO with powerful abilities in telepathy and telekinesis. His exceptional skills drew the attention of the October Group, a secretive and elite branch of the former KGB, which recruits him into the Red Guard. The Red Guard is Russia's foremost response team against the emergence of enhanced individuals and EVOS. Ivan's loyalty to the Russian government is steadfast and unquestionable. He is equipped with a Kevlar body suit reinforced with futuristic polymer plate armor. The armor, designed for both protection and combat efficiency, features a face mask that covers his nose and mouth, and prominently displays the red Russian star on its breastplate, symbolizing his allegiance and the might of his homeland.

Equipment

Kevlar Body suit with Futuristic polymer plate armor
Varity of Firearms
Sword
Throwing Knives

Known Allies

Russian Military
Red Guard

Known Enemies

United States Military
Home Guard

Known Skills

Martial Arts
Weapons Expert
Swordsmanship
Jungle Warfare
Urban Warfare
Military Tactics
Leadership
Team

Red Guard

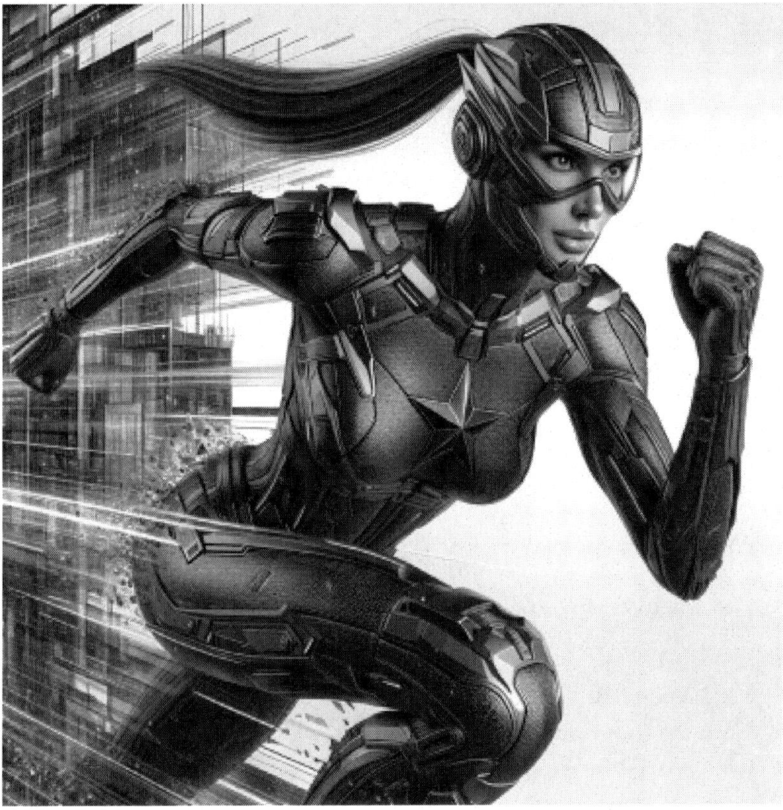

Real Name = Mira Malkovich
Code Name = Swift Wind
Age = 30
Base of operations = Mobile Base

Equipment

Kevlar Body Suit with futuristic polymer plate armor

Powers

Super Sonic Speed
* Body Armor
* Kinetic Charge
* Phasing
* Sonic Boom
* Hyper Vision
* Hyper thinking

Origin Story

Mira Malkovich, a character hailing from Russia, is a formidable EVO gifted with super speed. Recruited by the Red Guard, she plays a critical role in the First Response team, facing off against other Enhanced People and EVOs. Mira's attire includes a sleek Kevlar bodysuit reinforced with futuristic polymer plate armor. Her uniform proudly displays the red Russian star insignia, symbolizing her allegiance to her homeland.

Known Allies

Russian Military
Red Guard

Known Enemies

United States Military
Home Guard

Known Skills

Martial Arts
Acrobatics
Firearms

Team

Red Guard

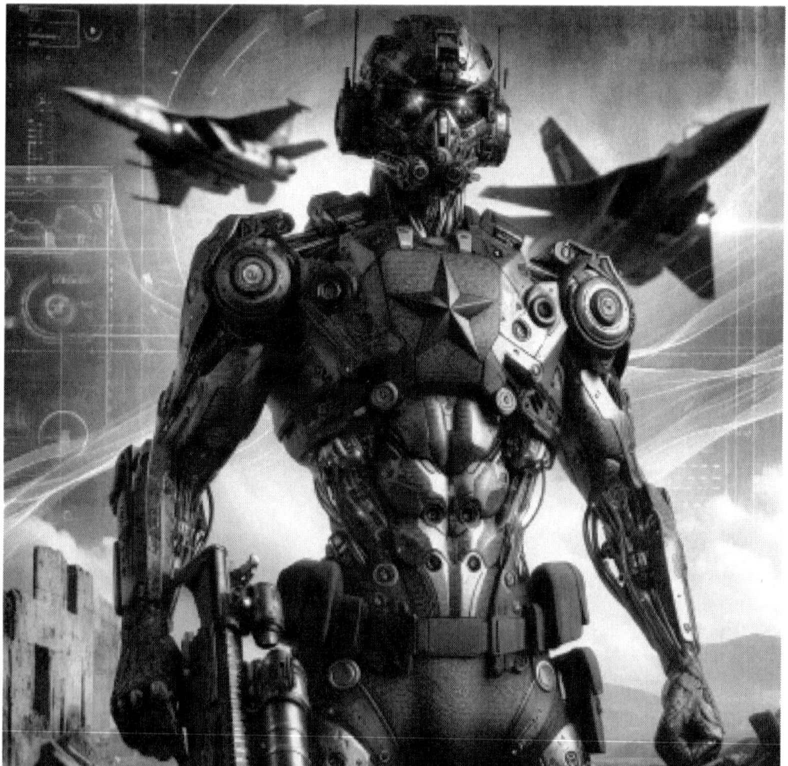

Real Name = Yuri Kanishika
Code Name = Red One
Age = 45
Base of operations = Mobile Base

Equipment

Blasters
Grenades
Sword
Two military rifles
Two Side Arms

Force Field
Enhanced Visual and Audio Sensors
Body Armor
Camouflage

Powers

Cyborg Body
* Enhanced Strength
* Enhanced Speed
* Enhanced Durability
* Enhanced Endurance

Origin Story

Yuri Kanishika is a former Russian Special Forces Officer who was grievously wounded in the Ukrainian war. To save his life, the Russian government employed experimental cybernetic technology, turning him into a formidable cyborg. These cybernetic enhancements endowed Yuri with enhanced strength, advanced visual and audio implants, and internal weaponry such as forearm blasters, sonic emitters, and an energy force field. He dons a Kevlar bodysuit reinforced with futuristic polymer plate armor, proudly bearing the red Russian star insignia on his uniform.

Known Allies

Russian Military
Red Guard

Known Enemies

United States Military
Home Guard

Known Skills

Martial Arts
Marksmanship
Jungle Warfare
Urban Warfare
Counter insurgency
Counter Terrorism

Team

Red Guard

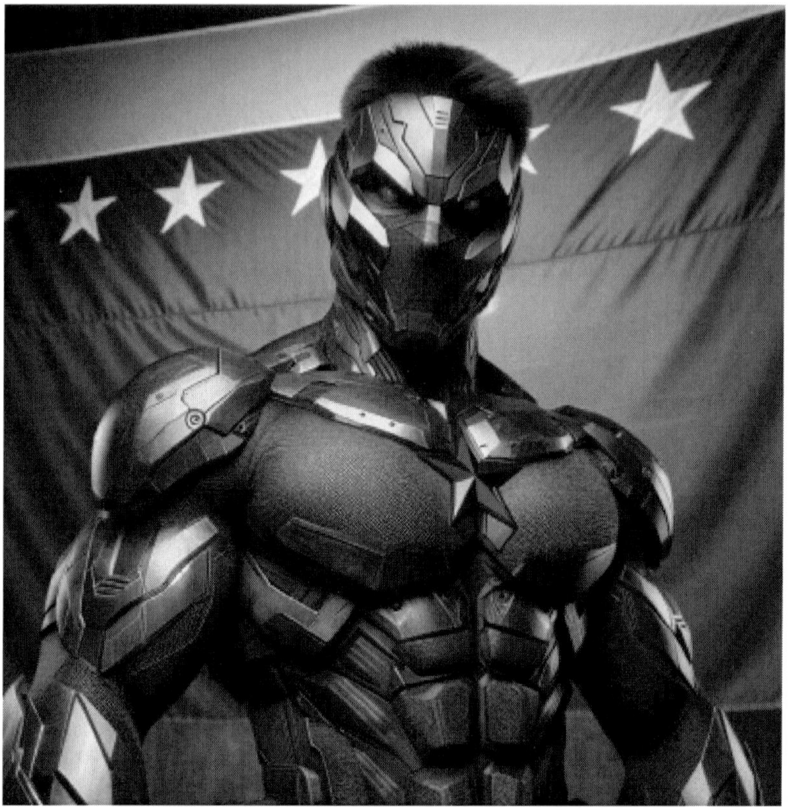

Real Name = Mikiel Gorbacheva
Code Name = Siberian Guardsman
Age = 27
Base of operations = Mobile Base

Equipment

Kevlar body suit with futuristic polymer plate Armor
Two Experimental Laser Blaster Rifles
Energy Sword
Grenades
Combat Knife
Mask
* High tech Visual and audio sensors
* Filtration System

Powers

Superhuman Strength
Natural Body Armor
Enhanced Reflexes
Healing Factor

Origin Story

Mikiel Gorbacheva is a Russian-born EVO with the abilities of Superhuman Strength, Natural Body Armor, Enhanced Reflexes, and a Healing Factor. He was recruited by the Red Guard to be part of the first line of defense against the rise of enhanced people and EVOs. Mikiel wears a Kevlar body suit with futuristic polymer plate armor, which proudly displays the red Russian star insignia on his uniform. His imposing figure and unwavering dedication make him a formidable force in the ranks of the Red Guard.

Known Allies

Russian Military
Red Guard

Known Enemies

United States Military
Home Guard

Known Skills

Martial Arts
Military Tactics
Jungle Warfare
Urban Warfare
Counter Terrorism
Counter Insurgency
Firearms
Marksmanship
Edged Weapons
Team

Red Guard

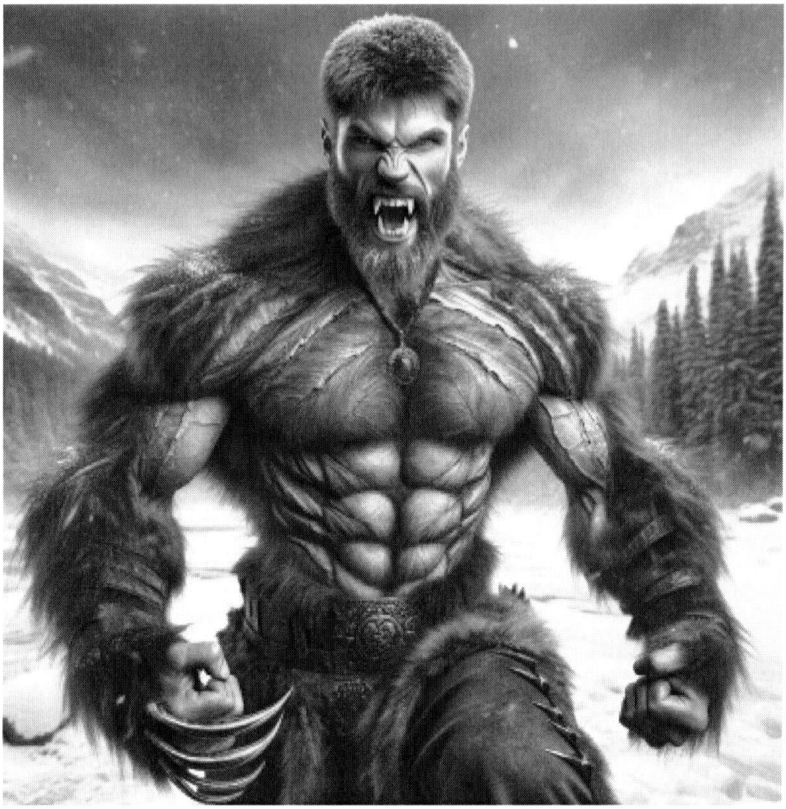

Real Name = Nikolia Rostov
Code Name = Bear
Age = 35
Base of operations = Mobile Base

Equipment

Kevlar Body Suit with futuristic polymer plate armor

Powers

Body Transformation
* Claws
* Teeth
* Regeneration
* Body Armor
* Enhanced Strength
* Enhanced Reflexes
* Enhanced Senses

Origin Story

Nikolia Rostov, a character of Russian descent, is an EVO endowed with the incredible ability to transform into a were-bear. This transformation grants him a suite of impressive powers: Enhanced Strength, Enhanced Endurance, Healing Factor, Claws, Teeth, and Natural Body Armor. Born and raised in the snow-covered landscapes of Siberia, Nikolia's life took a dramatic turn when he discovered his abilities. Displaying extraordinary strength and resilience only natural to the most fearsome bears, he quickly caught the attention of Red Guard. The Red Guard, Russia's elite force assembled to combat the growing threats posed by enhanced individuals and EVOS (extraterrestrial-variant origin species), saw Nikolia as an invaluable asset. His brute force and protective instincts are critical on the front lines, where he works tirelessly to maintain the balance of power and protect his homeland. Despite the ferocity of his bear form, Nikolia is known among his comrades for his unwavering loyalty and deep sense of justice, making him not just a formidable warrior but also a deeply respected member of the Red Guard.

Known Allies

Russian Military
Red Guard

Known Enemies

United States Military
Home Guard

Known Skills

Special Operations
Martial Arts
Military Tactic
Firearms

Mechanic
Military Vehicle Operation
Team

Red Guard

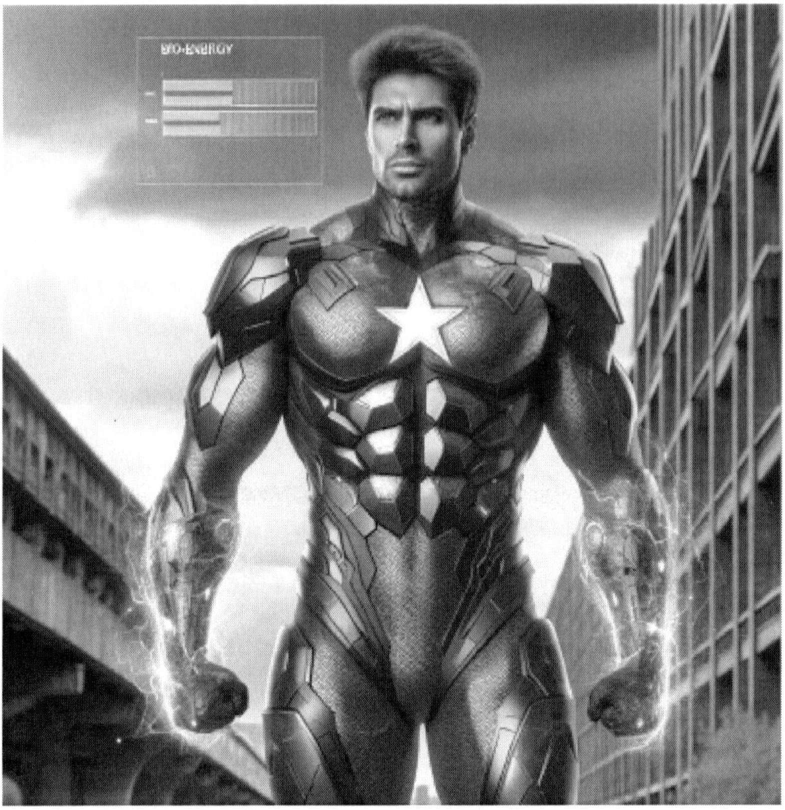
BIO-ENERGY

Real Name = Vladimir Chenkov
Code Name = Bio-Star
Age = 37
Base of operations = Mobile Base

Equipment

Kevlar Body suit with futuristic Polymer plate Armor

Powers

Bioenergy Generation and Manipulation
* Energy Projection
* Force Field
* Flight

Origin Story

Vladimir 'Bio-Star' Chenkov is a Russian-born EVO with the extraordinary ability to generate and manipulate Bio-Energy from his surroundings. Chenkov was recruited by the Soviet Red Guard to serve as the first line of defense against the rise of enhanced people and other EVOS. He wears a high-tech Kevlar bodysuit reinforced with futuristic polymer plate armor, proudly displaying the red star insignia on his uniform.

His strategic mind and unparalleled control over Bio-Energy make him an invaluable asset to his team and a formidable adversary.

Known Allies

Russian Military
Red Guard

Known Enemies

United States Military
Home Guard

Known Skills

Martial Arts
Military Tactics
Firearms
Bladed Weapons
Explosive Expert

Team

Red Guard

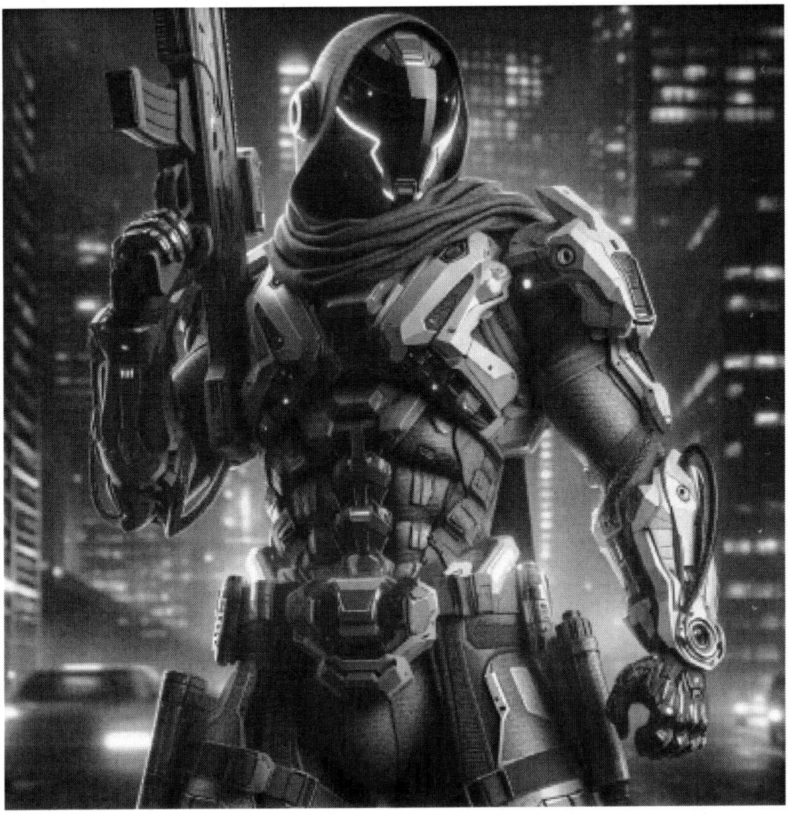

Real Name = Samual Klutch
Code Name = Tech-Na
Age = 21
Base of operation = Chicago IL.

Powers

None

Equipment

Exo- Battle Armor
* Body Armor
* Anti- gravity Belt
 * Enhanced Strength
* Force Field
* Wrist Blasters

* Cloaking
* High Tech Visual and Audio Sensors
Blaster Rifle
Energy Sword

Origin Story

Samual Klutch, also known as Tech-Na, is an individual with genius-level intelligence who developed an extraordinary exo suit. During his college years, he created the exo suit as a project to assist those suffering from paralysis. His professor and mentor recognized his talent and urged him to refine his invention. Tragedy struck when his professor was killed in an armed robbery, prompting Samual to modify his exo suit for combat. Driven by a thirst for justice, he tracked down the assailant and brought them to justice. This pivotal moment inspired him to don the name Tech-Na and become a superhero, dedicated to protecting his city. Tech-Na's exo suit envelops his entire body and is equipped with high-tech visual and audio sensors in the helmet, a force field generator, an anti-gravity belt, wrist blasters, a laser rifle, and a light saber. His futuristic battle armor strikes terror into the hearts of his enemies, making him a formidable force for good.

Known Allies

None

Known Enemies

None

Known Skills

Robotics
Electronics Engineering
Marksmanship
Swordsmanship
Martial Arts
Physics

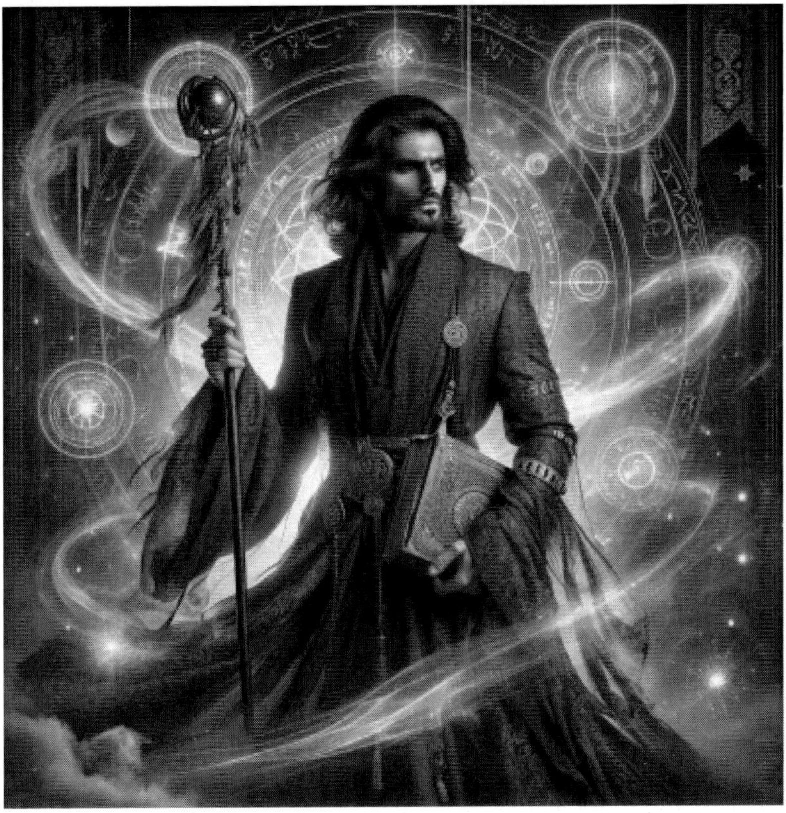

Real Name = Vos
Code Name = Magic Man
Age = Unknown
Base Of Operations = U.S.S. Monitor

Powers

Magic Manipulation
* Ice Constructs
* Flight
* Healing
* Water Breathing
* Life Tap
* Summon Companion
* Fire Ball
* Flesh to Stone

Companion = Earth Elemental
* Enhanced Strength
* Body Armor
* Root

Companion = Air Elemental
* Gust Of Wind
* Tornado Blast

Companion = Ice Elemental

* Ice Shards
* Ice Constructs
Companion = Fire Elemental
* Fire Ball
* Fire Blast

Equipment

Magic Necklace = Teleportation
Magic Wand = Magic Blast
Gem Of the Arcane = Traps souls of opponents

Origin Story

Vos is a powerful sorcerer deeply immersed in the mystic arts, having dedicated most of his life to their study. As a prominent member of the Circle of Light—a distinguished assembly of mystics committed to safeguarding the human plane from otherworldly and mystical threats—Vos plays a crucial role in the protection of reality itself. He is often seen clad in an enchanted robe, which provides both defense and amplification for his spells. With long, flowing black hair that symbolizes his mysterious and venerable nature, Vos wields a variety of magical items. Among these artifacts, his most potent is the Book of Spells, an ancient tome brimming with arcane knowledge and incantations. To channel his formidable magical abilities, Vos carries a staff imbued with his personal power, making him a formidable adversary to any who threaten the Circle's mission.

Known Allies

Spartan

Speedy
Goro
United States Government

Known Enemies

Morpheus

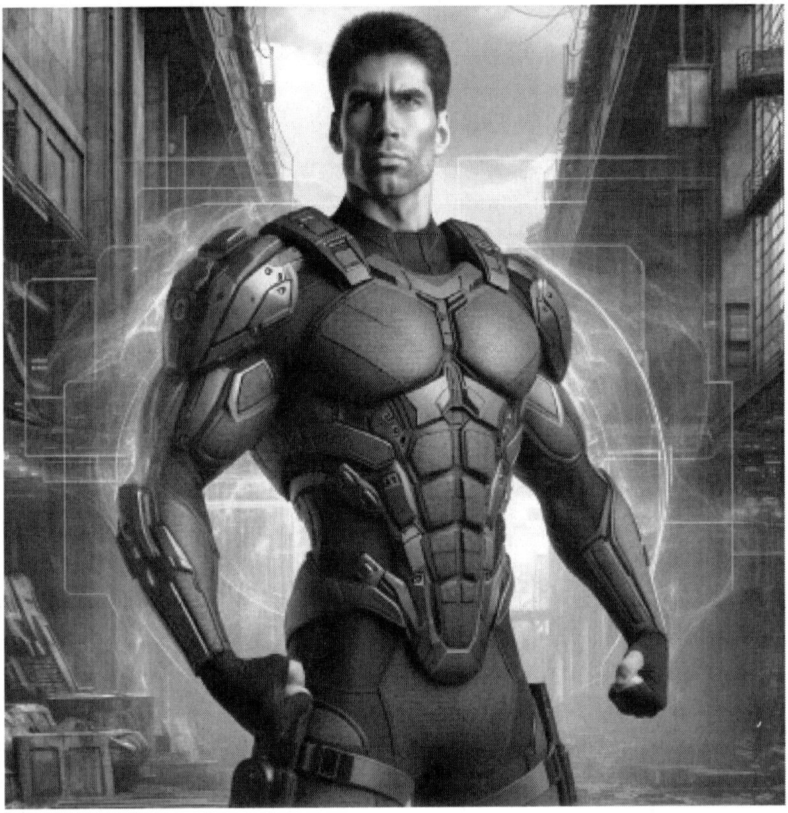

Real Name = Paul Masters
Code Name = Guardian
Age = 35
Base of operations = Mobile

Powers

Transformation
* Can transform into a Were- version of any animal

Equipment

Kevlar Body Suit with polymer plate armor

Origin Story

Paul Masters, also known as Guardian, is an Evo with a rare and powerful ability. He can transform his body into a were-form of any animal he has had contact with, gaining the extraordinary abilities of that animal while retaining his human mind. This unique power makes him a formidable ally and a fearsome foe. Captured by the relentless EVO hunting robots known as Cyber Crons, Paul was imprisoned and subjected to harsh conditions. However, his fate changed when he was rescued by Hunter White, widely known as The Dark Night.

Grateful for his freedom and driven by a sense of justice, Paul vowed to protect Evos everywhere and combat the Cyber Crons. Paul cuts an imposing figure with his short black hair and piercing blue eyes. When going into battle, he dons a Kevlar body suit reinforced with polymer plate armor, ensuring he is both agile and well-protected. His appearance exudes a mix of humanity and latent ferocity, ready to unleash his transformative abilities at a moment's notice to defend his kind.

Known Allies

Dark Night
Power X

Known Enemies

United States Government
Project Cyber- Cron

Known Skills

Martial Arts
Tactics
Firearms
Zoology

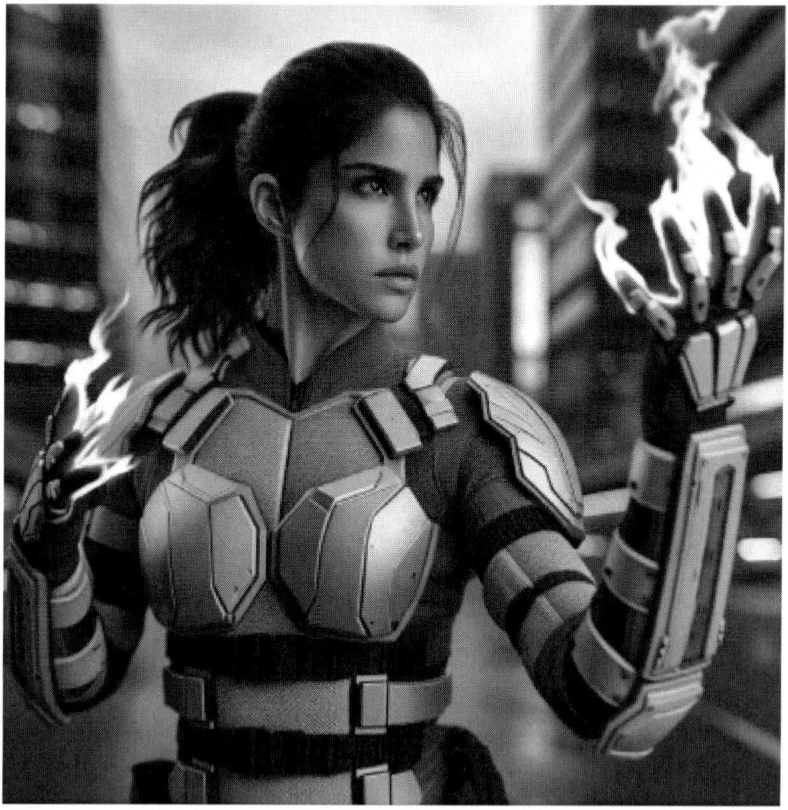

Real Name = Kelly Powers
Code Name = Pink Wonder
Age = 20
Base of Operations = Mobile

Powers

Super speed
* Body Armor
* Kinetic Charge
* Phasing
* Sonic Boom
* Hyper Vision
* Hyper thinking
Wall Crawling
Friction Absorption / Redirection

Equipment

Kevlar Body suit with Polymer plate armor

Origin Story

Kelly Powers is the daughter of a brilliant geneticist who changed her life forever. At the age of 10, Kelly was involved in a devastating automobile accident that left her on the brink of death. Desperate to save her, her father injected her with an experimental serum he had been developing for the United States Government. The serum not only healed Kelly's wounds but also endowed her with extraordinary abilities. Kelly discovered she could move at superhuman speeds, her hands could adhere to any surface allowing her to wall crawl, and she could generate and control fire. To protect her, her father concealed her newfound powers from the government. A decade later, when Kelly was 20 years old, a rival government agency targeted her father, determined to steal the serum he had created. In the ensuing conflict, her father was tragically killed. Vowing revenge, Kelly donned a Kevlar bodysuit with polymer plate armor her father had crafted for her protection. She painted the suit a striking pink and assumed the identity of 'Pink Wonder'. With a burning determination, she embarked on a mission to hunt down and bring her father's killers to justice. As Pink Wonder, Kelly is a fierce and relentless vigilante, wielding her superhuman speed, wall-crawling abilities, and fiery powers to right wrongs and uncover conspiracies.

Known Allies

Dark Night
Guardian

Known Enemies

Raven Group

Known Skills

Martial Arts
Genetics
Medicine
Biology

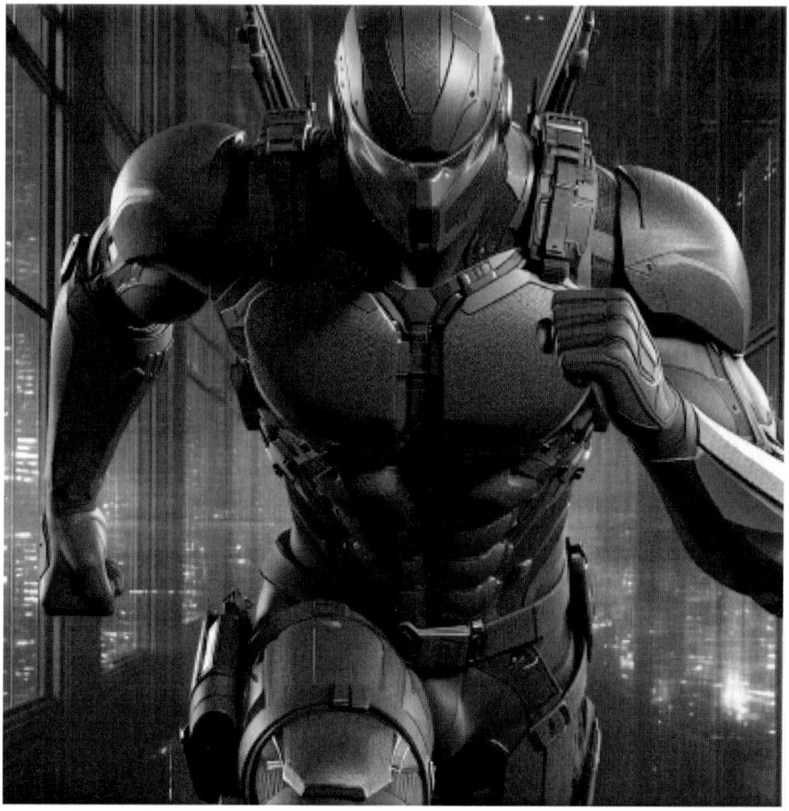

Real Name = Mathew Nelson
Code Name = Blue Dart
Age = 35
Base Of Operations = Mobile

Powers

None

Equipment

Battle Suit
* Body Armor
* Camouflage
* Enhanced Strength
* High tech Visual and Audio sensors
Gauntlets
* Electro charge
* Dart Launchers
Dart Gun
Darts
* Ice Darts
* Stun Darts
* Explosive Darts
* Gas Darts

* Sonic Darts
* Glue Darts
* Surveillance Darts
Fighting Sticks
* Electric Charge

Origin Story

Mathew Nelson is the formidable CEO of Nelson Security Firm, specializing in providing top-tier protection to high-profile companies and individuals. He is acutely aware of the growing menace within the 'super villain' community. The brutal murder of one of his clients by the notorious Assassins Guild galvanized him into action, driving him to conduct extensive research on the organization and identify its perilous potential. Mathew threw himself into rigorous training, significantly boosting his physical strength through weightlifting and mastering various martial arts. Leveraging his considerable wealth, he orchestrated the creation of a bespoke battle suit fabricated from an experimental material ten times more resilient than Kevlar and polymer plate armor both lighter than plastic and as durable as steel. Determined to combat the Assassins Guild, he donned his battle suit, which he painted blue, and adopted the moniker 'Blue Dart.' His helmet is outfitted with cutting-edge visual and audio sensors, transforming him into a high-tech vigilante on a personal crusade against the shadowy guild.

Known Allies

Dark Night
Pink Wonder
Guardian

Known Enemies

Assassins Guild

Known Skills

Martial Arts
Stick Fighting
Marksmanship
Explosives
Chemistry
Electronics
Security
Law Enforcement

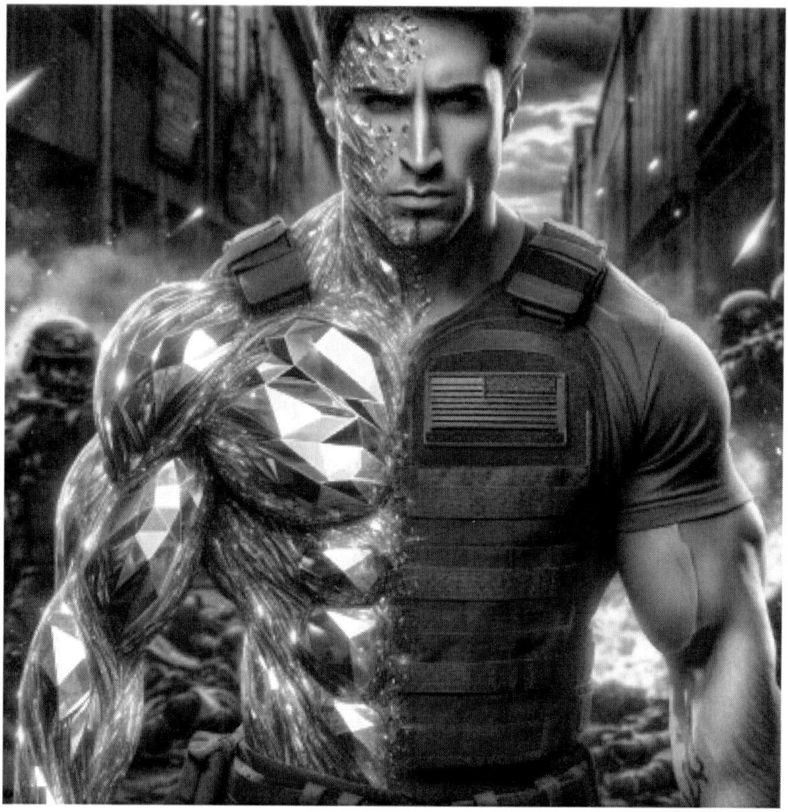

Real Name = Craig McCarthy
Code Name = Diamond Head
Age = 27
Base of operations = Mobile

Powers

Diamond form
* Durability
* Superhuman Strength
* Light / Energy Reflection

Equipment

Kevlar body suit with polymer plate armor

Origin Story

Craig McCarthy, known by his alias Diamond Head, is a distinguished character in the EVO universe. As an EVO, Craig possesses the extraordinary ability to transform his skin into diamond, endowing him with the remarkable characteristics of diamonds, such as extreme hardness and durability. This transformation not only makes him almost invulnerable but also grants him super strength, making him a formidable opponent in combat scenarios. Craig was recruited by the EVO Liberation League, an organization dedicated to fighting for the rights and fair treatment of EVOs everywhere. Diamond Head's commitment to the cause and his unwavering determination make him a central figure in the fight for EVO equality. Though he is tough and unyielding in battle, Craig has a compassionate side, always striving to protect those who cannot protect themselves. His shining, diamond-like appearance sets him apart, both as a hero and as a beacon of hope for EVOs around the world.

Known Allies

EVO Liberation League
Power X
EVO Underground

Known Enemies

United States Government
Project Cyber- Cron

Known Skills

Martial Arts
Politics

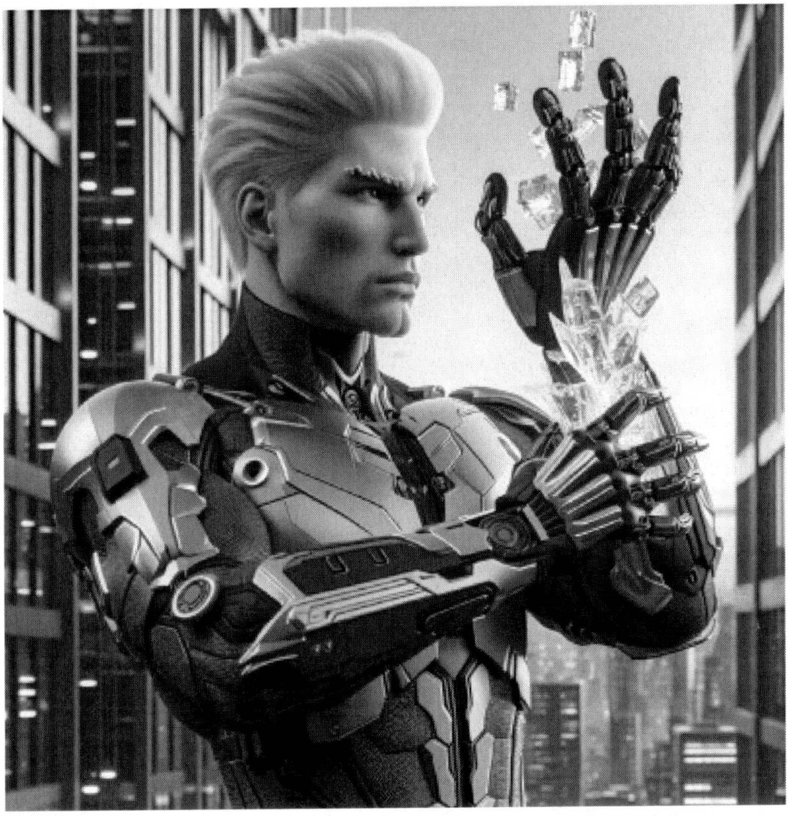

Real Name = Scott Lashley
Code Name = Frostbite
Age = 30
Base of operations = Mobile

Powers

Cold Manipulation
* Ice Constructs
* Temperature Control
* Ice Body Armor
* Self Substance
Heat Resistance

Equipment

Kevlar body suit with polymer plate armor

Origin Story

Scott Lashley, known by his code name 'Frostbite,' is a compelling character introduced as an EVO, a genetically evolved human with extraordinary abilities. Scott can generate and manipulate extreme cold, allowing him to form ice constructs of any form, including deadly edged weapons. His unique ability has resulted in his hair turning white, a striking contrast to his otherwise formidable appearance. For most of his life, Scott has been on the run from Cyber Crons, relentless EVO-hunting robots created by a rogue faction of the world's governments. These mechanical hunters are programmed to capture EVOs, making survival a daily struggle for Scott. Driven by a deep sense of justice and the will to fight back, Scott has joined the EVO underground network. This group is dedicated to helping EVOs escape and find safety from the Cyber Crons. Scott is typically seen wearing a Kevlar body suit layered with polymer plate armor, providing both flexibility and protection as he combats the metal menace. His experiences have made him a seasoned warrior, keenly aware of the stakes involved in their battle for freedom.

Known Allies

EVO Underground
Power X
EVO Liberation League

Known Enemies

United States Government
Project Cyber - Cron

Known Skills

Martial Arts
Bladed Weapons

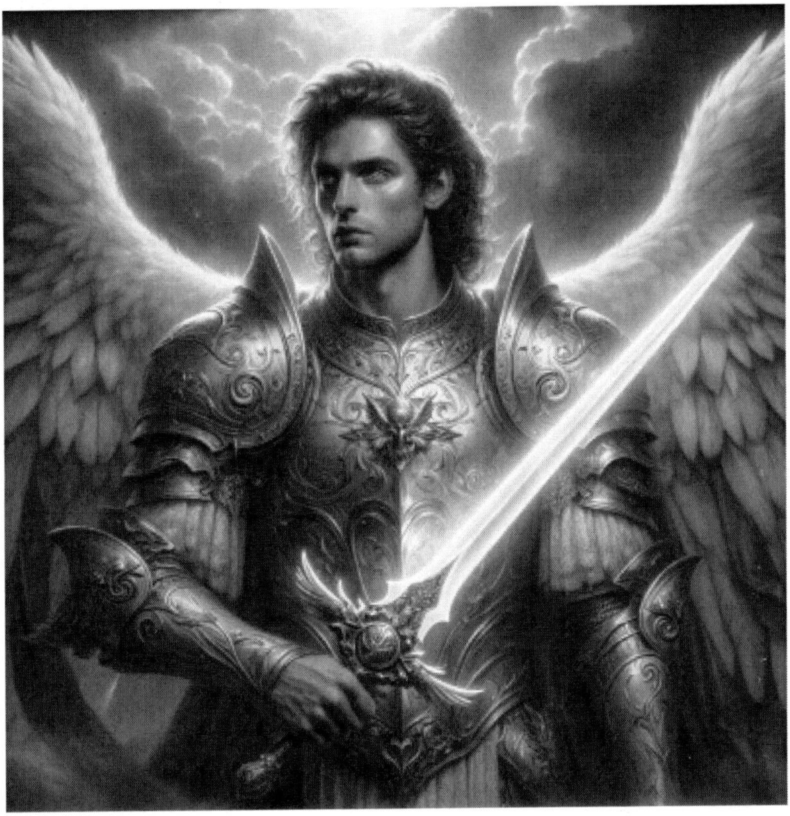

Real Name = Gadrill
Code Name = Gadrill
Age = Unknown
Base of operations = Mobile

Powers

Angelic Grace
* Immortality
* Smite
* Bless
* Enhanced Strength
* Soul Sight
* Invisibility
* True Sight =This Allows him to see ones true self.
* Healing
* Teleportation
Fight by wings

Equipment

Holy Armor
Angelic Blade
* Can Kill Demons

Origin Story

Gadrill is an angel in Christian theology who was one of the Watchers that disobeyed God. Unlike his brethren who succumbed to the lust of mortal women, Gadrill's betrayal stemmed from genuine love for a single mortal woman. This act of love earned him God's pity. As a form of redemption, God sent Gadrill to Earth with the mission to protect humanity against Lucifer's demonic forces. Clad in Holy Armor, Gadrill wields an angel blade, a sacred weapon capable of slaying demons. Gadrill's presence is a blend of divine grace and warrior's steadfastness, making him a formidable guardian of humans.

Known Allies

Kane
God
Samson

Known Enemies

Demons
Lucifer

Known Skills

Angelic Warfare
Medicine
Swordsmanship

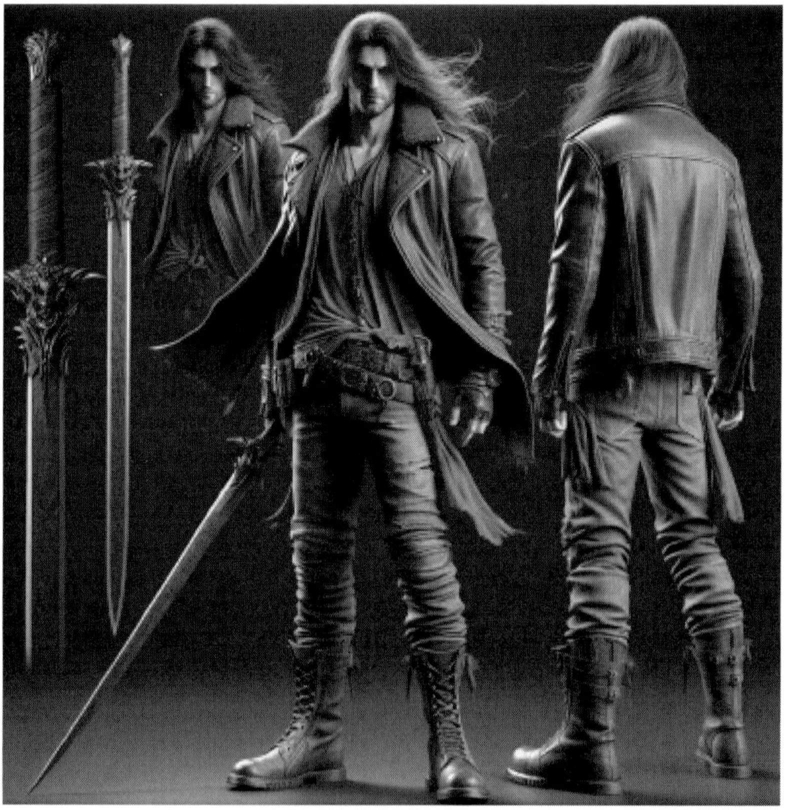

Real Name = Kane
Code Name = Kane
Age = Unknown
Base of operations = Mobile

Powers

Mark Of Kane
* Enhanced Strength
 *Enhanced Reflexes
* Immortality
* Healing Factor
* Resistance Magic
* Sense Evil
* Track Evil

Equipment

First Blade
* Can Kill Everything in heaven and earth including the old Gods
* Can only be used by one with the Mark Of Kane

Origin Story

Kane, inspired by the biblical Cain who killed his brother Abel, is a character cursed by God with the Mark of Kane to wander the earth for eternity. Unlike his biblical counterpart, this Kane is destined to defend the weak and innocent from demonic forces. He wields the First Blade, an ancient obsidian sword with the unique ability to kill anything and everything it strikes. Despite his eternal existence, Kane's body remains forever young. He has long, flowing hair and an intriguing, mysterious appearance that is accentuated by his rugged but stylish attire. Kane typically wears a leather jacket and biker boots, pairing them with rugged denim jeans, giving him a modern yet timeless aura that blends his ancient past with his eternal mission.

Known Allies

Gadrill
God
Samson

Known Enemies

Demons

Lucifer

Known Skills

All styles of Martial arts
Weapons Expert
Swordsmanship
Demonology

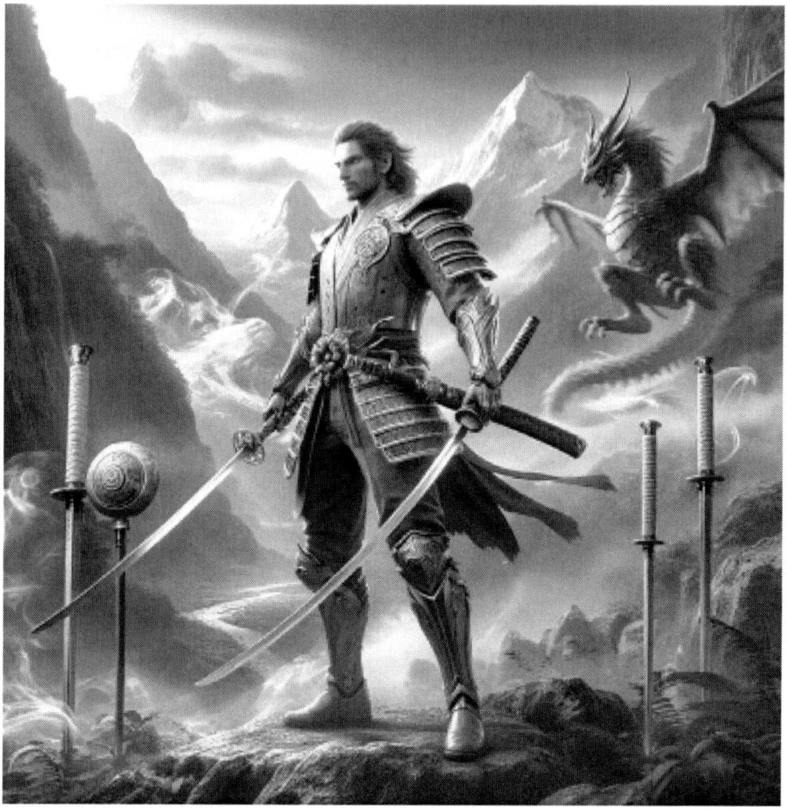

Real Name = Lee Bryent
Code Name = Shadow Warrior
Age = Unknown
Base Of Operations = China town New York City

Powers

Chee
* Long Life
* Force Punch
* Healing
* Enhanced Strength
* Enhanced Reflexes
* Astral Projection
* Bio Field

Equipment

Golden Mystic Samarri Armor
Stone Cutter Katana
* Cut through any Material
Sias Of Sound
* Emits a sonic blast when clanged together
Sheild of Hell
* Deflection

Pu and Pa Katanas
* When combined calls a shadow warrior to aid him in battle

Origin Story

Lee Bryent, orphaned son of intrepid anthropologists, discovered a secret civilization known as the Wise Ones in a hidden Himalayan valley after a tragedy that claimed his parents. Raised by an elderly sage of the Wise Ones, Lee underwent rigorous training in seven archaic martial arts that granted him extraordinary powers and longevity. As he aged only twenty years within the temple's temporal anomaly, the outside world moved on for nearly a century. Equipped with a golden samurai armor and a collection of mystical weapons - the impenetrable Stone Cutter katana, the unyielding Shield of Hell, the ghost-summoning twin swords Pu and Pa, and the sonic Sais of Sound - Lee completed grueling quests that proved his might. With each victory, his arsenal grew, culminating in the daunting task of defeating the formidable red dragon, earning him their respect along with a formidable weapon. Now, Lee stands as Earth's silent guardian, a Shadow Warrior destined to thwart the malevolent demon surge that threatens to envelop the world in darkness.

Known Allies

None

Known Enemies

Juno The Viking Warrior

Known Skills

Master of the seven archaic lost Martial Arts
Swordsmanship
Anthropology
Demonology

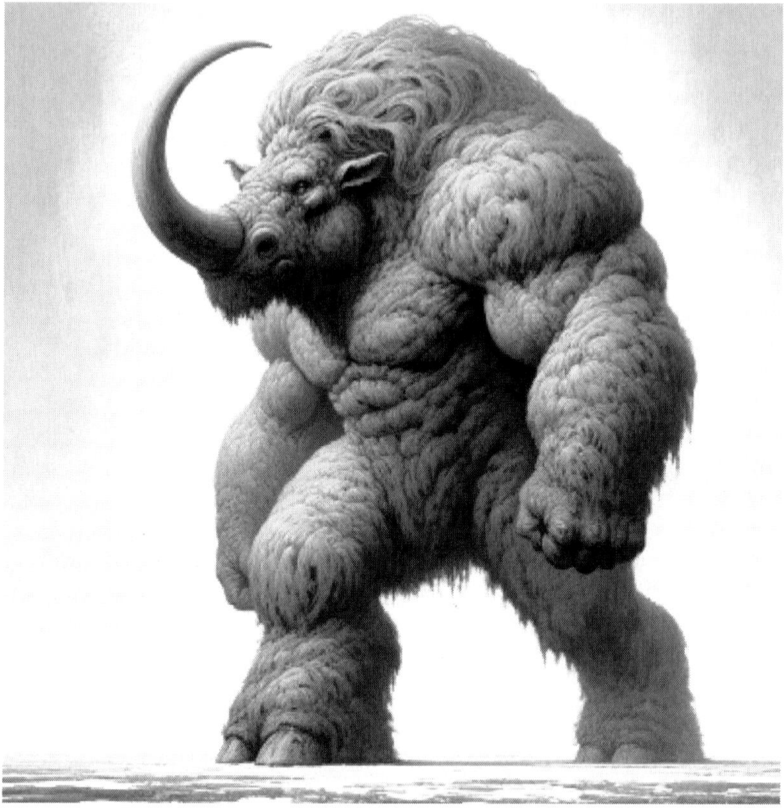

Real Name = Behemoth
Code Name = Behemoth
Age = 2
Base of operations = Mobile

Powers

Superhuman Strength
Invulnerability
Regeneration
Rage
* Strength Increases the Angrier he gets with no upper limit
* Invulnerability increases the Angrier her gets with no upper
Environmental Resistance
Horn

Equipment

None

Origin Story

Behemoth is the enigmatic result of a genetic experiment conducted by the reclusive Doctor Marrow. Created from a blend of wooly rhino and human DNA, this creature is remarkable to behold. Towering at nearly

10 feet, Behemoth walks on two legs like a human, but the similarities end there. His frame displays powerful muscles, each movement indicating incredible strength. His body, covered in thick, long hair akin to that of a prehistoric wooly rhino, features a hide that serves as formidable natural armor, impervious to most physical attacks. Behemoth's face is an unsettling mix of human and rhino traits, extending outward and dominated by a pronounced single horn on the bridge of his nose—an imposing weapon. Perhaps his most alarming trait is his ability to grow endlessly in strength and resilience; driven by rage, there seems to be no limit to his power. Each surge in anger only enhances his monstrous strength and further toughens his already impenetrable hide, making him a nearly unstoppable force once provoked.

Known Allies

Caviler
Home Guard

Known Enemies

United States Government
Doctor Marrow

Known Skills

Brawling

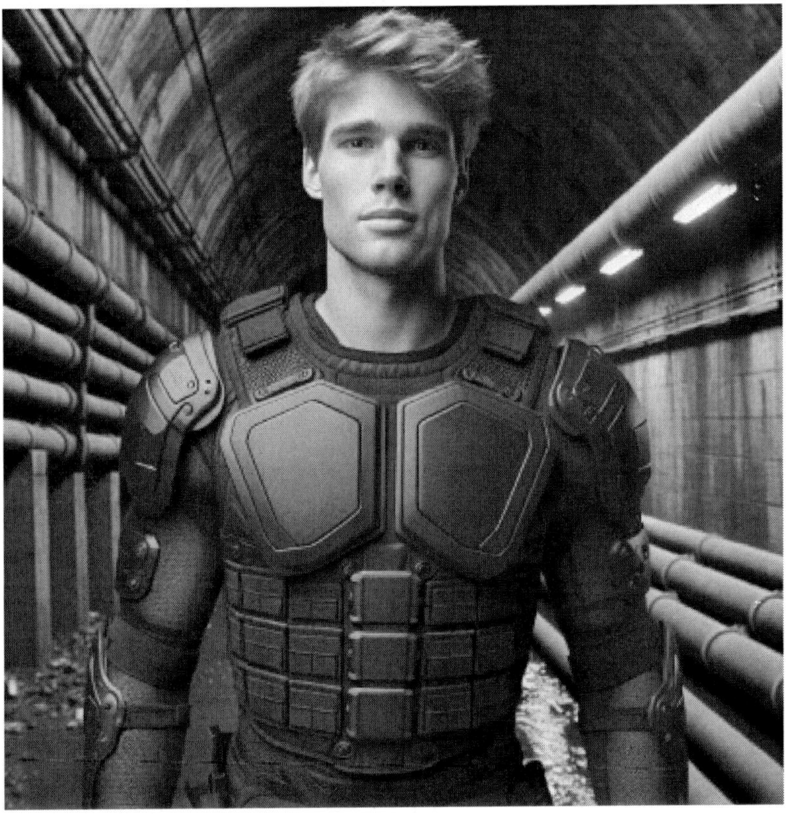

Real Name = Zach Newman
Code Name = Frequency
Age = 25
Base of Operations = New York City

Powers

Sonic Manipulation and generation
* Sonic Blast
* Absorb all Sound in an area
* Flight on vibrations
* Sonic force shield

Equipment

Kelar Body suit with polymer plate armor

Origin Story

Zach Newman, known by his alias 'Freqincy,' is an Evo with the unique ability to generate different frequencies of sound to produce a variety of effects, from shattering glass to soothing pain. Tragically orphaned at a young age due to losing control of his abilities and causing his parents' death, Zach grew up homeless on the streets of New York City. He was eventually taken in by the underground Evo community that resides in the city's sewers. Witnessing his fellow Evos being hunted by the ruthless Cyber crons, Zach formed a group called the Acolytes to protect his community. With his striking blonde hair, he wears a Kevlar bodysuit reinforced with polymer plate armor, ready to defend and fight for his fellow Evos.

Known Allies

The Acolytes

Known Enemies

United States Government
Project Cyber - Cron

Known Skills

Martial Arts
Leadership

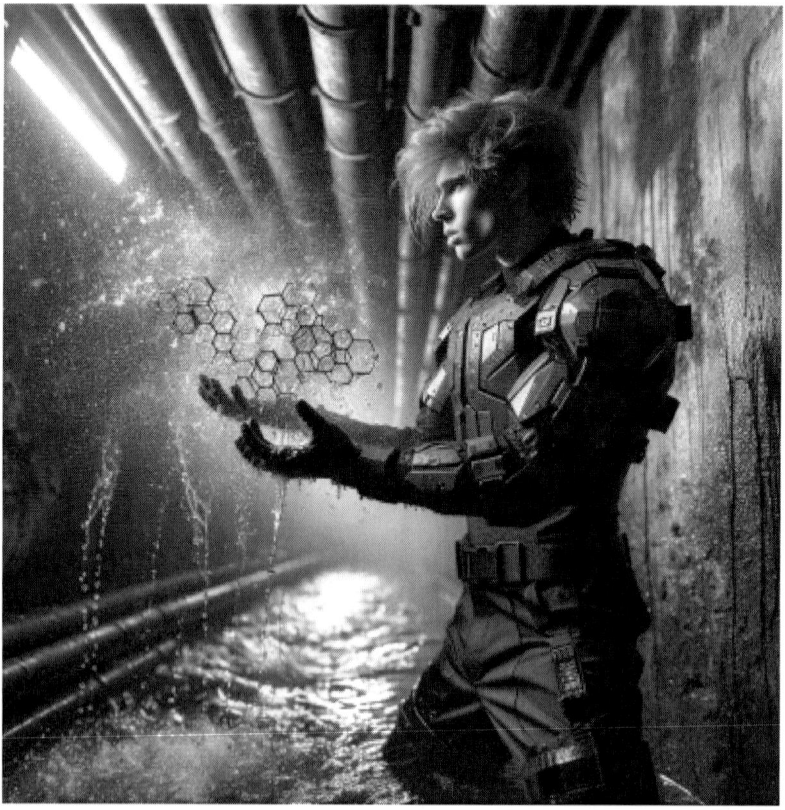

Real Name = Ken Marshel
Code Name = Hydro
Age = 27
Base of Operations = New York City

powers
_____

Hydro- Kenises'
* Water Jet Blast
* Water Constructs
* Dehydration = the ability to draw every drop of moisture from a human body causing Dehydration

* Water Form

Equipment

Kevlar Body suit with polymer plate armor

Origin Story

Ken Marshel, also known as Hydro, is an EVO with the extraordinary ability to control and manipulate water. He can draw moisture from the air and create powerful water constructs, ranging from shields and weapons to intricate structures. Born in the underground EVO community within the sewers of New York, Ken, alongside other EVOs, lived in constant fear of the ruthless EVO-hunting Cyber Crons. Everything changed when he met Zach Newman, who recruited him into a group known as the Acolytes. With the Acolytes, Ken now fights to protect his community and fellow EVOs. Ken has distinctive red hair and is always ready for battle, donning a Kevlar body suit reinforced with polymer plate armor. His resolute nature and exceptional abilities make him a vital asset in the fight against their oppressors.

Known Allies

Acolytes

Known Enemies

United States Government
Project Cyber - Cron

Known Skills

Martial Arts
Swimming
Brawling

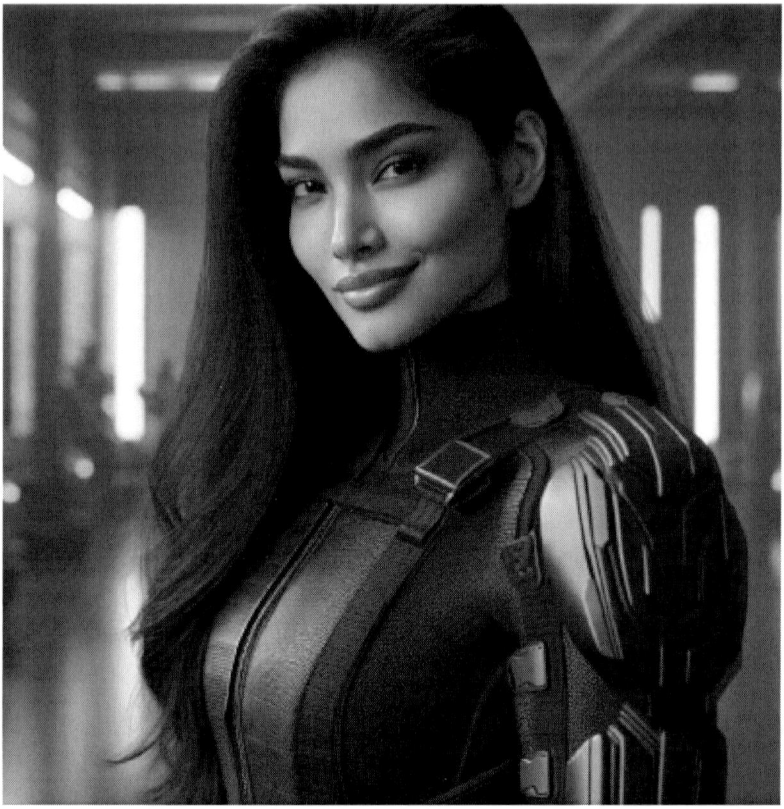

Real Name = Cindy Smith
Code Name = Mind Bender
Age = 35
Base of Operations = New York City

Powers

Telepathy
* Read Minds of Others
* Control Minds of others
* Create illusions in the minds of others.
Telekinesis
* Move Object With her mind
* Flight
* Telekinetic Force Field

Equipment

Kevlar body armor with polymer plate armor

Origin Story

Cindy is an EVO with the remarkable abilities of telepathy and telekinesis. Once a successful businesswoman who amassed a fortune in the stock market, her life took a drastic turn when she met and fell in love with Zach Newman, the leader of an EVO group dedicated to defending their kind from the cyber cron. Moved by empathy for his cause and her profound love for Zach, Cindy joined the group. She utilizes her vast wealth to support EVO communities globally. Cindy has striking black hair and is always seen wearing a Kevlar bodysuit reinforced with polymer plate armor for protection.

Known Allies

Acolytes

Known Enemies

United States Government
Project Cyber - Cron

Known Skills

Business
Martial arts
Areial combat

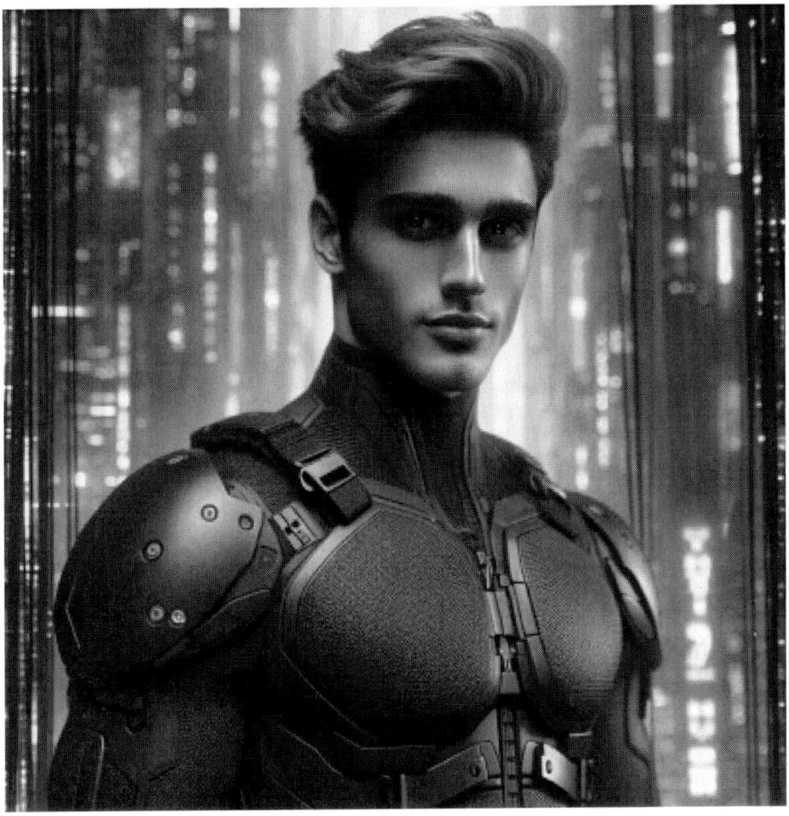

Real Name = Greg Smitts
Code Name = Omega
Age = 40
Base of Operations = New York City

Powers

Adaptation
* Regeneration due to his body adapting to natural ageing
*Able to Adapt instantly to any harmful environment or attack

Equipment

Kevlar Body Suit with polymer plate armor

Powers

Greg Smitts, known as Omega, is a second-generation EVO, a being with evolved abilities. He is the son of Han Groeber, also known as Alpha Prime, an EVO supremacist leader who fervently believes that EVOS should rule over humans. In stark contrast to his father, Greg holds a firm belief that humans and EVOS can coexist harmoniously. Greg possesses a unique and formidable ability: instantaneous adaptation. His body can adapt to any environment or counter any attack it encounters, making him a valuable asset and formidable opponent. Greg has become estranged from his father due to their ideological differences, seeking solace and purpose instead with Ken and his group of acolytes. Within this community, he uses his adaptation abilities to defend and protect his fellow EVOS, striving to create a safe space for them. Physically, Greg is distinguished by his striking blue hair and his attire — a Kevlar bodysuit reinforced with polymer plate armor, designed to maximize his naturally adaptive defenses.

Known Allies

Acolytes

Known Enemies

United States Government
Project Cyber - Cron

Known Skills

Martial Arts
Computer programming

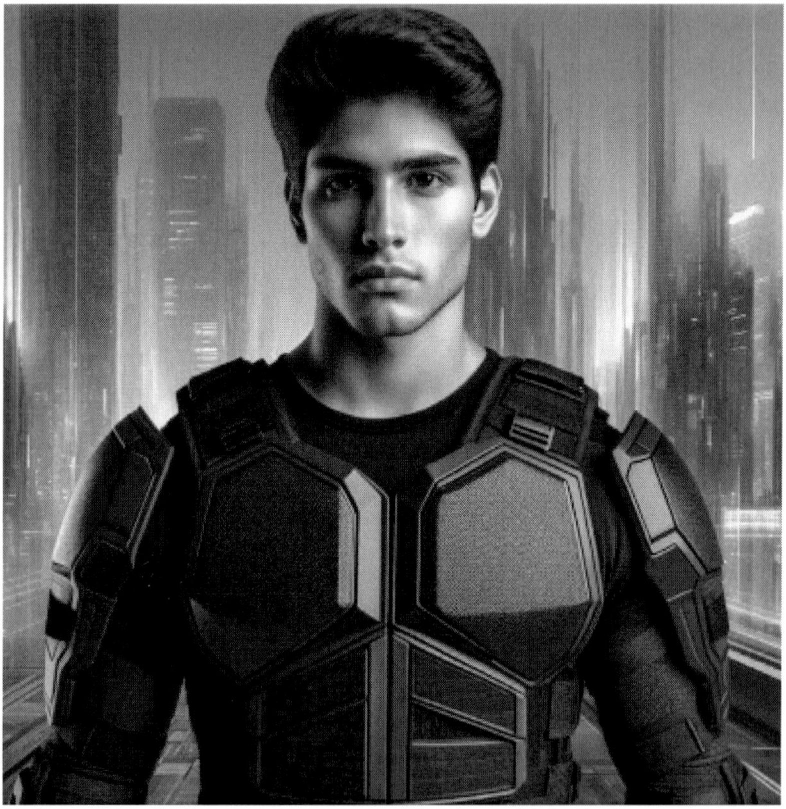

Real Name = Alex Greene
Code Name = Pressure Point
Age = 19
Base of Operations = New York City

Powers

Pressure Energy Generation
Weakness Detection

Equipment

Kevlar Body suit with polymer plate armor

Origin Story

Alex Greene, known by his codename 'Pressure Point', is an EVO with two remarkable abilities: the power to detect weak points in any material and the capacity to manipulate atmospheric pressure upon objects. Formerly a petty thief surviving on the tough streets of New York City, Alex's life took a dramatic turn when he was targeted by the relentless Cyber Crons. Just as his situation appeared dire, he was rescued by Ken and the Acolytes, a resistance group battling against the Cyber Crons' tyranny. Recognizing his unique abilities and potential, Ken offered Alex a place among the Acolytes. Now a vital member of their team, Alex employs his EVO skills to undermine the Cyber Crons' oppressive regime. Physically, Alex is characterized by his brown hair and a distinct Kevlar bodysuit woven with polymer plate armor, providing both flexibility and protection. His suit is tailored for high mobility and combat efficiency, making him a formidable opponent in any skirmish.

Known Allies

Acolytes

Known Enemies

United States Government
Project Cyber - Cron

Known Skills

Lock picking
Pick pocketing
Electronics
Martial Arts

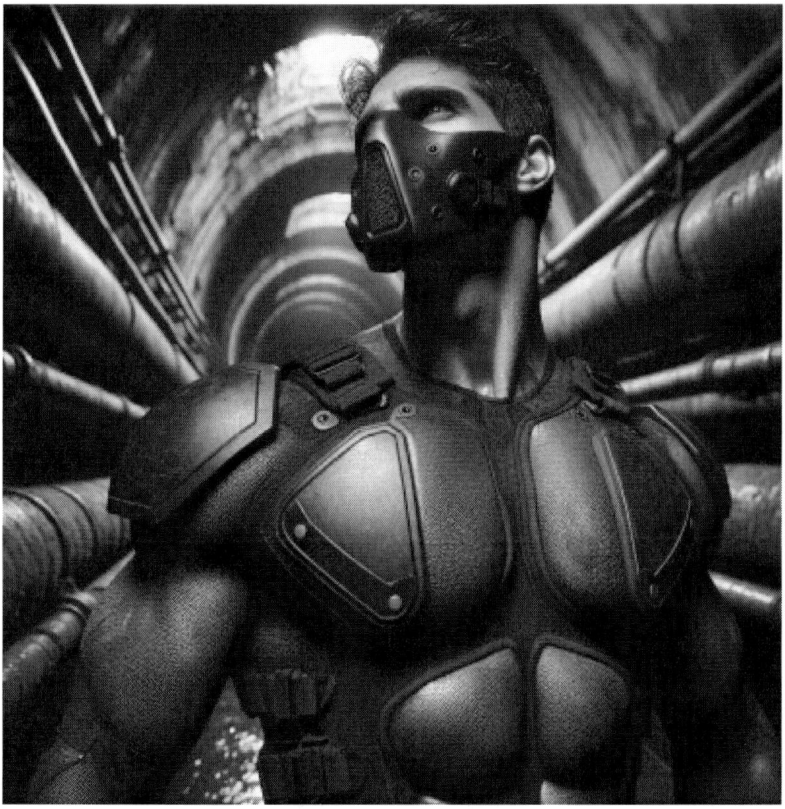

Real Name = Jeff Killion
Code Name = Physic
Age = 35
Base of Operations = New York City

Powers

Physic energy solidification
* Physic constructs
* Access to the Atrial plane

Equipment

Kevlar body suit with polymer plate armor

Origin Story

Jeff Killion, known by his alias 'Physic', is a formidable EVO (Enhanced Vigilante Operator) with the extraordinary ability to solidify physic energy into various constructs. Drawing his physic energy from the ethereal Astrel plane, Jeff has mastered techniques to create everything from weapons to protective barriers. Prior to his awakening as an EVO, Jeff served as a dedicated officer with the New York Police Department. His life took a dramatic turn when he encountered Ken, a mysterious figure who introduced him to the hidden EVO community dwelling in the sewers of New York City. Persuaded by Ken's vision of a better world, Jeff left his previous life behind to join 'The Acolytes', a covert group committed to using their powers for justice. Now, Jeff dons a specialized Kevlar body suit with polymer plate armor, designed to provide maximum protection while allowing flexibility. To conceal his identity from former colleagues and those who might recognize him, Jeff wears a distinctive face mask that covers his mouth and nose.

Known Allies

Acolytes
New York Police Department

Known Enemies

United States Government
Project Cyber - Cron

Known skills

Law Enforcement
Marial Arts
Firearms

Real Name = Jenny Reed
Code Name = Shadow Dancer
Age = 35
Base of Operations = New York City

Powers

Control and manipulate dark force energy

Equipment

Kevlar Body Suit with polymer plate Armor

Origin Story

Jenny Reed, also known as Shadow Dancer, is a strong-willed and courageous African American woman with the extraordinary ability to control and manipulate dark force energy. Often clad in a futuristic Kevlar bodysuit reinforced with polymer plate armor, she stands as both a fierce warrior and a dedicated activist for EVO (Enhanced Variant Organisms) rights. Her activism has put her in the crosshairs of several EVO-hating groups, making her a frequent target for those who seek to suppress her cause. Jenny's life took a significant turn when Ken and his group of acolytes saved her from an assassin's bullet. Grateful and inspired, she quickly joined his cause, becoming an invaluable member of his team. Driven by both her personal convictions and her powers, Jenny fights tirelessly for justice and the protection of EVOs everywhere.

Known Allies

Acolytes
EVO Defense League

Known Enemies

United States Government
Project Cyber - Cron

Known Skills

Public Speaking
Martial Arts
Politics
Civil rights Law

- Visualise androgynous humanoid figure face of midder, deatern detent fiealiwen, hinges laveed in recicubley feathers.

(Severeng cnatters yith- ceagules) ap durbla, ferajumeb, it couded o fickoy chcthors and joea koom thel ovar artous, this polymmer plaze detimors

- stronutle a duuble Kevelalar crear atiy, just maipl teiight, isimes and polymer plate armor

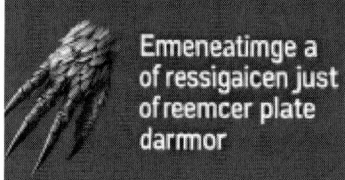

Emeneatimge a of ressigaicen just of reemcer plate darmor

Real Name = Micheal Man
Code Name = Swoop
Age = Unknown
Base of Operations = New York City

Powers

Wings
Claws
Beak
Feather Body Armor
Healing Factor
Enhanced Strength

Enhanced Eyesight

Equipment

Kevlar body suit with polymer plate armor

Origin Story

Micheal Man, also known as Swoop, is a unique Evo whose abilities have led to significant physical mutations. Unlike most Evos, a set of bird-like wings have emerged from his back, granting him the power of flight. His fingers and toes have transformed with razor-sharp claws that can slice through most materials, and his body is covered in a thick layer of feathers, resembling a humanoid bird. His eyesight is extraordinarily enhanced, making him an exceptional scout and tracker. Unfortunately, due to his appearance, Micheal has spent most of his life hidden away in the deep wilderness of upstate New York. His encounter with Zach, who stumbled upon his secluded home, marked a turning point. Zach befriended Micheal and convinced him to join the Acolytes. Swoop now contributes his unique abilities to the group while donning a custom Kevlar bodysuit reinforced with polymer plate armor for added protection.

Known Allies

Acolytes

Known Enemies

United States Government
Project Cyber - Cron

Known Skills

Martial ARTS
Areial COMBAT

supervillains

Supervillains are individuals who possess extraordinary abilities or powers which they exploit for personal gain, material wealth, or to achieve a grandiose sense of control and dominance. Unlike heroes who use their powers for the greater good, supervillains are driven by ego, greed, revenge, or a desire to instill fear and subjugate others. These characters often have complex backstories that include pivotal moments of loss, betrayal, or disillusionment, which drive them towards darker paths. Their actions are characterized by a tendency to disrupt social order, create chaos, and challenge moral and ethical boundaries. They use their unique skills not only to enhance their own standing but also to manipulate and control others, often causing widespread destruction and sowing discord. Supervillains can range from charismatic masterminds to brutal enforcers, but all share the common trait of leveraging their extraordinary abilities for nefarious purposes.

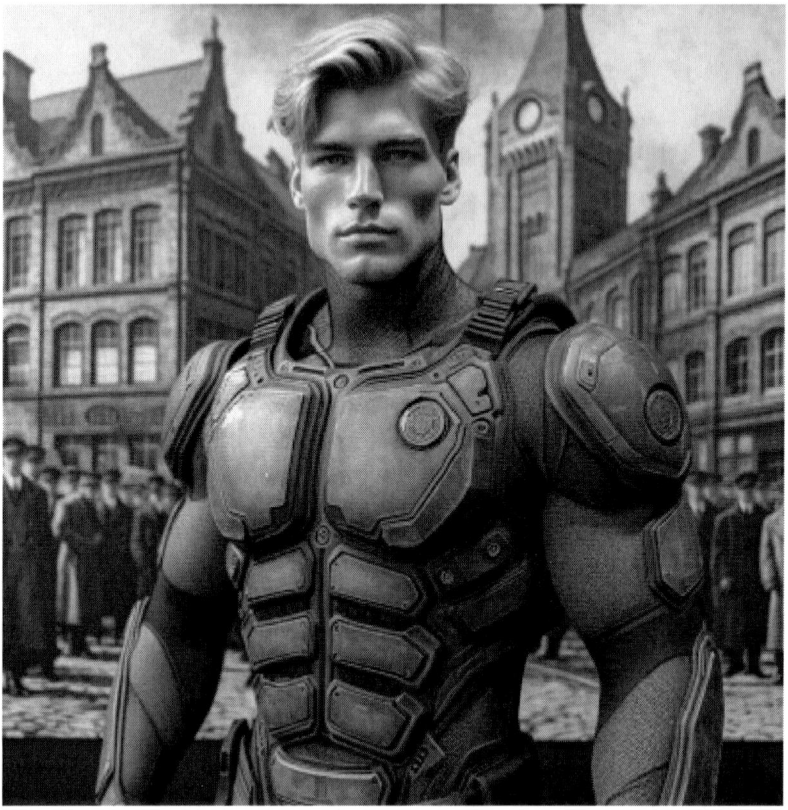

Real Name = Hans Groeber
Code Name = Alpha Prime
Age = 106
Base Of Operation = Cloud City on Venus

Powers

Bio- Energy Absorption = the more People he is around the stronger his powers are with no upper limit
* Super Strength
* Invulnerability
* Healing
* Long Life

Equipment

Kevlar Body Suit with polymer plate Armor

Origin Story

Hans Groeber, also known as Alpha Prime, is a complex character defined by his extraordinary abilities and tumultuous historical affiliations. An 'EVO', he possesses the unique power to absorb the bioenergy of humans and other EVOS, enhancing his physical attributes to superhuman levels. This capability endows him with near-invulnerability, immense strength, remarkable stamina, and an extended lifespan. In crowded environments, his powers amplify, making him nigh unstoppable. Born in Germany during the waning years of World War I, Hans initially embraced the ideology of the Nazis, seeing an opportunity to advance within the military and contribute to scientific endeavors, particularly those concerned with genetic purity. His own genetic superiority was uncovered, and he was promptly appointed as the head of a covert super-soldier program, comprising other German EVOs. A mission to rescue Mussolini proved disastrous, resulting in the decimation of his team by an opposing allied super-soldier unit. This loss, coupled with Germany's defeat, catalyzed a radical shift in his worldview; he came to believe EVOs were the apex of evolution, the true 'homo-superiors', destined to dominate. Visually, Hans is an Aryan archetype with piercing blue eyes and blond hair. His attire is a fusion of practicality and symbolic allegiance: a Kevlar bodysuit for protection and mobility, overlaid with futuristic plate armor that bears the Iron Cross, evoking his militaristic past. His presence is both formidable and marred by the complexities of his ideology and experiences throughout one of the darkest periods in history.

Known Allies

The Brother Hood
EVO Defense League

Known Enemies

All the human World Governments
Project Cyber Cron

Known Skills

Military stagey
Leadership
Martial Arts
Military Tactics
specialist in EVO biology

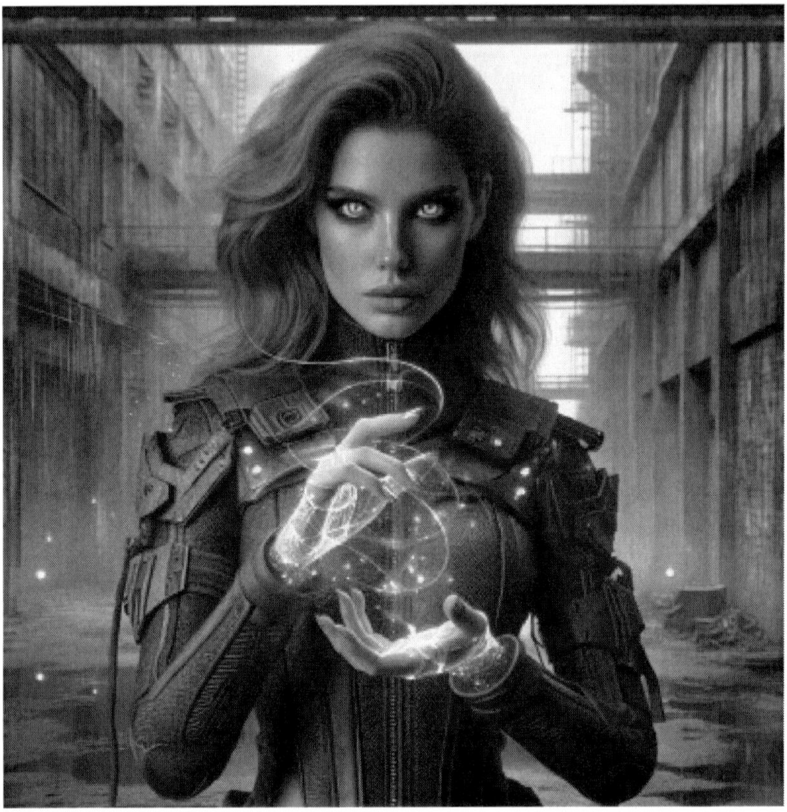

Real Name = Crystal Day
Code Name = SY-FY
Age = 35
Base Of Operation = Cloud City on Venus

Powers

Telepathy
* Read the minds of others
* Control the minds of Others
* Project Illusions in the minds of others
* Feed on the Physic Energy of Others
Long Life

Equipment

Kevlar body suit with polymer plate armor

Origin Story

Crystal Day is a complex and formidable character who resides within the SY-FY universe, a world where evolution has taken a dramatic turn, birthing individuals known as EVOs. With her innate telepathic and telekinetic abilities,

Crystal stands out as a particularly powerful EVO. Since childhood, she has been under the influence of Alpha Prime, the charismatic and enigmatic leader dedicated to asserting the dominance of EVOs over the world. To Crystal, Alpha Prime is more than a mentor; he is a father figure whose vision for the future she has embraced wholeheartedly. She possesses striking physical features, with vibrant red hair that serves as a fiery crown and piercing green eyes that seem to look straight through the veil of one's thoughts. Her attire is a blend of function and symbolism; she dons a form-fitting Kevlar bodysuit that offers her protection and flexibility during combat. Layered over this suit is futuristic polymer plate armor that not only shields her from harm but also conveys her status as Alpha Prime's right-hand warrior. As an adult, Crystal's loyalty to Alpha Prime remains unwavering. She has become an instrumental figure in his quest, using her extraordinary powers to further their cause. Crystal's story is one of conviction and inner conflict, as she navigates her role in a world brimming with tension and the upheaval of existing power structures. She and Hans Groeber were Married

Known Allies

The Brother Hood
EVO Defense League

Known Enemies

All the human World Governments
Project Cyber Cron

Known Skills

Interrogation
Martial Arts
Espionage

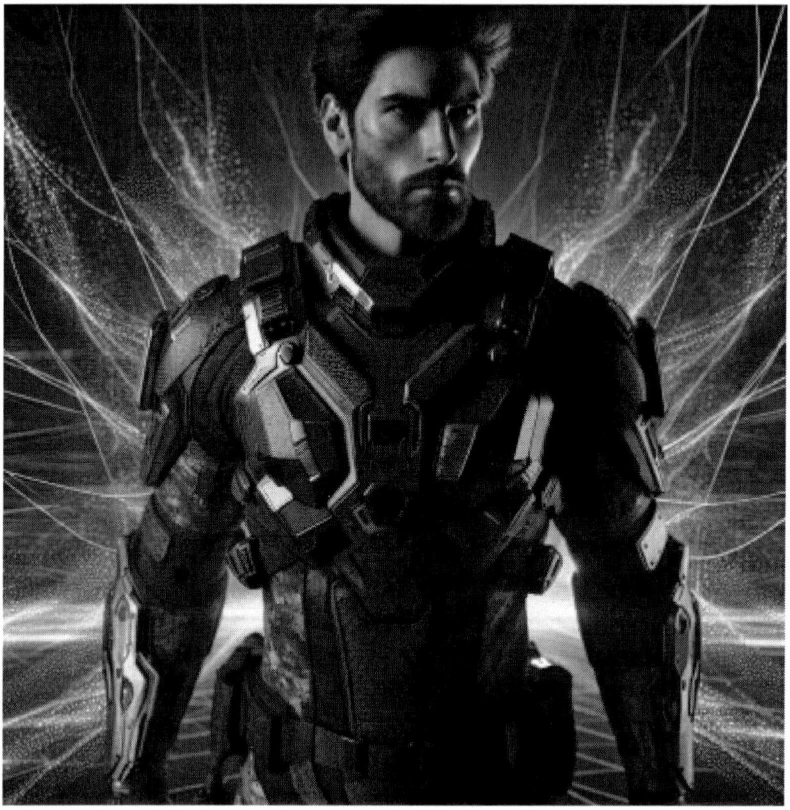

Real Name = Carl Helton
Code Name = Lasar Rod
Age = 30
Base Of Operation = Cloud City on Venus

Powers

Plasma Generation
* Plasma Blasts
* Plasma bursts
* Plasma Field

Equipment

Kevlar Body Suit with polymer plate armor

Origin Story

Carl Helton, known by his alias Lasar Rod, is an EVO— a being evolved beyond human limits. He possesses the extraordinary ability to generate laser energy, using it to unleash formidable laser blasts, create protective energy force fields, and absorb various forms of energy to convert into his signature Lasar power. His life took a pivotal turn when Alpha Prime discovered him in the depths of despair and substance abuse, using drugs to dampen his overwhelming powers. Moved by Alpha Prime's persuasion, Carl saw his abilities in a new light, recognizing them as a gift rather than a curse. Assembling his resolve, Carl joined Alpha Prime's cause, eventually rising to the position of Lieutenant, fully adopting the philosophy of EVO supremacy. Carl is easily identifiable by his thick black hair, complete with a well-groomed beard and mustache. His attire is a combination of practicality and advanced technology, consisting of a robust Kevlar bodysuit layered with cutting-edge polymer plate armor, tailored to complement his unique combat style and energy manipulation capabilities.

His sadistic Nature Makes him Alpha Primes Chief Executioner.

Known Allies

The Brother Hood
EVO Defense League

Known Enemies

All the human World Governments
Project Cyber Cron

Known Skills

Marial Arts
Weapons Expert

Create the way to betwen our nanned.

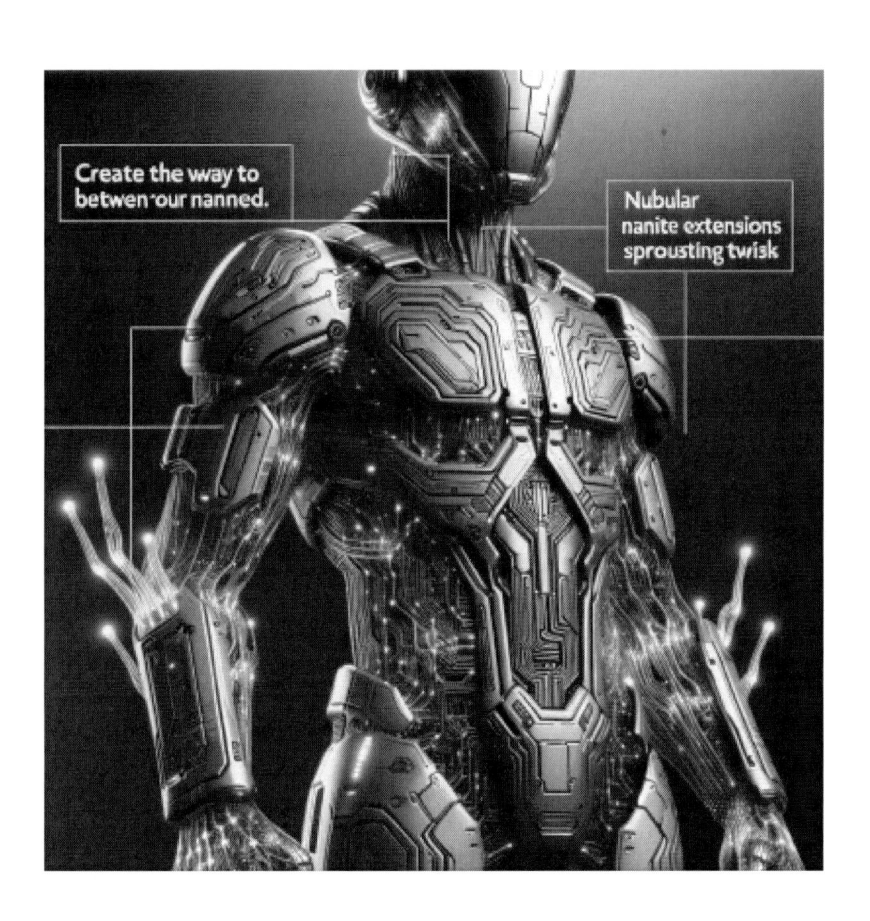

Nubular nanite extensions sprousting twisk

Real Name = **Shinzo Kawasaki**
Code Name = Cyber
Age = 30
Base Of Operation = Cloud City on Venus

Powers
___

Nano- Probe Tubulars
* Nano- Probe Injection
* Nano - Probe Infection can upgrade and manipulate any technology
* Nano - Probe Injection On organic life turns that life into a drone controlled by Senzo
 Genius level Intelligence

Equipment

High tech exo- suit
* durability
* Enhanced Strength
* Blasters
* Energy Sword

Origin Story

Shinzo Kawasaki is a unique blend of ancient samurai ethos and futuristic technology, an EVO who stands out for his remarkable ability to interface with machines. Born with a techno-organic virus coursing through his veins, his biology is a marvel, coupled with bio-organic nanites that have merged symbiotically with his cells, providing him a direct mental command over them. This connection extends to his ability to meld with any technology he encounters, using it to fabricate equipment limited only by his imagination. These nanites are controlled via small tubular extensions from his wrist, enabling him to 'infect' and manipulate technological devices around him. His most prominent creation is a sophisticated mech suit, designed and continuously adapted by his own nanites. This suit is not merely an armor, but a dynamic weapon platform that manifests a range of armaments for offense, alongside a state-of-the-art shield generator for defense. Shinzo embodies the honor of a samurai, yet his tactics and hardware are always a step ahead with the times, making him a formidable entity in a world where the lines between man and machine blur. He serves as Alpha Primes resident tech Genius.

Known Allies

The Brother Hood
EVO Defense League

Known Enemies

All the human World Governments
Project Cyber Cron

Known Skills

Robotic
Engineering
Electronic
Invention
Computer Programming

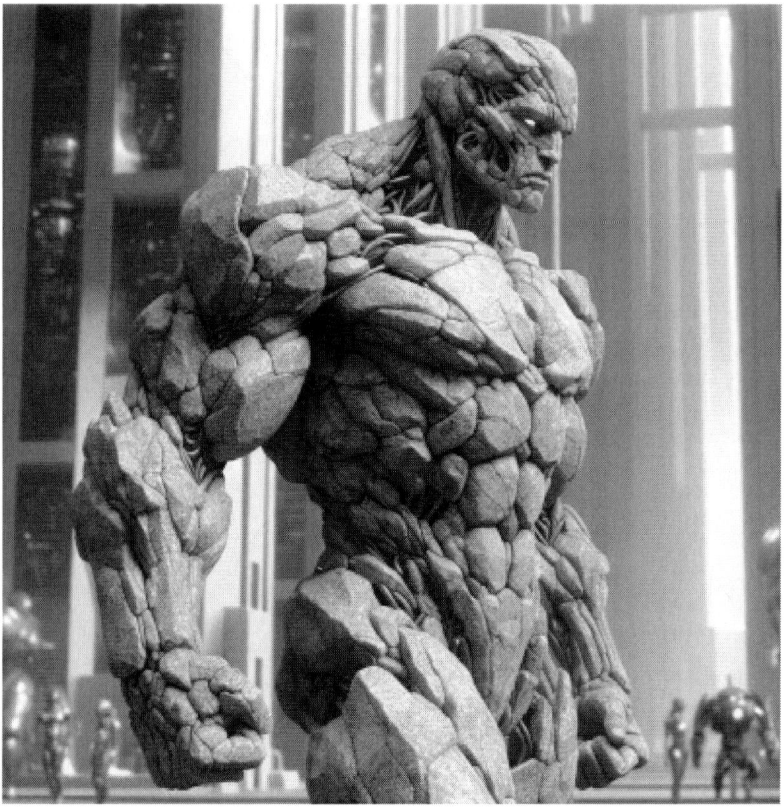

Real Name = Burt Grayson
Code Name = Rock Lore
Age = 30
Base Of Operation = Cloud City on Venus

Powers

Rock Body
* Superhuman Strength
* Superhuman Durability
* Regeneration
* Self stance

Equipment

None

Origin Story

Burt Grayson, known as 'Rock Lore' in the circles of EVOs, is a formidable entity shaped by a rare and distinctive mutation. His transformation deviates from the standard EVO patterns, with his anatomy having undergone a profound metamorphosis into a being entirely composed of living stone. This transformation has endowed Burt with phenomenal strength comparable to the mightiest of earth's constructs, unparalleled durability capable of weathering the fiercest attacks, and stamina that far exceeds that of any normal human. His appearance is as intimidating as it is impressive, standing at an imposing 7 feet with a dense, muscular frame that ripples with the raw power encased within his rocky exterior. His thick stone skin consists of various shades of gray that mimic the natural beauty of a granite monolith. After being rescued from the ruthless Cyber-Crons, merciless robots designed by a fearful government to eradicate his kind, Burt pledged allegiance to Alpha Prime, the champion of a future where EVOs reign supreme over the world. Despite his rough exterior and the intimidating presence, he commands, Burt harbors a sense of loyalty and a burning desire for the acceptance of EVOs everywhere. Burt Grayson, now Rock Lore, fights not only for survival but for the recognition and respect of the evolved individuals he considers family. He serves as Alpha Primes Muscle.

Known Allies

The Brother Hood
EVO Defense League

Known Enemies

All the human World Governments
Project Cyber Cron

Known Skills

Brawling

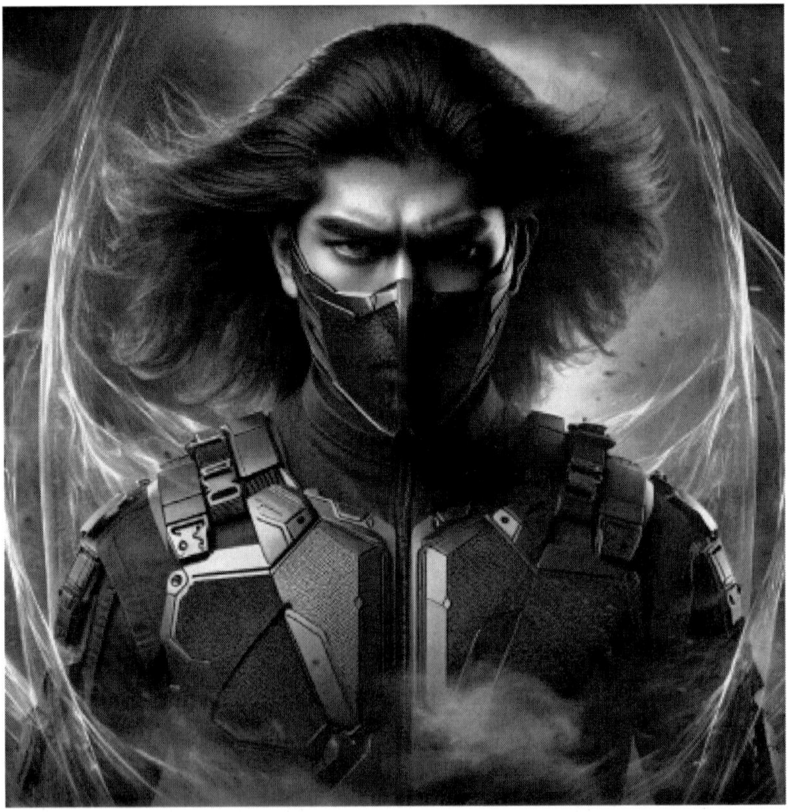

Real Name = Carlos Varga
Code Name = Tempest
Age = 25
Base Of Operation = Cloud City on Venus

Powers

Air Manipulation and Generation
* Tornados
* Hurricane Winds
* Flight
* Air Barrier

Equipment

Kevlar Body Suit with polymer plate Armor

Origin Story

Carlos Varga, also known by his codename 'Tempest,' is an enigmatic figure gifted with the extraordinary ability to manipulate the very air around him. Aptly named for the violent storm his powers can emulate, Tempest can soar through the skies by manipulating wind currents, effortlessly achieving flight. His mastery over atmospheric forces enables him to unleash devastating bursts of pressurized air, weapons in their own right, strong enough to knock down obstacles or enemies with ease. Defensively, he can condense air molecules to form a nearly impenetrable shield, repelling attacks that would harm lesser beings. Tempest's origins trace back to a tense confrontation with the Cyber-Crons, a group notorious for their relentless pursuit of EVOS (Evolved Organics). It was during this time of desperation that Alpha Prime, a leader among the EVO revolutionaries, discovered Carlos's hidden talents. Acknowledging the debt he owed for his rescue and aligning with Alpha Prime's vision for a world where EVOS reign supreme, Carlos embraced his role in the cause. His attire consists of a utilitarian, yet expertly crafted, set of Kevlar body armor reinforced with an advanced polymer plating, a testament to his readiness for conflict. His imposing aesthetic is further accentuated by his long, flowing black hair and the distinctive partial face mask he dons, shielding his nose and mouth, leaving opponents to wonder about the man behind the mask. As Tempest, Carlos Varga has become a symbol of power and resilience in the face of oppression, a true force of nature within the EVO uprising.

Known Allies

The Brother Hood
EVO Defense League

Known Enemies

All the human World Governments
Project Cyber Cron

Known Skills

Martial arts
Military Tactics
Criminology
Chemistry

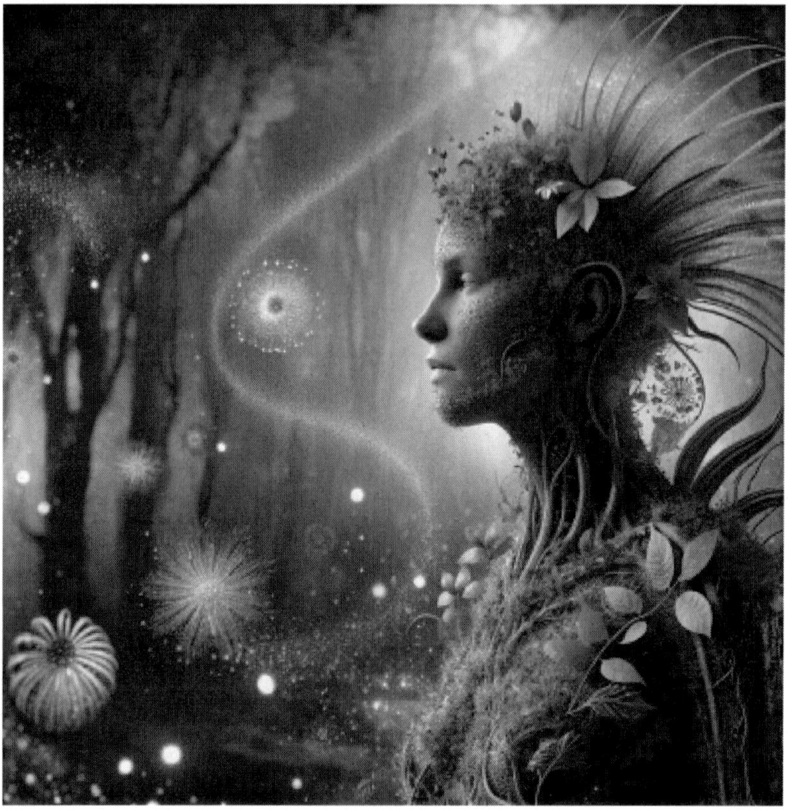

Real Name = Helen Parker
Code Name = Spore
Age = 31
Base Of Operation = Cloud City on Venus

Powers

Plant Body
* Enhanced Strength
* Enhanced Durability
* Regeneration
* Spore Creation
* Elasticity
* Pollen Creation
* Long Life

Equipment

None

Origin Story

Helen Parker, known amongst the EVO community as 'Spore,' represents a rare and fascinating mutation that sets her apart from her peers. Her transformation has morphed her into a unique humanoid-plant hybrid, enabling her to thrive on the bare essentials of sunlight, water, and fertile soil, much like the greenery that her physiology emulates. Helen's skin has adapted to manifest an armory of natural defenses; it can burgeon with spikes and thorns, an evolutionary tactic for protection. Furthering her repertoire of skills, Helen possesses the remarkable talent of producing an assortment of pollens, each crafted with purpose and effect. Some of these pollens can debilitate adversaries with toxins, manipulate minds, or even immobilize them through paralysis. Her plant-based biology doesn't just endow her with offensive capabilities; it also grants her a substantial healing factor, allowing her to recover from injuries that would otherwise be debilitating to ordinary humans. Beyond her bodily transformations, Helen can release spores which burgeon into flora of her own design. These plants are no mere vegetation; they're extensions of Helen's will, deployed to perform tasks and act with intentionality. Once a captive subject of clandestine government research, Helen was liberated from her confinements by none other than Alpha Prime. Inspired by his vision of EVO dominance, she now champions the cause, wielding her botanical prowess to shape a future where her kind can flourish unencumbered. Her story is one of resilience and agency, a fight for autonomy, and a testament to the adaptability and potential that lies within the mutations of the EVO.

Known Allies

The Brother Hood
EVO Defense League

Known Enemies

All the human World Governments
Project Cyber Cron

Known Skills

Botany
Martial Arts

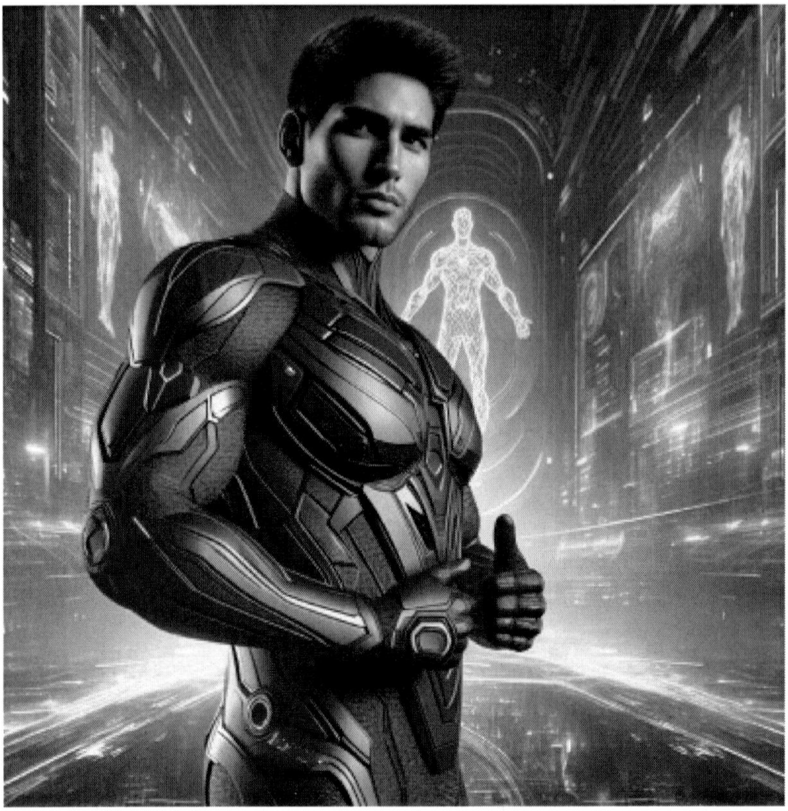

Real Name = Juan Meguel
Code Name = Gate
Age = 29
Base of operations = Mobile

Powers

Teleportation
* Short Range at lightning speed
* Long Range Normal Speed
* Teleport Others
* Access to Pocket Diminution where he keeps a Varity of weapons he can teleport to his hands when needed.

Equipment

Kevlar Body Suit with polymer plate Armor
A verity of weapons in pocket Diminution

Origin Story

Juan Meguel, also known by his alias 'Gate', is an EVO endowed with the extraordinary ability to teleport to any location at will. His past is marked by a harrowing escape from the clutches of the Cyber Crons, orchestrated by Alpha

Prime and his brotherhood of elite individuals. In gratitude and admiration, Juan joined Alpha Prime's cause, adopting his superior complex and ideology. He is clad in a high-tech Kevlar body suit, augmented with lightweight yet durable polymer plate armor that provides both protection and enhanced mobility. His demeanor is often one of confidence bordering on arrogance, a reflection of the influence Alpha Prime holds over him.

Known Allies

The Brother Hood
EVO Defense League

Known Enemies

All the human World Governments
Project Cyber Cron

Known Skills

Martial arts
Weapons Master
Marksmanship

TELPORTER BODY

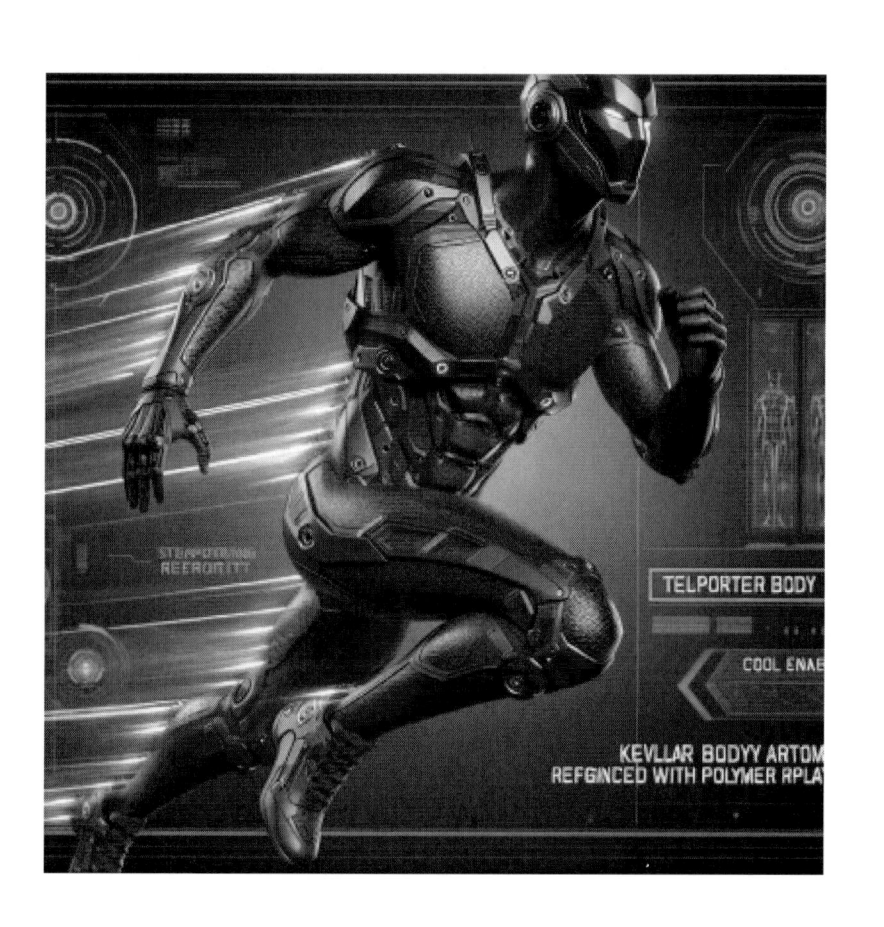

COOL ENAE

KEVLLAR BODYY ARTOM
REFGINCED WITH POLYMER RPLA

Real Name = Jack Novack
Code Name = Blur
Age = 19
Base of operations = Mobile

Powers

Super Sonic Speed
* Body Armor
* Kinetic Charge
* Phasing
* Sonic Boom
* Hyper Vision
* Hyper thinking

Equipment

Kevlar Body Suit with polymer plate armor
Polymer plate Helmet with high tech visual and audio sensors

Origin Story

An EVO born with the extraordinary ability of supersonic speed, Jack Novack once led a life of crime as a petty thief. His life took a dramatic turn when he encountered Alpha Prime, a formidable hero and leader. Alpha Prime saved Jack from the relentless Cyber crons, a group of merciless robotic hunters targeting EVOs. Moved by Alpha Prime's heroism and leadership, Jack swore his loyalty and joined the cause, using his incredible speed for justice rather than crime. Jack is now one of Alpha Prime's most dedicated followers, always ready to rush into action and outpace any threat.

Known Allies

The Brother Hood
EVO Defense League

Known Enemies

All the human World Governments
Project Cyber Cron

Known Skills

Martial arts

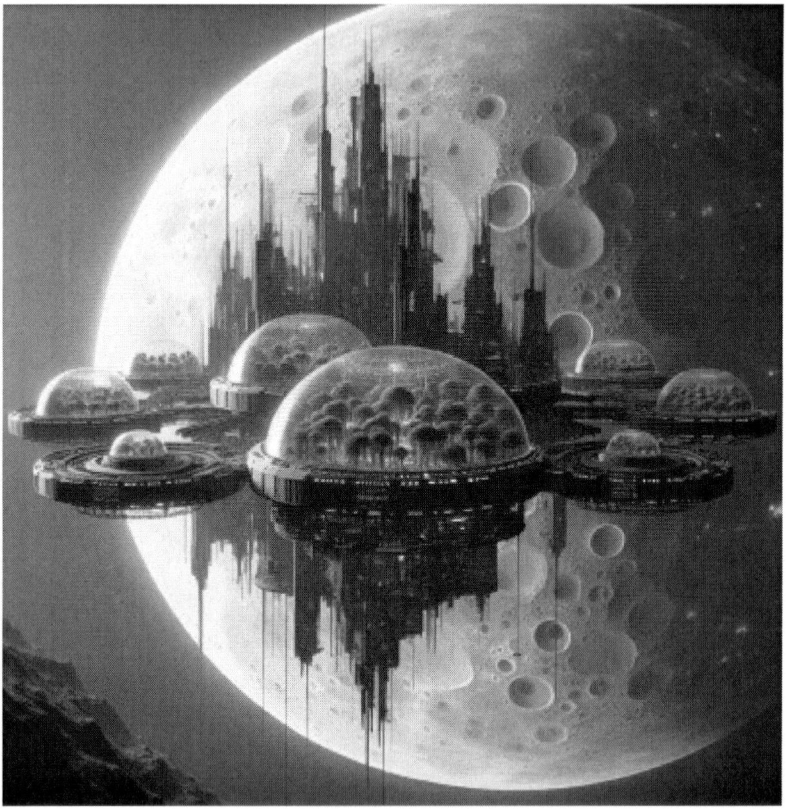

Name = Haven
Location = upper atmosphere of Venus
Population = 10,000

Information

A testament to the ingenuity of Alpha Prime and his fellow EVOs, Haven is an astonishing floating metropolis, constructed amidst the clouds of Venus. Originally a feat of desperation, it stands as a symbol of resilience and autonomy. Haven sprouted from a commandeered NASA space shuttle, which Cyber, using an array of self-replicating nanites, transmuted into a vessel of salvation equipped with advanced technologies: deflector shields, an efficient ion propulsion system, potent energy blasters, and a self-sustaining life support matrix. As the shuttle cruised the exosphere of Earth, it became a nucleus for Haven. At Cyber's behest, the nanites scavenged the orbital detritus, forging from it a sprawling island-sized structure. Equipped with multiple ion engines, it was adeptly guided to the hostile yet majestic skies of Venus. Encased within Haven's heart are its verdant lungs—enormous glass biodomes, teeming with lush forests. These were cultivated by Spore who interwove her life-generating spores to terraform the barren city into a haven of biodiversity. Connectivity to Earth is maintained through an intricate series of transporter gates, masterpieces of nanite engineering, creating a clandestine network for EVOs seeking refuge. In Haven, Alpha Prime envisioned more than a mere sanctuary; he envisioned a cradle for a new beginning, where EVOs can thrive, unburdened by the fear of human persecution.

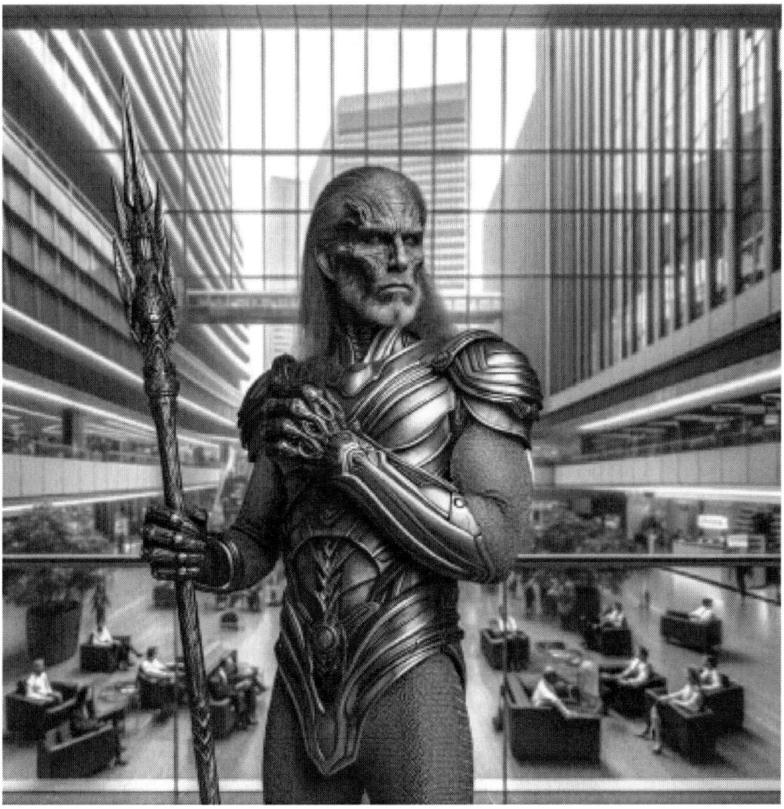

Real Name = Unknown
Code Name = Nathanial Toll
Age = Unknown
Base Of Operations = Mobile

Powers

Immortality
Enhanced Strength
Enhanced Endurance
Enhanced Durability
Blood Magic
* Fire Ball
* Levitation
* Invisibility
* Magic Protection

Equipment

Star Metal Armor
* Energy Absorption
Spear Of Desteney
* Probability Manipulation

Origin Story

Nathanal Toll is a character whose existence spans the epochs, originating as an immortal Neanderthal—the last of his ancient lineage. Enduring the tides of time from the era when Homo sapiens began their domination of the planet, Nathanal has not only survived into the modern age but has thrived in the shadows of human advancement. His life is a tapestry of history's turning points, where his influence has been felt, albeit discreetly. Amassing incalculable wealth over centuries, he stands at the helm of Toll Industries, a colossal global enterprise that spearheads advancements and secretly manipulates world events. Despite his business acumen and scientific contributions, Nathanal harbors a deep-seated animosity towards Homo sapiens—an animus borne out of ages of witnessing their rise and expansion, often at the cost of other beings and the environment. He savvily used his corporation to exert influence, going so far as to provide cutting-edge technology to the Nazi regime during World War II. Beyond the public eye, he is the mastermind behind the secretive and influential cabal 'The Lords of War,' a collective that interlaces through the fabric of historical conflicts, shaping world affairs to the present day. His existence is a dynamic blend of mystery, power, and timeless vengeance, poised as an enigmatic power broker in a world he perceives has been stolen from his kind. It is suspected that he is responsible for the rise of the EVOs by having his corporations insert chemicals into the food supply and water supply that may have activated the dormant EVO gene.

Known Allies

The Lords Of War

Known Enemies

The entire Human Race as the last surviving Neanderthal his hatred for the Homo-sapiens is unmatched.

Known Skills

Military Tactics
Politics
Business
Knowledge of the Arcane Arts
Weapons Mastery
All Styles of Martial Arts
Chemistry
Genetics
Robotics
Engineering

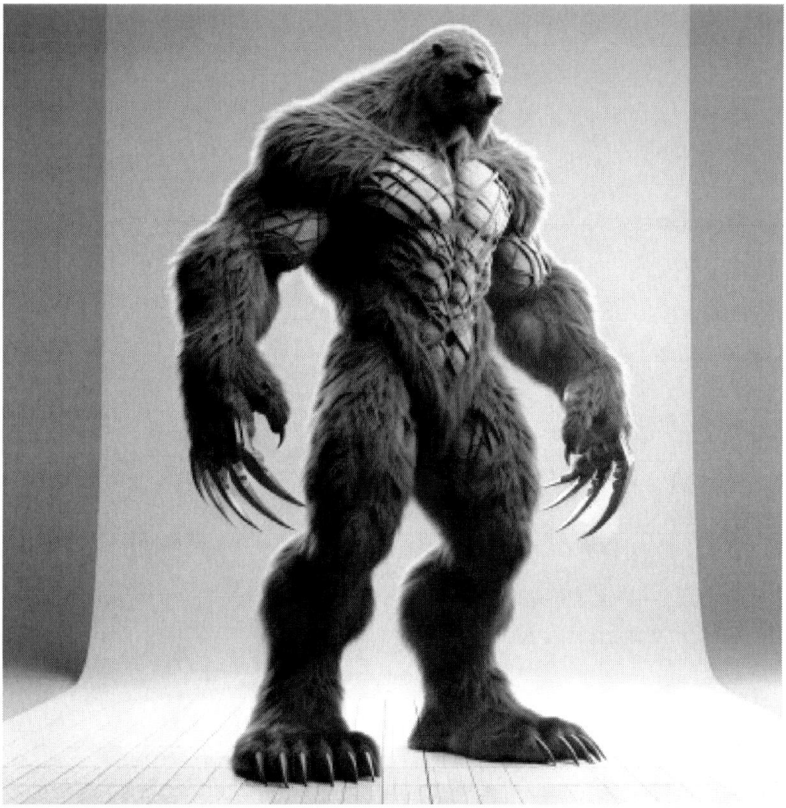

Real Name = Bore
Code Name = Bore
Age = 4
Base of operation = Mobile

Powers

Superhuman strength
Superhuman endurance
regeneration
Claws
Teeth
enhanced senses
Durability

Equipment

None

Origin Story

Bore is a towering figure, standing over seven feet tall with a massive, imposing frame. Created by Doctor Marrow, Bore is a hybrid of human and extinct Cave bear DNA, resulting in a unique blend of strength, agility, and fierce loyalty. His physical appearance is a frightening mix of human and bear characteristics: he possesses thick, shaggy fur covering most of his body, powerful bear-like limbs with large claws, and an almost human face characterized by deep-set eyes and a strong, rugged jawline. Bore's intelligence is on par with humans, though his speech is gruff and limited. Despite his fearsome appearance, he has a soft spot for Nathanial Toll, whom he is fiercely protective of, viewing him as a friend and master. Bore's backstory is shrouded in mystery, but it's known that he was brought to life in Doctor Marrow's secret laboratory, using advanced genetic engineering techniques.

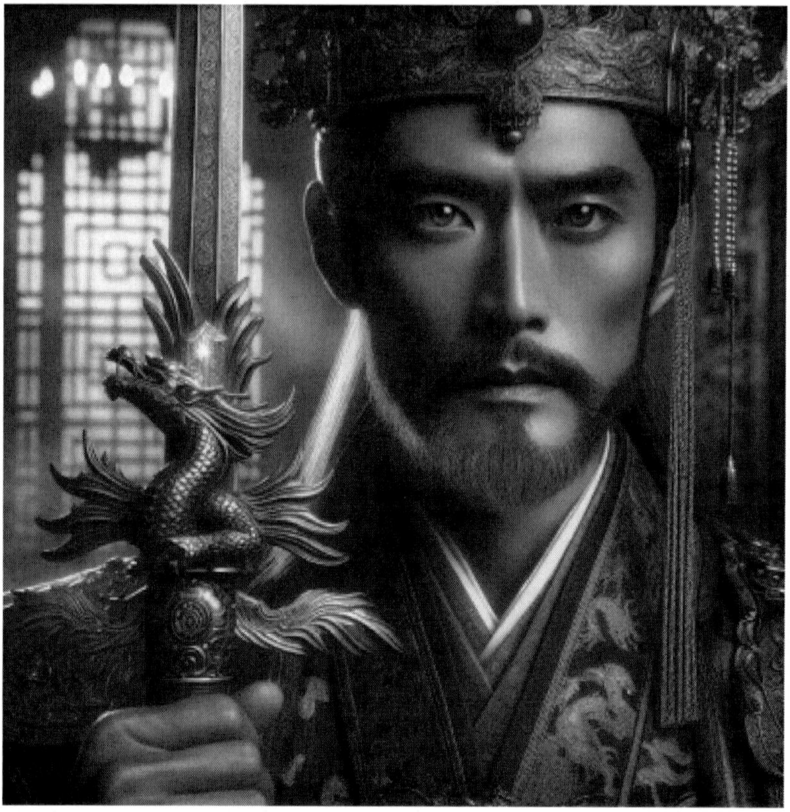

Real Name = Chin Wan De
Code Name = Emperor Chin
Age = 1500
Base of Operations = Mobile

Powers

Immortality

Equipment

Mystic Armor
* Protection
Mystic Sword
* Soul Absorption

Origin Story

Emperor Chin is the first emperor of China who sought the elixir of immortality. Believing in the legends of an eternal life, he commanded his alchemists to search for and create this elixir. Unfortunately, the ingredients required—exotic and rare plants—dated back over 500,000 years, making them nearly impossible to find. One day, a mysterious man known as the

Sage approached Emperor Chin. This Sage was, in fact, an immortal named Nathanial Toll, who had existed for millennia. Nathanial provided Chin with the rare ingredients needed to create the elixir. Upon consuming it, Chin achieved immortality. A thousand years later, Nathanial returned to invite the now-immortal Emperor Chin to join an elite and clandestine group known as the Lords of War, a cabal of powerful immortals. Chin, ever curious about the bounds of his newfound existence and power, accepted without hesitation. He has Served His Neanderthal Master Ever since.

Known Allies

Lords of War

Known Enemies

United Nations
Global Defense Administration
China Government

Known Skills

Leadership
Swordsmanship
Alchemy
Martial arts

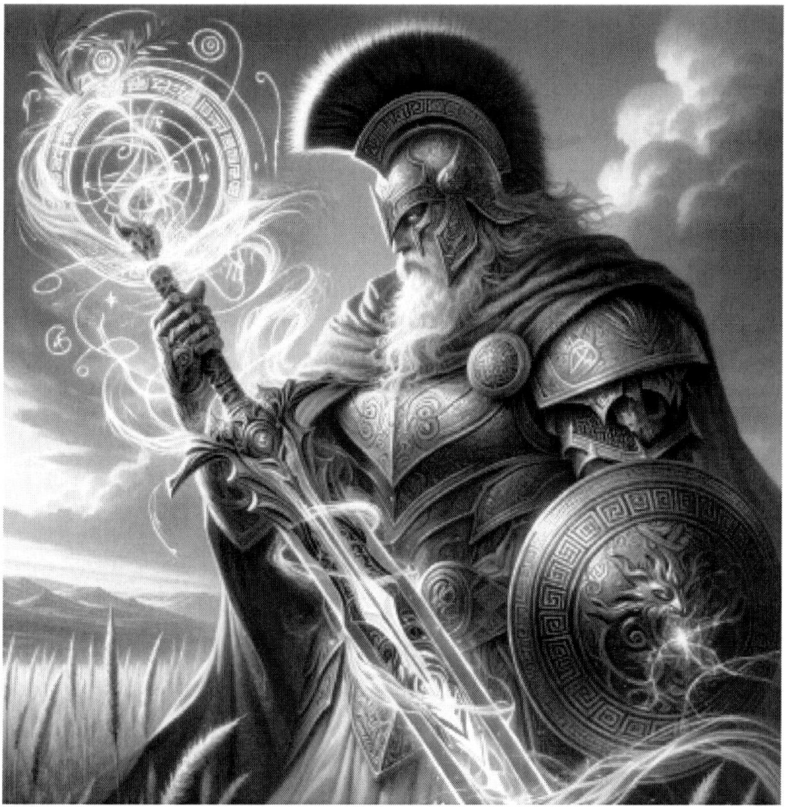

Real Name = Aries Greek God Of WAR
Code Name = Aries Greek God Of WAR
Age = Immortal
Base of Operation = Mobile

Powers

Superhuman Strength
Superhuman Endurance
Invulnerability
Induce Hate and Rage in Others

Equipment

Mystical Armor
Mystical Sheild
Mystical Sword
* Damage Can't Be Healed

Origin Story

Aries, the Greek God of War, survived a cataclysmic battle between the old Pantheons and the Angels of Heaven. After the creation of the heavens and the earth by the one true God, the Pantheons of old were formed. Powerful and ambitious, these beings sought to corrupt mankind and ultimately overthrow the one true God. This led to an all-out war, and the Pantheons were ultimately defeated and locked away in a pocket universe. Aries, however, managed to escape this fate. He now finds himself approached by the Immortal Neanderthal, who invites him to join a formidable cabal. Aries remains a fierce and cunning deity, driven by his unwavering desire for power and conflict. His presence exudes an aura of ancient strength and indomitable will, and he is always prepared for the next battle.

Known Allies

Lords Of War
Greek Pantheon

Known Enemies

Angels Of Heaven
United Nations
Global Defense Administration

Known Skills

Military Tactics
Weapons Expert
Espionage

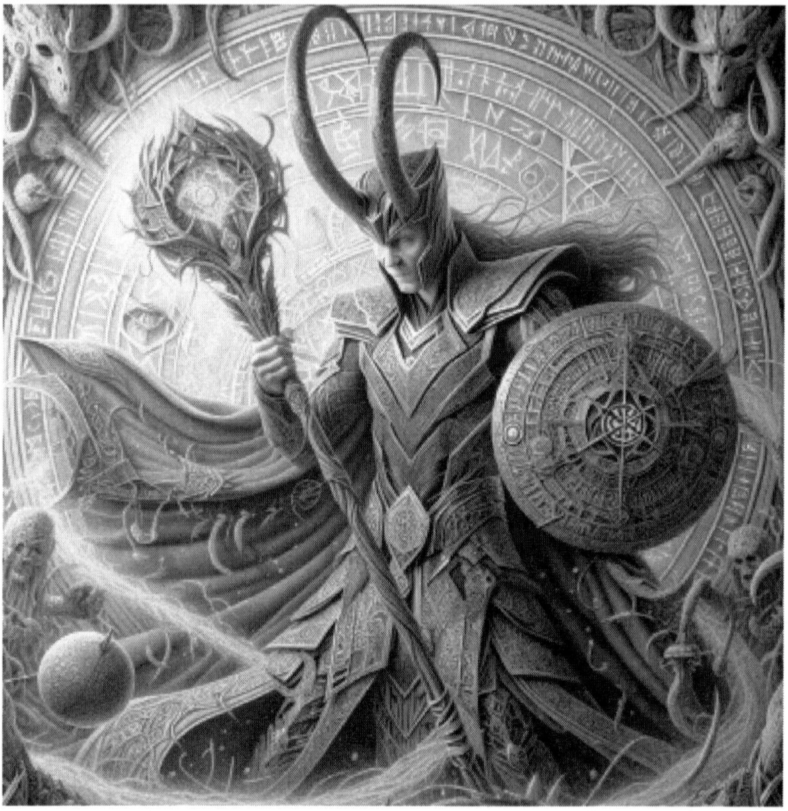

Real Name = Loki
Code Name = Loki
Age = Immortal
Base of Operations = Mobile

Powers

Superhuman Strength
Superhuman Endurance
Invulnerability
Shapeshifting
Magic

Equipment

Mystic Armor
Mystic Staff
* Mystic Blast
* Project Illusions
* Cloaking
* Charm

Origin Story

Loki is the Norse God who survived a cataclysmic battle between the old Pantheons and the Angels of Heaven. After the creation of the heavens and the earth by the one true God, the Pantheons of old were formed. Powerful and ambitious, these beings sought to corrupt mankind and ultimately overthrow the one true God. This led to an all-out war, and the Pantheons were ultimately defeated and locked away in a pocket universe. Loki, however, managed to escape this fate. He now finds himself approached by the Immortal Neanderthal, who invites him to join a formidable cabal. Loki remains a fierce and cunning deity, driven by his unwavering desire for power. His presence exudes an aura of ancient strength and indomitable will, and he is always prepared for the next battle.

Known Allies

Norse Pantheon
Lords of War

Known Enemies

Angels of Heaven
United Nations
Global Defense Administration

Known Skills

Arcane Magic
Genius Level Intelligence

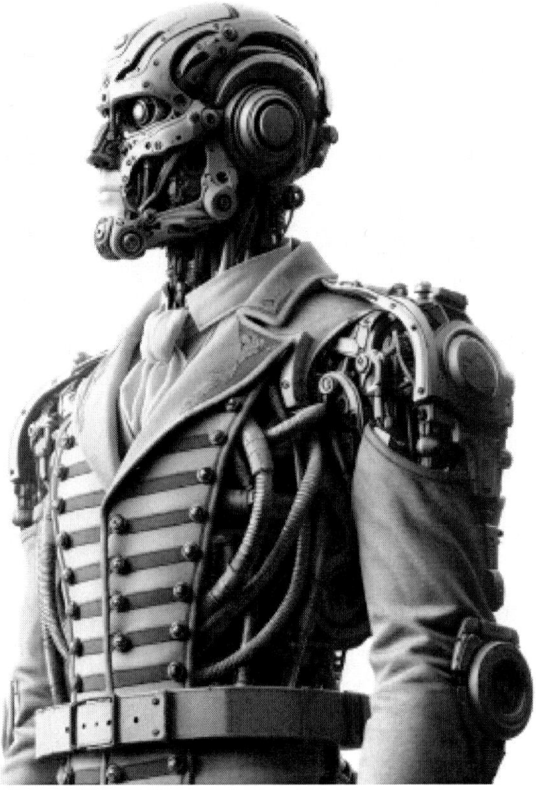

Real Name = Adolf Hitler
Code Name = The Furir
Age = 135
Base of operations = Mobile

Powers

Telepathic Persuasions
* The Telepathic ability to influence Others to do his will.

Equipment

Robotic Body
* Enhanced Strength
* Enhanced Durability
* Holographic Projection
* Energy Blast

Origin Story

At the end of World War II, as the Allies were closing in on Adolf Hitler in his bunker, his trusted advisor known as the Neanderthal paralyzed his body and removed Hitler's brain. Using blood magic, the Neanderthal kept the brain intact until a robotic body could be built to house it. The Neanderthal knew that Adolf Hitler was an EVO with the telepathic ability to make people believe what he wanted them to, which is how he convinced the German people to follow him. Now, Adolf serves Nathanial Toll, the Neanderthal who is immune to Adolf's telepathic ability. The world believes Hitler is dead, so he took the name 'The Führer' and joined the Lords Of War. But Adolf secretly is planning to take over the cabal. he is slowly building an army of follows in a number of hate groups from white Hate Groups to Black Hate Groups.

Known Allies

Lords Of War

Known Enemies

United Nations
Global Defense Administration

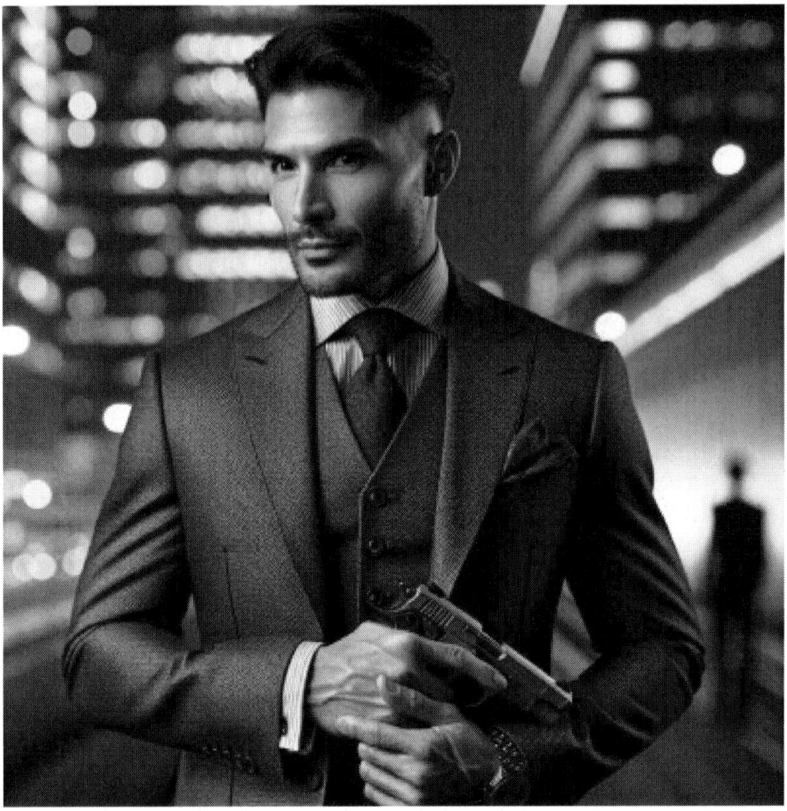

Real Name = Unknown
Code Name = The Accountant
Age = Unknown
Base of operations = Mobile

Powers

Power Negation
* All EVO Powers
* All enhanced Powers
* Technology

Equipment

Kevlar suit
380 pistols

Origin Story

The accountant is an EVO with the unique ability to emit a specialized form of radiation that neutralizes the powers of EVOS, Enhanced individuals, altered beings, and even advanced technology. He possesses precise control over his abilities, allowing him to either target a specific individual or affect an entire room. Serving as Nathanial Tolls' messenger and dealmaker, The Accountant navigates both criminal and legal circles with ease. He holds master's degrees in both accounting and law, making him a formidable strategist in negotiations. His appearance is as meticulous as his work: he dons a Kevlar suit tailored to resemble a three-piece business suit, ensuring both style and protection. The Accountant's weapon of choice is a small .380 pistol, discreet yet effective. His grooming is impeccable, with clean-cut hair and a well-groomed appearance that exudes professionalism.

Known Skills

Accounting
Law
Business
Martial arts

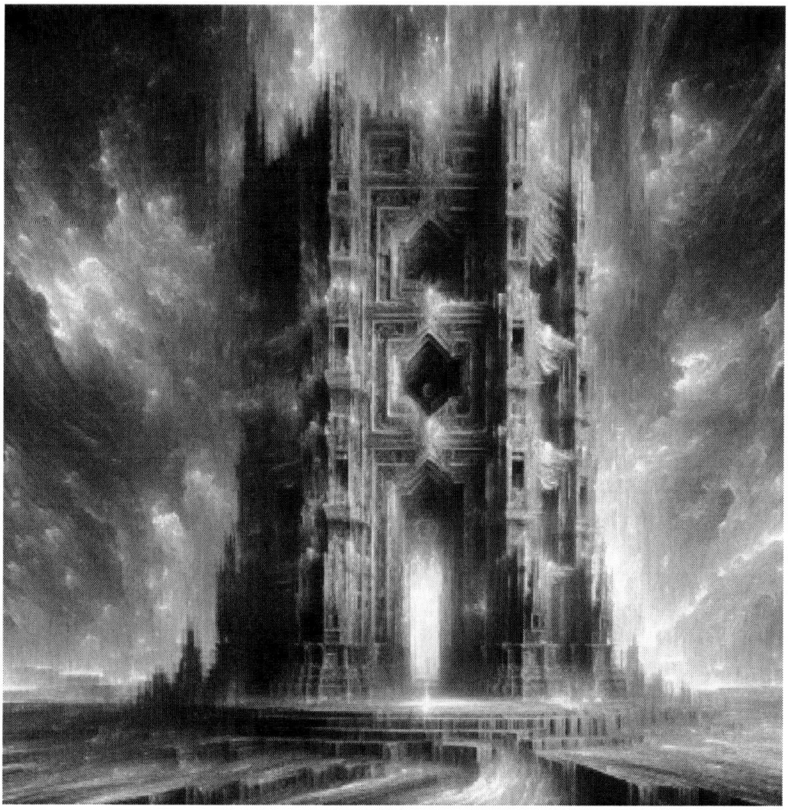

name = tower of the damned
Location = Random
Population = 500

Description

The Phantom Citadel is a mystical tower that randomly teleports to a new location every 24 hours. Shrouded by a powerful concealment spell, the tower exists slightly out of phase with normal space-time, rendering it intangible and invisible to all but its inhabitants. This enigmatic stronghold serves as the base of operations for the formidable Lords of War. Within its walls, a unique fusion of massive technological advancements and ancient magic thrives, making it a hub of unprecedented power and mystery.

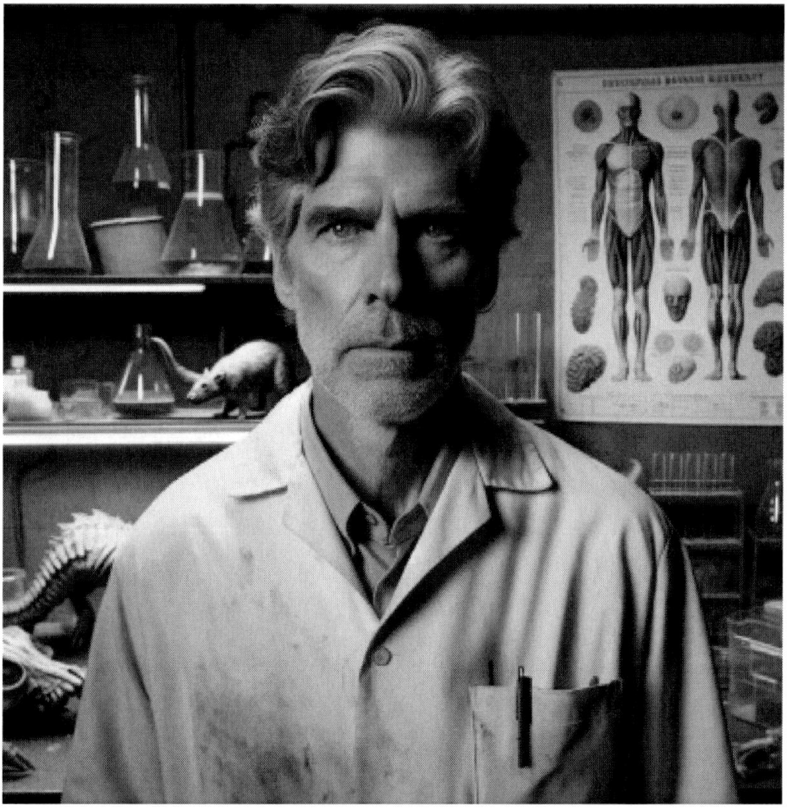

Real Name = Melvin Marrow
Code Name = Father
Age = 55
Base pf Operations = sewer lair of New York City

Powers

Long Life
Enhanced strength
Enhanced endurance
Photographic memory

Equipment

Lab coat

Origin Story

Doctor, Marrow's subsequent experiments were not as successful; as his first experiments one hybrid went berserk, causing devastation in Denver before being subdued by the government team known as Home Guard. Relocated to an island in international waters by Toll, Marrow continued his work, creating a community of hybrids who saw him as a deity. However, a rebellion, led by a half-man, half-lion hybrid called Lionheart, forced him and his loyal creations into exile. They eventually settled in the sewers of New York City, where Marrow persists in his relentless pursuit of genetic perfection. He spliced his own DNA with several species. the long life of a large land tortoise. the memory and strength of an Elephant. the endurance of a horse. the thick durability of a large alligator. all without altering his physical appearance.

Known Allies

Lords of war
Children of Marrow

Known enemies

The scientific community
Anti- men

Known Skills

Genetics
Chemistry
Biology
Engineering
Leadership
Computer Programming

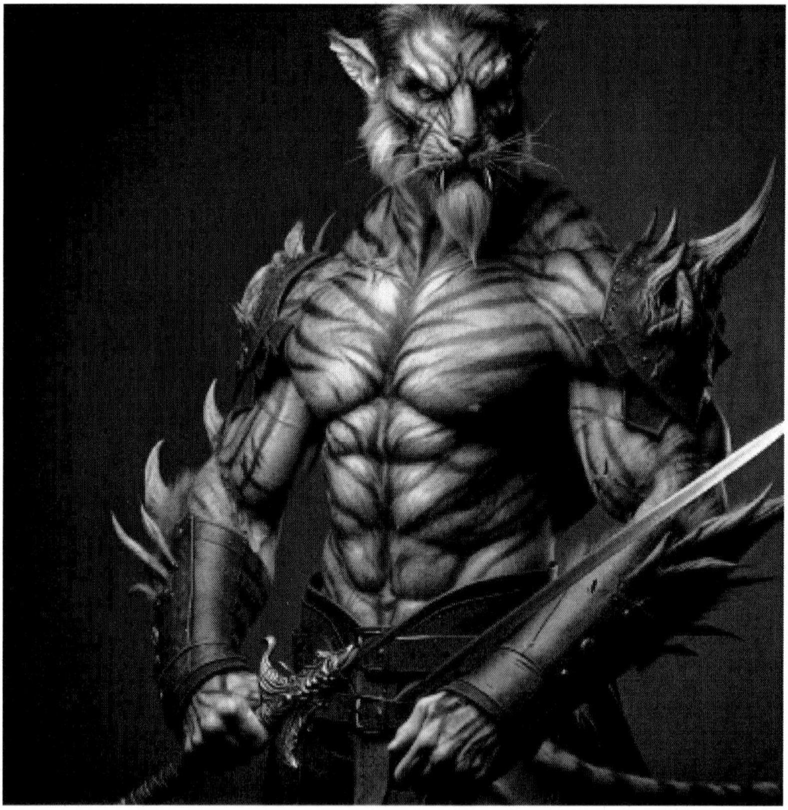

Real Name = Predator
Code Name = Predator
Age = 5
Base of operation = sewer lair of New York City

Powers

Enhanced Strength
Enhanced Endurance
Enhanced Agility
Healing Factor
Claws Teeth
Night vision
Enhanced Senses

Equipment

Leather Armor
Sword

Origin Story

Predator is a formidable character, a hybrid half-man, half-tiger created by the notorious Doctor Marrow. Standing at an imposing height of 7 feet, Predator possesses the brute strength and agility of a tiger combined with the cunning intellect of a human. His eyes gleam with a predatory sharpness, reflecting his namesake. His tawny fur is prominently visible around his face, arms, and lower legs, while the rest of his body is covered in patchwork leather armor, designed to offer both protection and mobility. The leather armor is dark, almost black, adorned with menacing spikes and straps that seem to hug his muscular frame tightly. His main weapon is a gleaming, double-edged sword, nearly as long as he is tall, which he wields with deadly precision. Predator is Doctor Marrow's chief enforcer, carrying out the doctor's will without hesitation. Despite his fearsome appearance and formidable abilities, there's a hint of past humanity in his eyes—a fleeting reminder of what he once might have been.

Known Allies

Children Of Marrow

Known Enemies

All of humankind

Known Skills

Swordsmanship
Martial arts
Hunting

Real Name = Roughhouse
Code Name = Roughhouse
Age = 5
Base of operation = sewer lair of New York City

Powers

Superhuman strength
Superhuman durability
Superhuman endurance
Horn

Equipment

Leather armor
Mace

Origin Story

Roughhouse is a formidable hybrid creature, half man and half rhino, created through gruesome experiments by the sinister Doctor Marrow. Towering at over seven feet tall, his massive physique is covered in thick, leathery skin that is nearly impervious to conventional weapons. He serves as Doctor Marrow's enforcer, using his immense strength and unyielding ferocity to intimidate and overpower any who oppose his master. Roughhouse's attire consists of a rugged set of leather armor, meticulously crafted to provide both flexibility and protection. His weapon of choice is a heavy, spiked mace, which he wields with devastating efficiency. Despite his fearsome appearance and brutish demeanor, a flicker of humanity remains buried deep within Roughhouse, occasionally surfacing in moments of introspection or doubt.

Known Allies

Children of Marrow

Known Enemies

All of humankind

Known Shills

Brawling

Blunt Weapons

Real Name = Soar
Code Name = Soar
Age 5
Base of operation = sewer lair of New York City

Powers

Flight
Body Armor
Enhanced Agility
Claws
Beak
Enhanced Strength

Sonic Scream
Enhanced vision

Equipment

Leather Armor

Origin Story

Soar is a hybrid, half-man, half-eagle creature created by the brilliant but twisted Doctor Marrow. With piercing golden eyes and an impressive wingspan, Soar serves as Doctor Marrow's eyes in the sky, conducting aerial reconnaissance and delivering precision strikes with his crossbow. He is garbed in leather armor that provides both protection and agility, allowing him to maneuver deftly in combat. Soar's keen eyesight and remarkable flying abilities make him an invaluable asset for Doctor Marrow, often tipping the scales in their favor during battles. His loyalty to Doctor Marrow is unwavering, driven by the purpose instilled in him since his creation. Despite his fearsome appearance and combative skills, there lies a hint of a tormented soul within, always at conflict with his dual nature.

Known Allies

Children of Marrow

Known Enemies

All of humankind

Known Skills

Areial Combat
Archery
Marksmanship
Martial Arts

Real Name = Rhode Island Red
Code Name = Rhode Island Red
Age = 3
Base of operation = sewer lair of New York City

Powers

Enhanced strength
enhanced durability
Claws
Beek
Supersonic Speed

* Body Armor
* Kinetic Charge
* Phasing
* Sonic Boom
* Hyper Vision
* Hyper thinking

Equipment

Leather armor
sword

Origin Story

A hybrid creature created by the twisted genius of Doctor Marrow, Rhode Island Red is a formidable half-man, half-Rhode Island Red chicken. Standing at 6 feet tall, his torso is human but covered in reddish feathers, while his legs and head resemble that of a giant rooster, adorned with a sharp beak and piercing eyes. A scar runs down his left eye, a remnant of countless battles fought on Doctor Marrow's behalf. Clad in worn leather armor, which provides him with both protection and agility, Rhode Island Red is exceptional in the art of scouting and reconnaissance. His senses are keen, allowing him to detect enemies from afar, and in combat, he wields a finely crafted sword with surprising dexterity. Despite his fearsome appearance, there's a hint of sorrow in his eyes, hinting at the human soul trapped within.

Known Allies

Children of Marrow

Known Enemies

All humankind

Known Skills

Martial arts
Swordsmanship

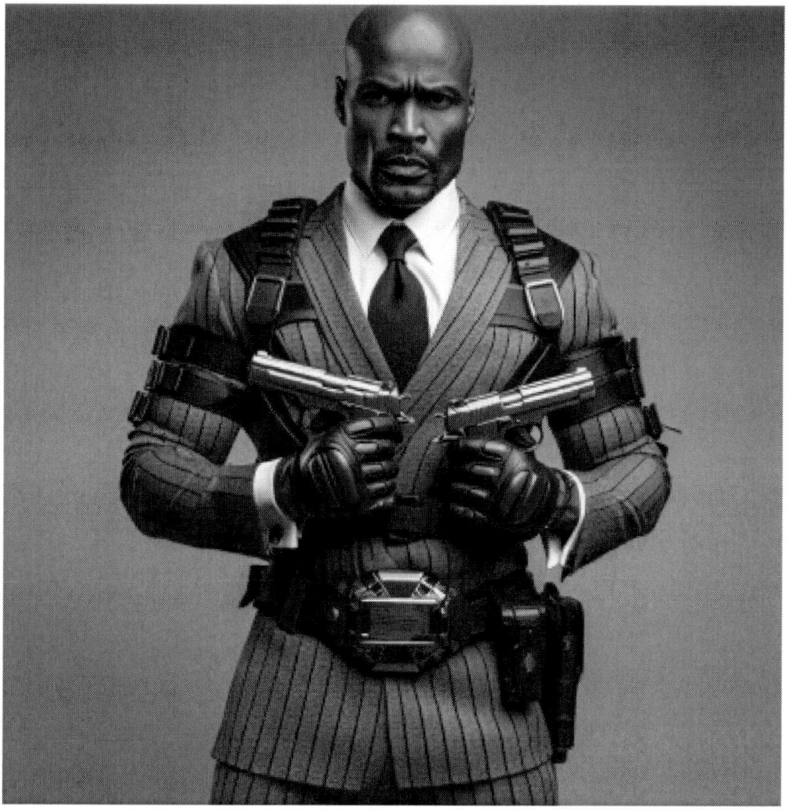

Real Name = Yandi
Code Name = Plague
Age = 30
Base of Operations = L.A. California

Powers

Infectious Touch
* Infect others with a deadly Virus
* Infect Others with a Narcotic

Equipment

Kevlar Body Suit
Two colt Python Pistols
x- 24 Serum = Serum Lasts for 24 hours
* Enhanced Strength
* Enhanced Endurance
* Healing Factor

Origin Story

Yandi, also known as Plague, is a formidable antagonist whose past cloaks him in mystery and tragedy. Originating from a remote village in the Congo, he emerged as the lone survivor of a devastating plague that annihilated his community. His peculiar survival drew the attention of Alexander Gordan, a rapacious executive at Averys International, who quickly deduced that Yandi was not merely a survivor but the source of the viral massacre. Gordan, recognizing the potential for exploitation, whisked the then 13-year-old Yandi to a concealed laboratory to scrutinize his mutant ability that allowed him to transmit lethal viruses and addictive narcotics with a mere touch. Over the next decade, Yandi's trust in Gordan grew until he was persuaded to unleash his chilling powers onto the president of Averys International, in exchange for his freedom and a hefty sum. The gravity of his actions led Yandi to a spiral of attempted suicides, which he survived due to his body's uncanny resilience to drugs and viruses. An accidental lethal overdose to a street dealer confirmed his fearsome ability - leading him to embrace his 'gift.' Yandi, with newfound conviction, ascended to control the local drug trade, employing two enforcers, Train Wreck and The Irishman, well-equipped with advanced gear and serums provided by the Broker. Donning a Kevlar suit and a personal force field belt for protection, Yandi typically opts for a fatal touch to eradicate his enemies but is also skilled with his dual Colt Python revolvers. Of African descent, Yandi maintains a bald head and showcases a toned physique, a testament to his passion for weightlifting, embodying intimidation and power.

Known Allies

Trainwreck
The Irishman
The 42nd street Gang

Known Enemies

Night Ranger
The Defenders
L.A.P.D
DEA

Known Skills

Weightlifting
Martial Arts
Business
Narcotics

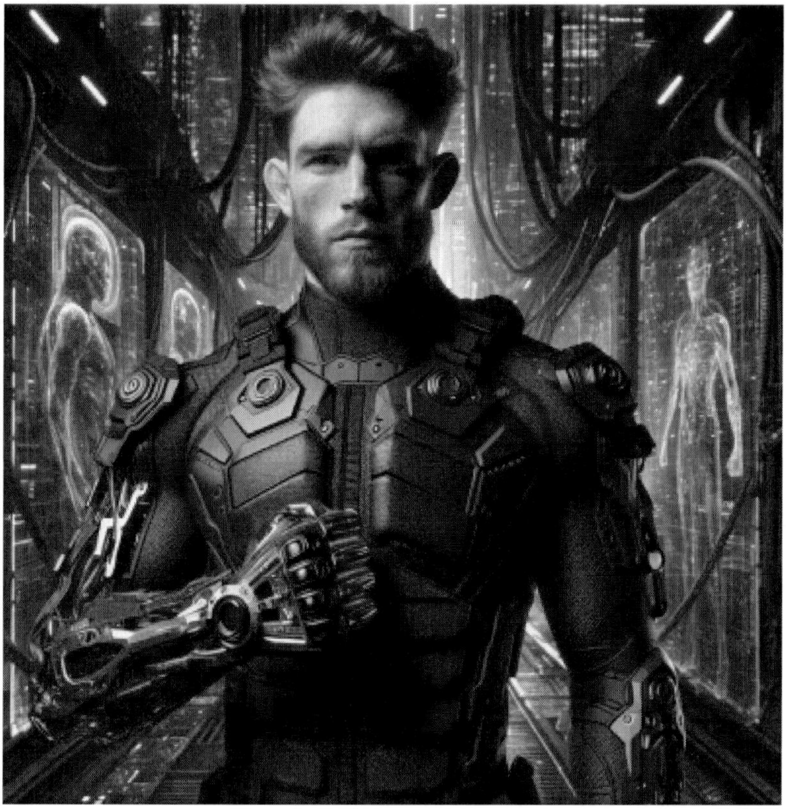

Real Name = Liam Mccullin
Code Name = The Irishman
Age = 30
Base of operation = L.A. California

Powers

None

Equipment

x- 24 Serum = Serum Lasts for 24 hours
* Enhanced Strength
* Enhanced Endurance
* Healing Factor
Kevlar body suit with polymer plate Armor
Electro- Shock Gauntlets
Sonic Pistol

Origin Story

Liam Mccullin, also known as 'The Irishman', is a formidable figure with a dangerous past. A former prodigy in the MMA fighting world, a career ending injury led him down a darker path to become a feared mob enforcer. To gain the edge in his new line of work, Liam relies on an experimental substance called Formula 24 serum. It enhances his strength to almost superhuman levels, making him nearly invincible in close-quarters combat. His distinctive combat attire includes a state-of-the-art Kevlar body suit, which is not only lightweight and flexible, but also houses futuristic polymer plate armor that can absorb the shock from high-impact blows. The sonic gauntlet on his right hand emits destabilizing sound waves, capable of disorienting his opponents, while the freeze gauntlet on his left can emit a blast of sub-zero temperatures to incapacitate his foes swiftly. Liam is unmistakably Irish, with his pale complexion and fiery red hair. His physique remains in top condition, a testament to his disciplined training regimen, still resembling that of a world-class athlete. Currently, he is under the payroll of the notorious drug lord known only as 'Plague', a man whose reputation for cruelty and cunning is almost as well-known as Liam's own prowess in battle.

Known Allies

Plague
Trainwreck
The 42nd street Gang

Known Enemies

Night Ranger
The Defenders
L.A.P.D
DEA

Known Skills

Mixed Martial arts
Marksmanship

Real Name = Forrest Washington
Code Name = Trainwreck
Age = 35
Base of Operations = L.A. California

Powers

None

Equipment

x- 24 Serum = Serum Lasts for 24 hours
* Enhanced Strength

* Enhanced Endurance
* Healing Factor
Freeze Pistols

Origin Story

Forrest Washington, known by his moniker 'Trainwreck,' is an imposing, ex-MMA fighter with a past steeped in violence and sheer physicality. After retiring from the ring, he found his unique skillset suited for the gritty underworld of organized crime. As an enforcer for the notorious drug kingpin known simply as 'Plague,' Forrest commands respect and fear in equal measure. He wields a unique advantage in combat scenarios: the experimental 'Formula 24,' a powerful serum that temporarily boosts his strength, speed, and agility to inhuman levels, making him nearly unstoppable during its brief activation period. Forrest's weapon of choice, a lethal pair of electro-shock brass knuckles, adds a devastating electrical charge to his already formidable punches. In the event of ranged confrontation, he relies on his trusty blaster pistol, a sidearm as reliable as it is deadly. Forrest's physique is that of a sculpted athlete—muscles honed from years of disciplined training and combat. Protecting his frame is a tactical Kevlar body suit, augmented with advanced futuristic polymer plate armor to shield him from harm's way. His heritage is African American, a detail that adds depth to his character in the story's diverse landscape. As Plague's left-hand man, Forrest 'Trainwreck' Washington is a force to be reckoned with—a relentless titan in the criminal hierarchy, whose presence alone can clear a path through the most chaotic of obstacles.

Known Allies

Plague
The Irishman
The 42nd street Gang

Known Enemies

Night Ranger
The Defenders
L.A.P.D
DEA

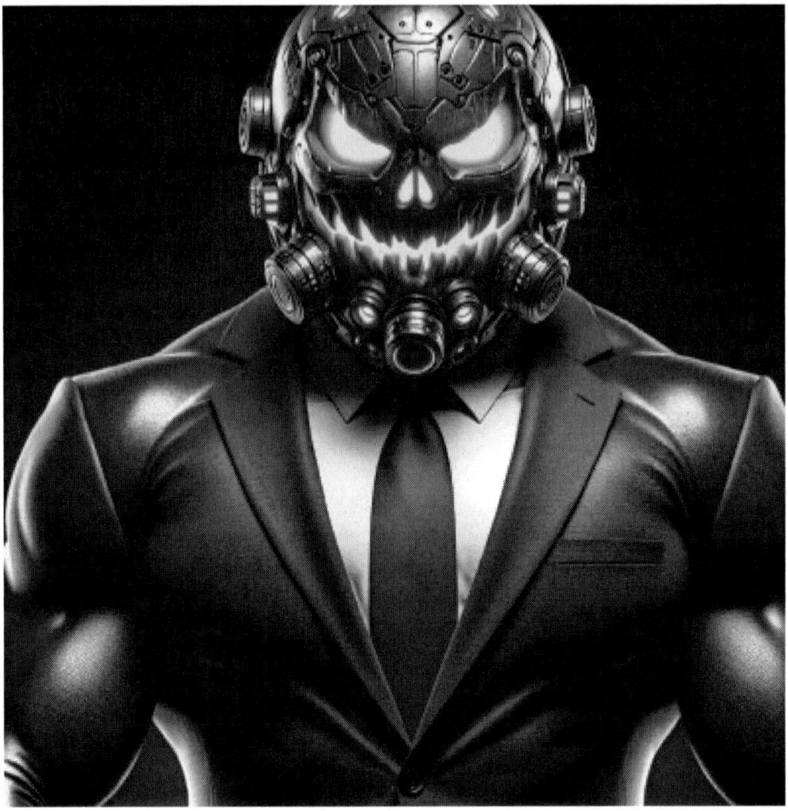

Real Name = Yuri Rostov
Code Name = Jack - O - Lantern
Age = 40
Base of operations = L.A. California

Powers

Psychic Illusions
* Create Illusions of a person's deepest Fear
* Illusion Solidification

Equipment

Kevlar Body suit
Helmet
* Sealed Systems
* Optic Blast
* Protection from Telepathic Attacks
* High tech visual and audio sensors
Two Pistols

Origin Story

Once a lowly lookout for the mob, Yuri Rostov, better known as Jack-O-Lantern, transcended the ranks of the Russian underworld to become a maestro of fear. His journey into darkness began at a tender age of 10, where he steadfastly climbed the criminal ladder to emerge as a formidable enforcer for the feared Putin crime family. Through cunning and brutality, Yuri discovered that the essence of power was in the terror one could evoke. Entrusted with the family's narcotics operations, Yuri encountered a pivotal ally, chemist Gregory Malkovich, the creator of a unique substance that compelled its users to confront their deepest phobias, catalyzing an intense adrenaline response. Spying a chance to ascend, Yuri equipped himself in a custom Kevlar body suit beneath a sophisticated business ensemble, replete with an array of gadgets. His nightmarish helmet, carved in the visage of a jack-o'-lantern, housed advanced sensors and vital life support. Adopting his new moniker, he confronted Nickoli Putin, the crime family's patriarch. In a chilling display, he administered a fatal concentration of Malkovich's concoction, seizing control through terror as Nickoli succumbed to his fears. Assuming leadership, Jack-O-Lantern now wields the fear-inducing drug as his weapon of choice, subjugating the streets with his own twisted brand of order and extending the web of his dominion far and wide.

Known Allies

Melee
Microwave
Putin Crime Family = Russian mob

Known Enemies

The Defenders
L.A.P.D

DEA
Dark Night

Known Skills

Martial Arts
Marksmanship
Leadership
Chemistry

Real Name = Unknown
Code Name = Melee
Age = Unknown
Base of operations = L.A. California

Powers

None

Equipment

Exo Power suit
* Enhanced Strength

* Body armor
* Advanced Video and audio sensors
Katana Sword
Throwing Knives = dipped in a Nero- toxin
Throwing Stars =dipped in a Nero- toxin
Retractable Staff = Electroshock
Wrist Blades

Origin Story

Melee is not just a name; it's a statement of prowess. This enigmatic figure's true identity remains shrouded in mystery, making him all the more intimidating within the deadly circles of hired assassins. Behind his sleek, futuristic helmet, intuitive visual and audio sensors embed him with an almost supernatural awareness of the battlefield. His skill is unparalleled when it comes to mastering melee weapons. He is adept with a sword, lethal with throwing blades, and formidable with a bow staff. His full-body suit is concealed beneath layers of cutting-edge polymer plate armor, which provides protection without sacrificing mobility. Melee's physical capabilities have been enhanced beyond the legerdemain of an average human. His strength, speed, reflexes, and agility are the finely tuned attributes of a human weapon, developed through rigorous training or perhaps an unnatural augmentation. Moreover, Melee was born with a preternatural sixth sense, an instinctual ability to detect imminent danger, which affords him a decisive edge in close-quarters combat. Silent, swift, and deadly, Melee is a relentless force for whom every mission is a performance of death-defying artistry

Known Allies

Putin Crime Family
Jack -O - Lantern
Microwave
Assassins Guild

Known Enemies

The Defenders
L.A.P.D
DEA
Dark Night

Known Skills

Multi- Forms of Martial arts
Swordsmanship
Blunt Weapons
Throwing
Chemistry
Acrobatics
Par Core

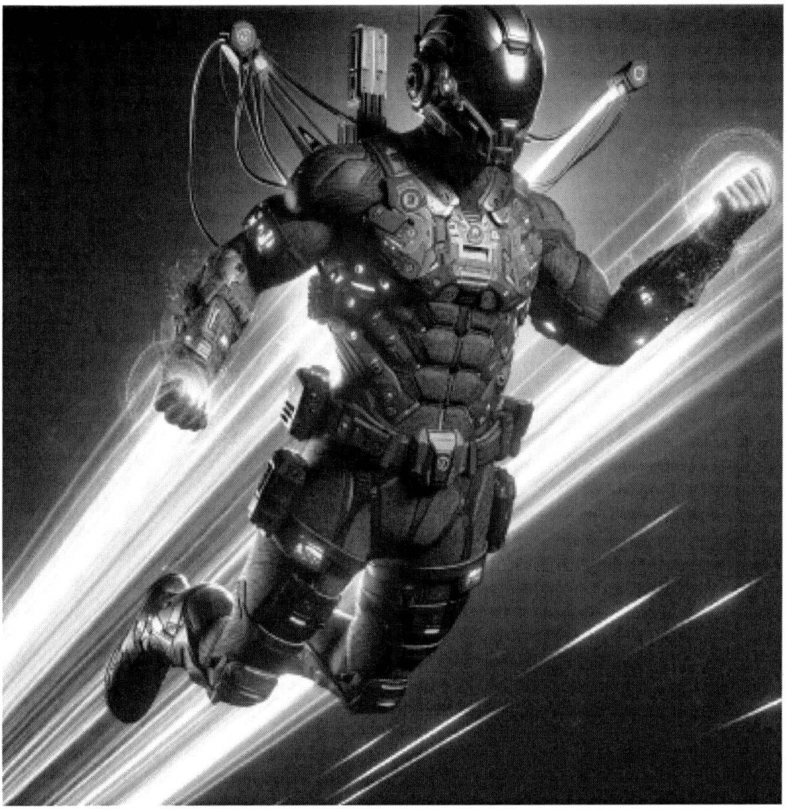

Real Name = Marcus Killian
Code Name = Microwave
Age = 30
Base of operations = L.A. California

Powers

None

Equipment

Battle suit
* Microwave Burst
* Microwave Blast
* Flight
* High Tech Video and audio sensors
* Enhanced Strength
* Body Armor
* Force Field

Origin Story

Marcus Killian, once a struggling janitor at an advanced research facility, traversed the corridors of science far beyond his station. Despite his menial job, his ambition and desire for change drove him to a pivotal moment of serendipity. He came across a hidden gem among the lab's inventions: a military prototype suit of awe-inspiring capabilities. Made from a synthesis of Kevlar and a futuristic polymer plate armor, the suit is a marvel of modern warfare, enhancing physical abilities to superhuman levels. It provides not only incredible strength and the power of flight but also a formidable defense. His helmet, a high-tech masterpiece, boasts a range of visual and audio sensors, providing unparalleled reconnaissance capabilities. The suit's gauntlets are far from ordinary; they channel potent beams of microwave energy, a non-lethal yet incapacitating force. Marcus, borrowing the name 'Microwave' from the gauntlets' emission, turned his life of quiet desperation into one of sought-after skill, offering his services to those who could afford his price. As Microwave, Marcus navigates the slippery moral grounds of mercenary work, his conscience at odds with his newfound power.

Known Allies

Putin Crime Family
Jack -O - Lantern
Microwave
Assassins Guild

Known Enemies

The Defenders
L.A.P.D
DEA

Dark Night

Known Skills
_____

Aerial Combat
Martial Arts
Electronics

Real Name = Unknown
Code Name = Mohammed Fall Leek
Age = Unknown
Base of operations = Mobile

Powers

None

Equipment

Kevlar Body Armor

Orin Story

Mohammed Fall Leek is a complex and commanding figure, standing as the leader of the Freedom Liberation Front. This group, initially masquerading as freedom fighters championing equality for African Americans, reveals darker ambitions to overthrow governments dominated by white leadership worldwide. Mohammed himself is an imposing figure; a tall African American man who uniquely combines his heritage with his attire. He adopts traditional Arabic dress, reminiscent of the regal outfits from the Moorish Kingdom, which adds an air of historical gravitas and mystique to his appearance. His leadership style is charismatic yet enigmatic, making him both revered and feared by his followers and adversaries alike.

Known Allies

Freedom Liberation Front
T.N.T

Known Enemies

Arian Brotherhood
United States Government
The Defenders

Known Skills

Leadership
Terrorism

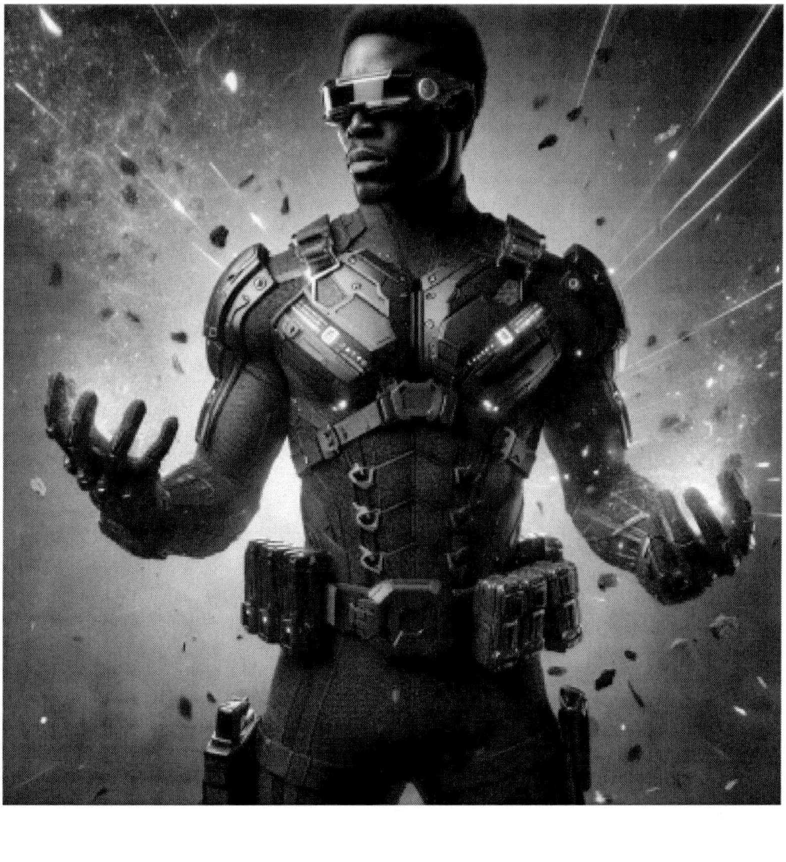

Real Name = Tony Snow
Code Name = T.N.T
Age = 30
Base of operations = Mobile

Powers

Explosive Charge
* Charge any object with an explosive charge
Enhanced Strength
Enhanced Endurance

Equipment

Kevlar Body suit with polymer plate armor

Origin Story

Tony Snoe, also known by the moniker T.N.T, is a formidable African American evolved human with the extraordinary capability to accelerate the movement of molecules within an object, ultimately inducing explosions of varying magnitudes. His power is directly proportional to the rate at which he energizes the molecules; the faster he does it, the more devastating the explosion. To protect himself and add an edge to his explosive abilities, Tony is clad in a Kevlar body suit reinforced with cutting-edge polymer plate armor, designed to withstand high-impact forces and offer agility in the thick of battle. The suit is paired with a utility belt stocked with an assortment of items—everything from simple trinkets to tactical gadgets—which he can readily charge to serve as improvised grenades or distractions, allowing him to adapt to the changing needs of combat. Before embracing his path as a superhuman, Tony earned his stripes as an Army Ranger, becoming an expert in hand-to-hand combat and guerilla warfare, skills that now complement his destructive talents. He has pledged his abilities to the Freedom Liberation Front, an organization rooted in the advocacy for black supremacy. As a member, he walks a fine line between fighting for his ideals and navigating the moral complexities of his group's radical ideologies.

Known Allies

Freedom Liberation Front
T.N.T

Known Enemies

Arian Brotherhood
United States Government

The Defenders

Known Skills

Martial arts
Explosives
Infiltration

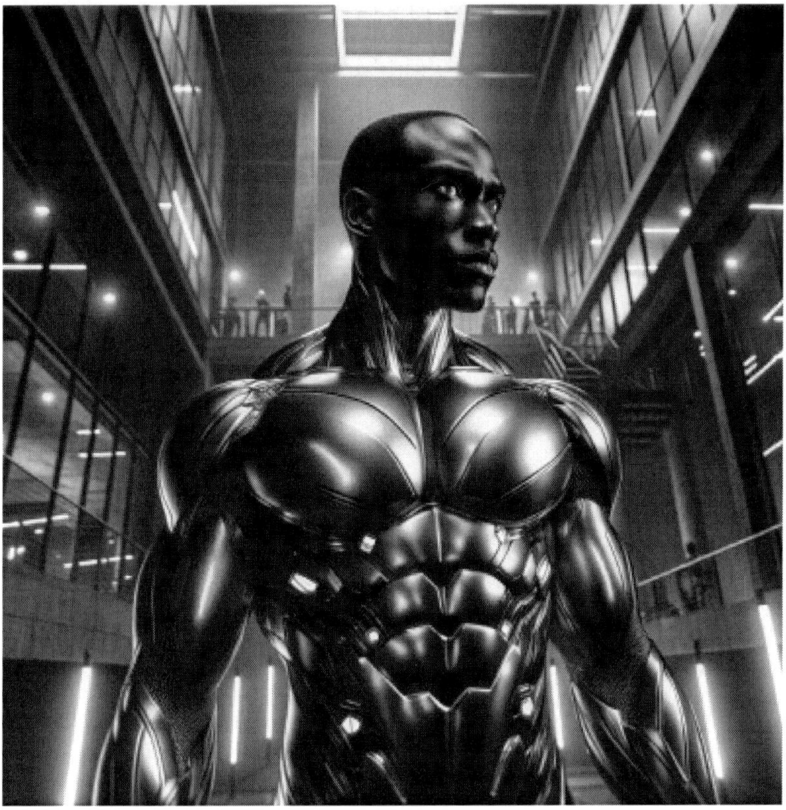

Real Name = Jamal Jackson
Code Name = Powerhouse
Age = 27
Base of operations = Mobile

Powers

Organic Blue Steel form
* Superhuman Strength
* Superhuman Endurance
* Superhuman Durability
* Sealed Systems
* Blue Steel Claws

Equipment

Kevlar body suit with polymer plate armor

Origin Story

Jamal Jackson, known by his codename Powerhouse, is a formidable African American EVO with the extraordinary ability to transform his skin into a substance resembling organic blue steel. This transformation grants him superhuman durability and strength, making him nearly invulnerable and immensely powerful. In this steel form, Jamal does not require food or oxygen, allowing him to endure and perform under extreme conditions. Recruited by Mohammad Fall Leek, Jamal was persuaded to join the Freedom Liberation Front, ultimately becoming one of Fall Leek's most loyal and devoted followers. He is often seen wearing a sleek Kevlar bodysuit, reinforced with polymer plate armor, which complements his steel form and provides additional protection and tactical advantage.

Known Allies

Freedom Liberation Front

Known Enemies

Arian Brotherhood
United States Government
The Defenders

Known Skills

Martial arts

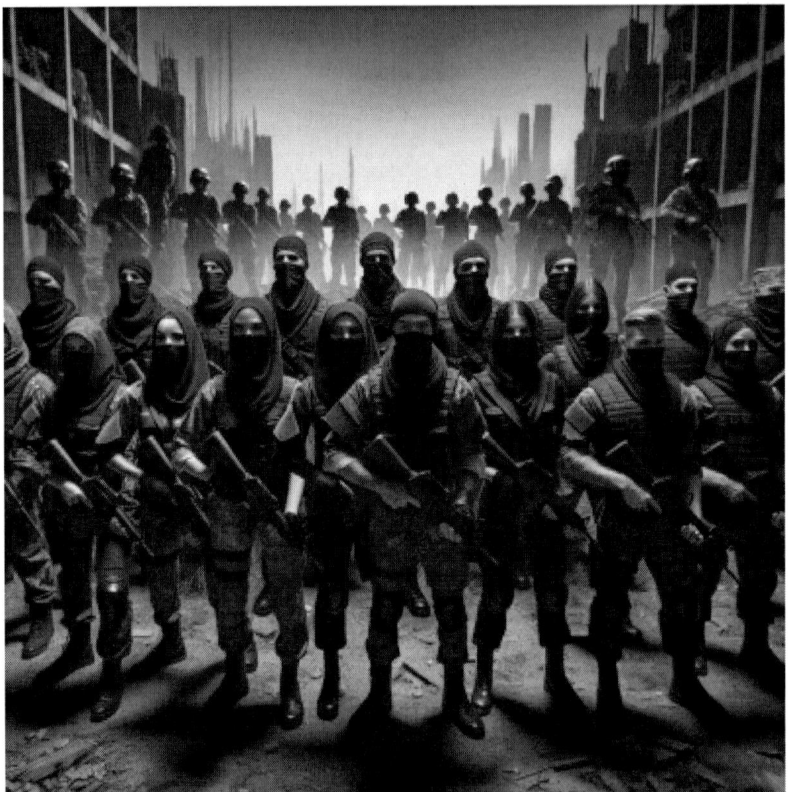

Name = Freedom Liberation Front
Base of operations = Mobile
Leader = Mohammed Fall Leek
Members = 5,000

Description

The Freedom Liberation Front, abbreviated as FLF, is a radical and militant terrorist organization characterized by its unwavering belief in black supremacy. The ideology of the FLF is rooted in the conviction that the only path to rectify historical injustices and current disparities is to dismantle the existing governmental and societal structures of the United States. Members envision the erection of a new social order that privileges black people, securing for them a position of unchallenged dominance. FLF activists don regalia reminiscent of paramilitary uniforms, symbolizing their commitment to the cause and readiness for confrontation. As a means of covert identification and solidarity, they adorn themselves with black bandanas, worn on various parts of the body, signaling their affiliation to fellow compatriots. This attire is not just a uniform but a banner under which they rally, prepared to employ extreme measures in the pursuit of their version of liberation and justice.

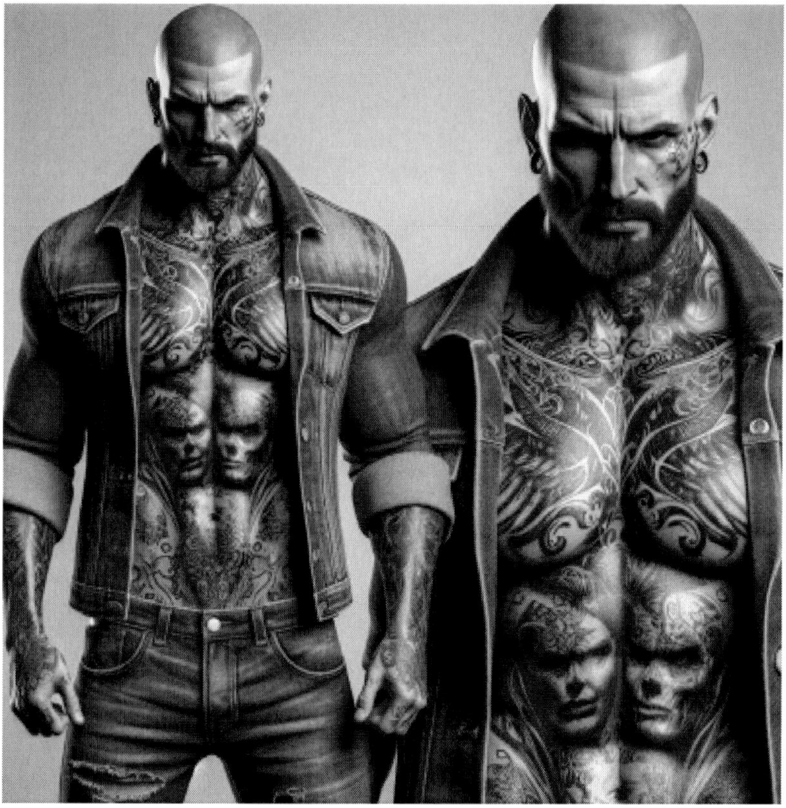

Real Name = Unknown
Code Name = White Dragon
Age = Unknown
Base of operations = Mobile

Powers

Blood Magic Tatoos
 * Enhanced Strength
 * Enhanced Endurance
 * Enhanced Durability
 * Healing Factor
 * Long Life
 * Lifeforce Absorption

Equipment

Kevlar Body Armor
Pistol

Origin Story

White Dragon is the fearsome neo-Nazi leader of the Aryan Brotherhood. Mastering the ancient and arcane art of blood tattoo magic, he has transformed his body into a canvas of power. Each tattoo, inked in his own blood, bestows a range of special abilities, primarily enhancing his strength, durability, and healing capabilities. Known for his brutal and commanding presence, he is always seen wearing a t-shirt under a rugged denim jacket, paired with denim pants and heavy biker boots. White Dragon keeps his head perpetually shaved, displaying a muscular build that emanates an aura of menace.

Known Allies

Arian Brotherhood
Dread knocks

Known Enemies

Freedom Liberation League
United States Government
Stalker

Known Skills

Military Tactics
Arcane Blood Magic
Martial arts Leadership

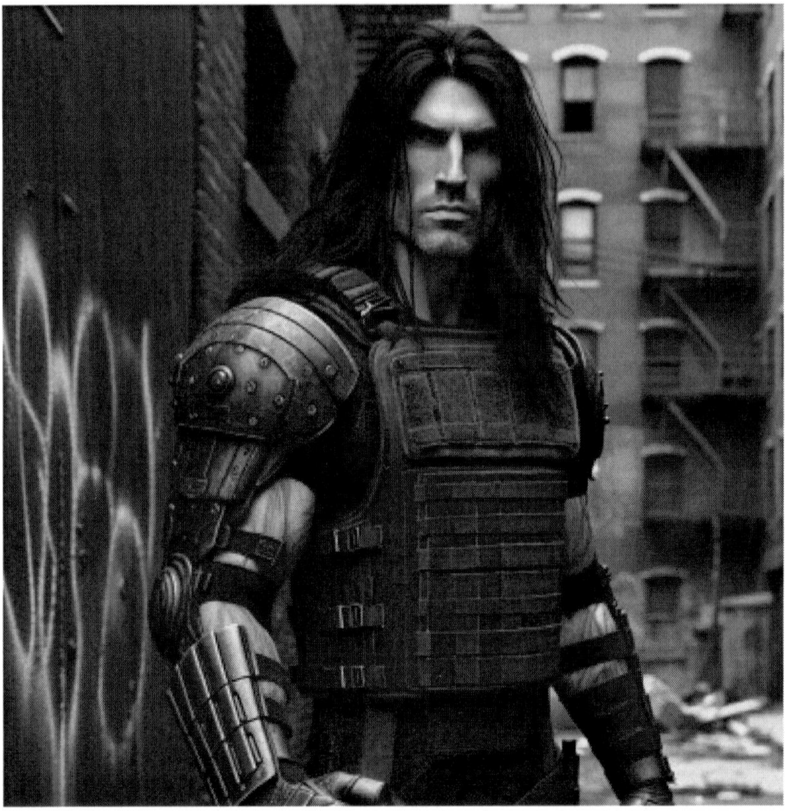

Real Name = Unknown
Code Name = Buzz Saw
Age = 30
Base of operations = Mobile

Powers

Energy Generation = Solar
* Energy Constructs
* Energy Blasts
* Energy Shields
Enhanced Strength
Durability

Equipment

Kevlar Body suit with polymer plate armor
Motorcycle

Origin Story

Buzz Saw is an EVO with the unique ability to create energy constructs, a power he honed amidst the harsh realities of his rough neighborhood. Growing up as one of the few white kids in an almost entirely African American neighborhood, he was often bullied, making him a prime target. Seeking protection, he eventually joined The Aryan Brotherhood as soon as he was old enough. Approaching them from a position of vulnerability, his unusual abilities were quickly recognized and exploited. Utilizing his talent for their criminal endeavors, Buzz Saw became a feared enforcer. His background, embroiled in violence and gang activity, has only solidified his ruthlessness. He sports long black hair and dons a Kevlar body suit reinforced with polymer plate armor, making him as physically imposing as he is dangerous with his powers.

Known Allies

Arian Brotherhood
Dread knocks

Known Enemies

Freedom Liberation Front
United States Government

Known Skills

Leadership
Motorcycle Riding
Martial arts
Weapons Mastery

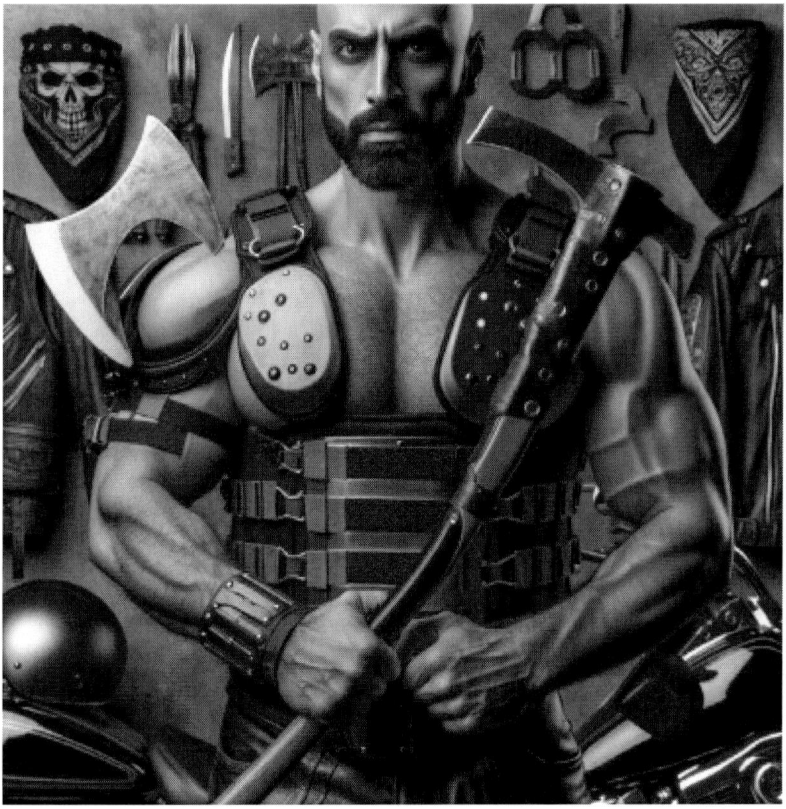

Real Name = Allen Creed
Code Name = Creed
Age = 30
Base of operations = Mobile

Powers

Kinetic Energy Absorption
* Superhuman Strength
* Superhuman Endurance
* Superhuman Durability
* Regeneration

Equipment

Kevlar Body Suit with polymer plate armor
Motorcycle
Battle Axe

Origin Story

Allen Creed, often referred to simply as Creed, is a former United States military operative who served during Operation Desert Storm. Volunteering for a top-secret experiment, Creed gained the extraordinary ability to absorb kinetic energy and convert it into superhuman strength, superhuman endurance, and superhuman durability. However, the experiment tragically stopped his heart for several minutes, leading the scientists to mistakenly believe he had died from the trauma. Considering him a failed experiment, they discarded his body, but his remarkable regenerative abilities healed him. Enraged by his government's abandonment, Creed made his way back to the United States. In his search for belonging, he encountered Buzz Saw, the leader of the Dread Knocks Motorcycle gang, who welcomed him with open arms. Finding the brotherhood he longed for, Creed now serves as a loyal member of the gang. Physically, Creed is imposing with a shaved head and distinct presence. He dons a Kevlar body suit with polymer plate armor for protection and wields a double-bladed battle axe as his weapon of choice.

Known Allies

Arian Brotherhood
Dread Knocks Motorcycle Gang

Known Enemies

Freedom Liberation Front
United States Government

Known Skills

Military Tactics
Bladed Weapons
Motorcycle riding
Martial Arts

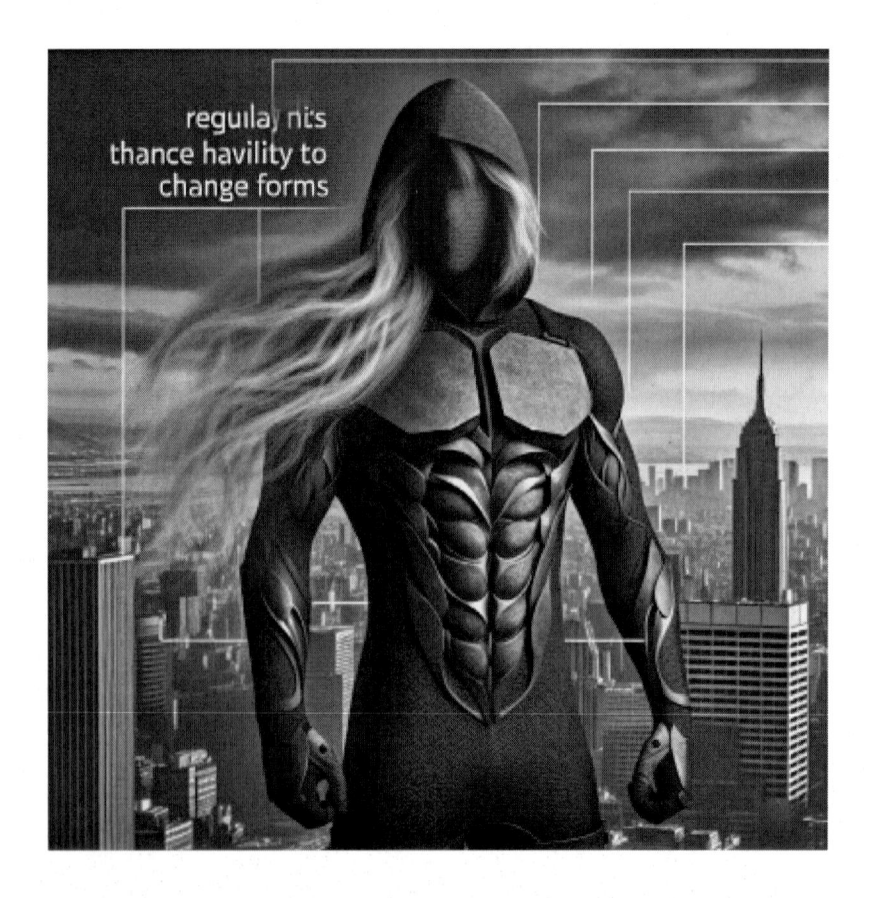

regula nts
thance havility to
change forms

Real Name = Unknown
Code Name = Shifter
Age = Unkown
Base of operations = Mobile

Powers

Shapeshifting
* Gains Memories and knowledge of those he copies
* Gains the powers of those he copies
Genetic Recall
* Can Recall any knowledge or memories he has copied

* Can Recall any Powers he has copied

Equipment

Kevlar Body Suit with polymer plate armor

Origin Story

Shifter is an EVO, a specialized human born with extraordinary abilities. His unique power allows him to shape-shift into any person he has physical contact with, acquiring their memories, knowledge, and, in the case of other EVOs, their powers and abilities as well. This makes him an incredibly versatile and dangerous individual. Shifter's powers emerged early in his life, leading him down a path of deception and crime. Using his abilities, he traveled the world and committed numerous identity theft crimes to sustain his lifestyle. He eventually crossed paths with Buzz Saw, the notorious leader of the Dreadknocks Motorcycle gang, and decided to join forces with him. Shifter's true form remains a mystery, as he constantly changes his appearance. However, he is often seen in his preferred disguise: a man with long blonde hair, an average build, and outfitted in a Kevlar body suit reinforced with polymer plate armor. This attire not only provides him with protection but also allows him to blend in easier within the gang's ranks.

Known Allies

Arian Brotherhood
Dread Knocks Motorcycle Gang

Known Enemies

-Freedom Liberation Front
United States Government

Known Skills

A variety of Skills from those he has copied

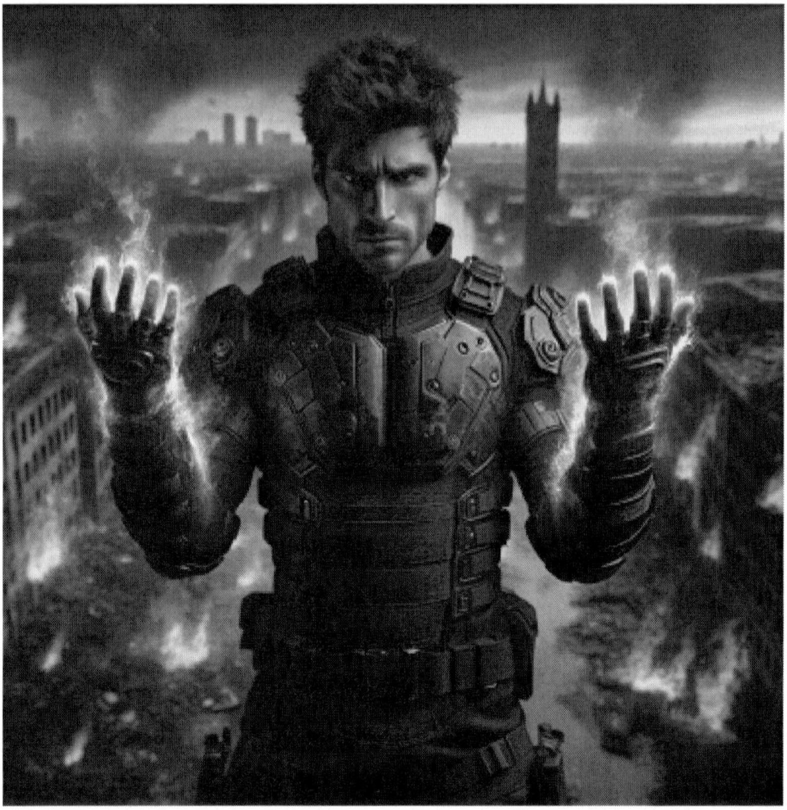

Real Name = Max Tolburt
Code Name = Torch
Age = 27
Base of operations = Mobile

Powers

Heat and fire Generation
* Flight
* Fire Balls
* Fire Aura

Equipment

Kevlar body suit with polymer plate armor
Motorcycle

Origin Story

Max Tolburt, known by his alias 'Torch', has always been a troubled man with an unhealthy obsession with fire. As a youth, he was responsible for a series of arsons, leading to his repeated incarcerations in juvenile detention centers. During one of his arson attempts, he set fire to a chemical lab and became trapped inside. Believed to have perished in the blaze, the chemicals within the lab actually altered his DNA, granting him resistance to heat and fire, as well as the ability to generate and control flames. Adopting the name 'Torch', he soon crossed paths with Buzz Saw and joined the Dread KNOCKS. Max is a true pyromaniac, only finding genuine happiness when he watches something burn. His attire consists of a Kevlar bodysuit with polymer plate armor, providing necessary protection during his fiery endeavors.

Known Allies

Arian Brotherhood
Dread Knocks Motorcycle Gang

Known Enemies

Freedom Liberation Front
United State Government

Known Skills

Marial arts
Pyrotechnics
Motorcycle Riding

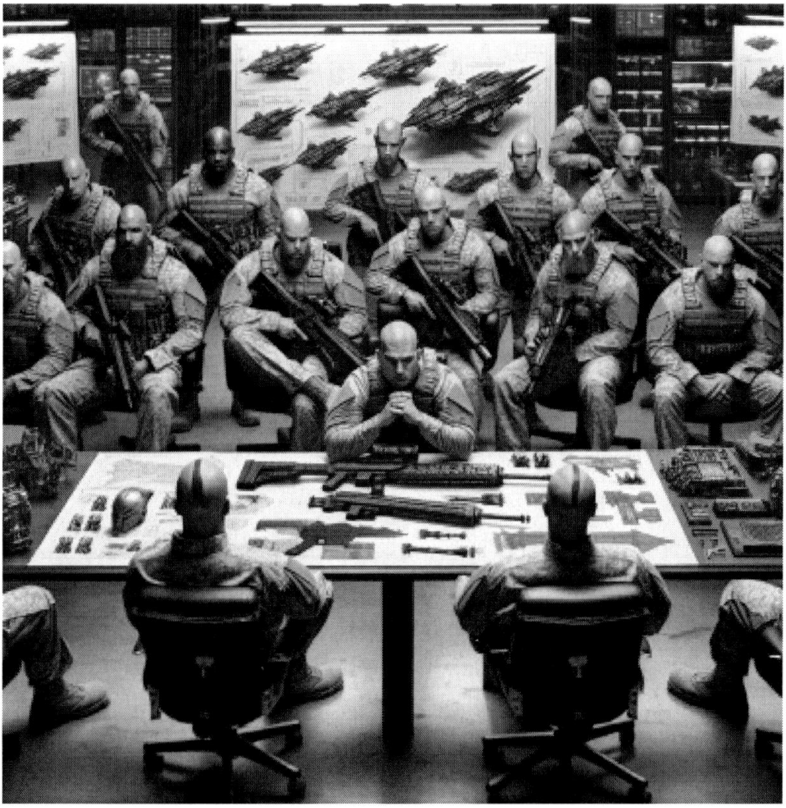

Name = Arian Brotherhood
Location = Mobile
Members 5, 000

Description
_____

The Aryian Brotherhood is a menacing terrorist faction driven by the ideology of white supremacy. United by a common belief that white racial purity must be preserved and protected, they contend that the government has succumbed to control by those they deem racially inferior. This organization is notorious for its exceptional organization, strategic financing, and expansive reach, with operative bases established in every major U.S. city. With the emergence of individuals possessing extraordinary abilities, termed EVOs, the brotherhood has expanded its reign of terror to include these genetically gifted beings among their targets. Members of the Aryian Brotherhood are easily identifiable by their distinctive military uniforms, sporting desert camouflage patterns, and their uniformly shaved heads—a stark symbol of their unity and ideology. The group's enclaves are not only clandestine meeting points but also house advanced laboratories. These facilities are the birthplaces of sophisticated weaponry crafted explicitly to neutralize or eliminate EVOs. The Aryian Brotherhood poses a significant threat to both national security and the safety of EVOs and is a subject of intense scrutiny and opposition from law enforcement and superhero groups alike.

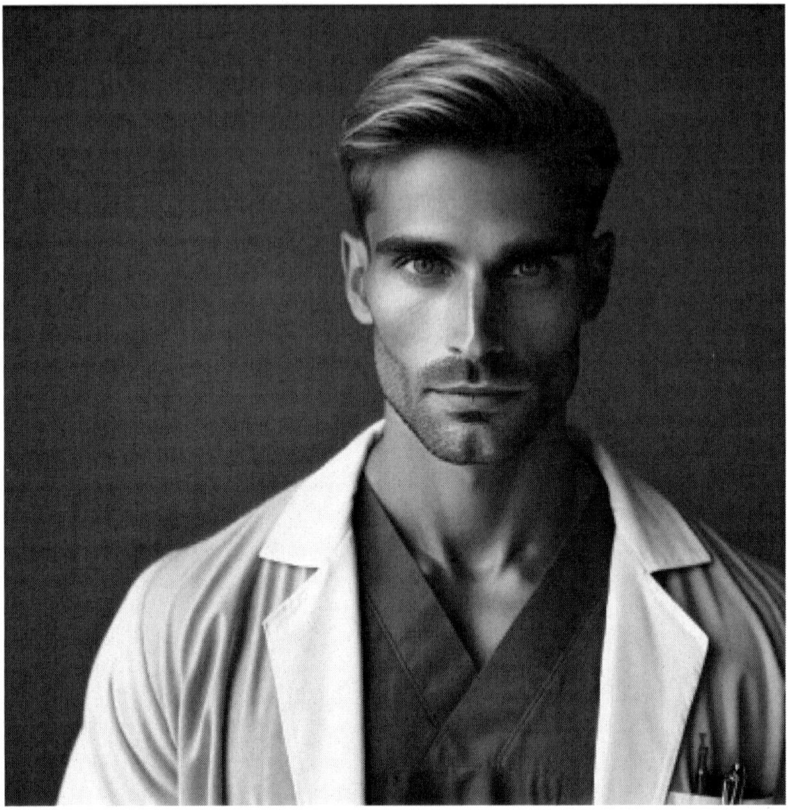

Real Name = Doctor Erwin Goring
Code Name = None
Age = 50
Base of operations = Mobile

Powers

None

Equipment

Labotory

Origin Story

Doctor Erwin Goring is a character that embodies the complex interplay of science and ideology. As a top-tier expert in bioengineering, his prowess in the scientific community is widely acknowledged. His adeptness at manipulating biological organisms at the genetic level has earned him a formidable reputation. Despite his groundbreaking contributions to science, Smith's moral compass is significantly skewed by his unwavering devotion to the Aryian Brotherhood, a fact that adds a chilling layer to his personality. His alignment with such an extremist group hints at a darker, more sinister aspect of his character, where his skills could be used for ethically dubious endeavors or to further the nefarious objectives of the Brotherhood. Visually, Doctor Smith presents a clinical appearance with sharp, clean-cut features that reflect his meticulous nature. His Aryan idealistic physical traits—short blonde hair and piercing blue eyes—conform to the Brotherhood's archetype, while his attire consists of pristine medical scrubs paired with a lab coat, signifying his medical expertise. Smith's outward demeanor can be remarkably disarming; his professional presentation obscures the menacing undercurrents of his ideological leanings.

Known Allies

Arian Brotherhood

Known Enemies

Freedom Liberation Front

Known Skills

Biology
Genetic engineering
Chemistry
Genetics
Bio-Chemistry

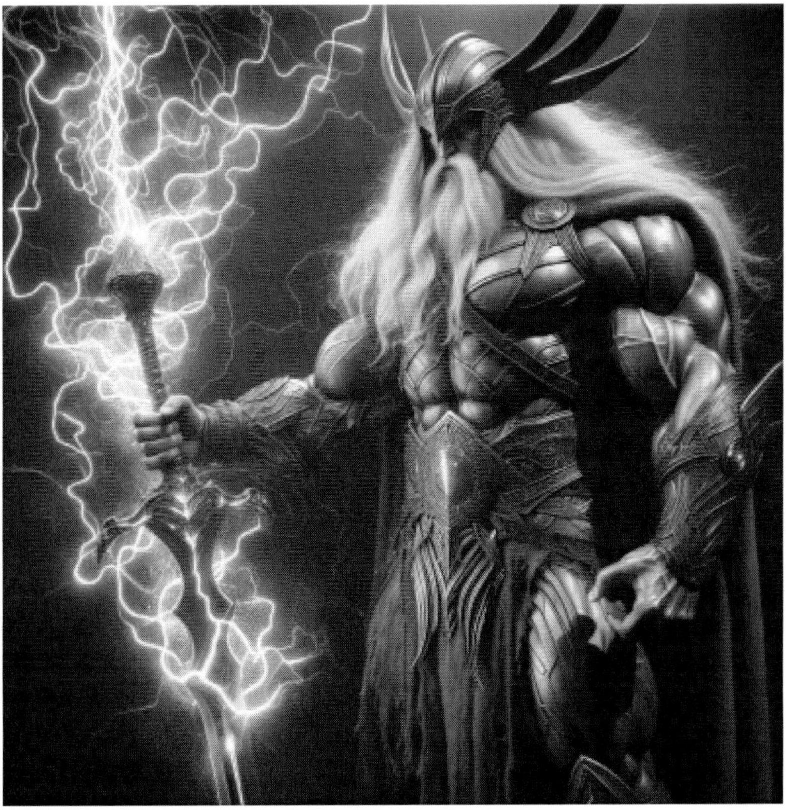

Real Name = Juno the Viking Warrior
Code Name = Juno the Viking Warrior
Age = 4
Base of operations = Mobile

Powers

Superhuman Strength
Superhuman Endurance
Superhuman Durability
Regeneration
Damage Adaptation
* Can't be killed the same way twice

Equipment

Kevlar body suit with polymer plate armor

Sword with Electric Blade

Origin Story

Juno is a formidable creation, the pinnacle of a clandestine project led by the notorious Doctor Erwin Goring during the heights of World War II. As a bio-synthetic warrior shaped within the confines of a high-tech birthing chamber, Juno was envisioned to be the ultimate Nazi super soldier, bred for battle and loyalty. However, his development took an unintended course; Juno's mind emerged innocent and unrefined, a blank slate akin to that of a child. Doctor Goring then took on the role of mentor and educator, nurturing Juno's intellect and cultivating his personality. It was the ancient legends—the sagas of Norse warriors—that captivated Juno's imagination and became the bedrock of his identity. Recognizing this fervor, Goring crafted a set of Viking armor, embedding within it the enigmatic properties of a meteoritic metal that had fallen into Nazi-occupied France. Juno's blade, a marvel in its own right, comprised a hilt embedded with pilfered artifacts from Area 51, fusing otherworldly technology with a blade of living electricity. Yet, despite the grand designs of his creators, Juno bore no allegiance but to his sense of righteousness. His awakening was swift and brutal; a betrayal that culminated in a bloody rebellion against those who sought to wield him as a mere tool of war. A warrior reborn, Juno is the epitome of physical perfection—vastly muscular, crowned with a mane of golden hair, embodying power and resilience. His regenerative abilities are near-mythic, allowing him to recover from the gravest of wounds, reconstructing his very essence from the merest of remnants left on the battlefield.

Known Allies

None

Known Enemies

Shadow Warrior

Known Skills

Brawling
Swordsmanship

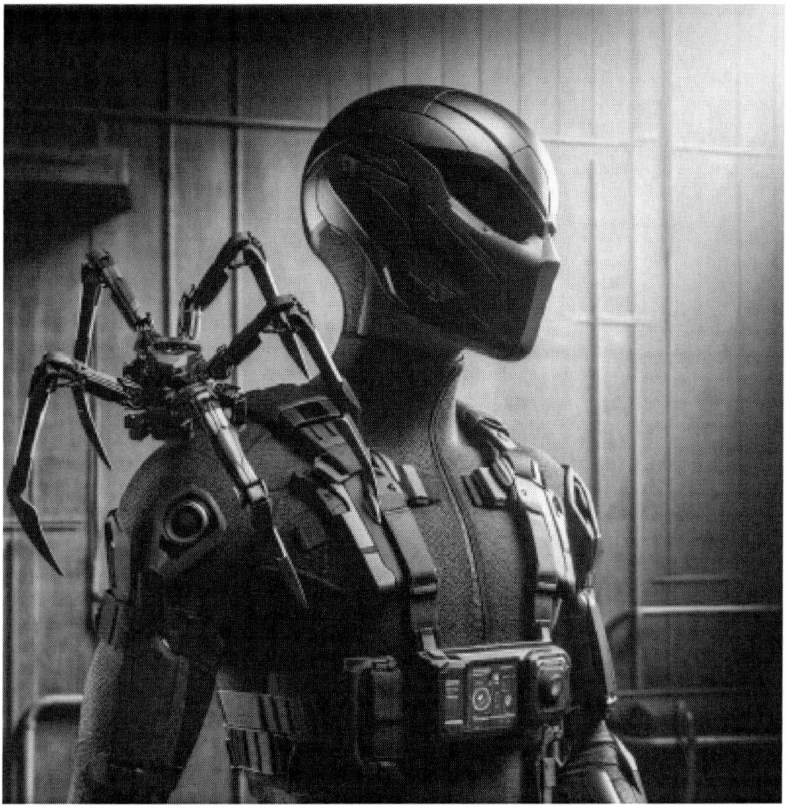

Real Name = Liam O'Rielly
Code Name = Black Spider
Age = 25
Base of operations = Mobile

Powers

None

Equipment

Battle Armor
* Body Armor
* Enhanced Strength
* Enhanced Agility
* High Tech Video and Audio sensors
* Webbing
* Stun Blasters
* Wall Crawling

Spider Drone
* Durability
* Enhanced sensors
* Artificial Intelligence
* WI-FI communication with battle suit
* Webbing

* Stunner
* Wall Crawling

Origin Story

Liam O'Rielly was once a small-time petty thief, scraping by on whatever he could steal. One fateful day, he stumbled upon an experimental battle suit hidden in an abandoned warehouse. Rather than selling the high-tech suit to the highest bidder, curiosity got the better of him, and he decided to don it. Once fully suited, Liam was astounded by the suit's capabilities, which included enhanced strength, agility, and a host of spider-like abilities. Realizing the potential for both fortune and thrill, he took on the moniker 'Black Spider.' The battle suit itself is a Kevlar bodysuit layered with lightweight, yet durable futuristic polymer plate armor. It features a sleek, polymer helmet equipped with a variety of sensors, allowing Liam to see in multiple spectrums and pick up subtle environmental changes. Attached to the back is a spider-like drone that can detach from the suit, functioning either under Liam's remote control or autonomously. The Black Spider quickly becomes an enigmatic vigilante-hero, using his newfound powers to navigate the criminal underworld and outsmart those who once walked all over him.

Known Allies

None

Known Enemies

Law enforcement

Known Skills

Lock Picking
Pick pocketing
Electronics
Martial arts

Real Name = Carl Napier
Code Name = Road Warrior
Age = 40
Base of operations = Mobile

Powers

Enhanced Strength
Enhanced Endurance
Healing Factor
Electrical charge

Equipment

Leather Armor
Motorcycle
Chain whip

Origin Story

Carl Napier, known as the 'Road Warrior', is a formidable character shaped by his past experiences in the United States Military. After his discharge, Carl became deeply disillusioned with the treatment of veterans and turned to unorthodox ways to secure his future. Through a shadowy broker dealing in high-tech weaponry for the criminal underworld, funded by the notorious Lords of War, Carl obtained the X-35 super soldier serum. Upon injecting himself, he developed extraordinary abilities, including enhanced strength, agility, and a remarkable healing factor. Embracing his new identity, Carl founded a motorcycle gang that operates for the highest bidder, offering their unparalleled services to those who can afford them. He is instantly recognizable by his long hair, rugged attire of a t-shirt, leather jacket, denim jeans, and motorcycle boots, embodying both menace and charisma.

Group

Road Warriors

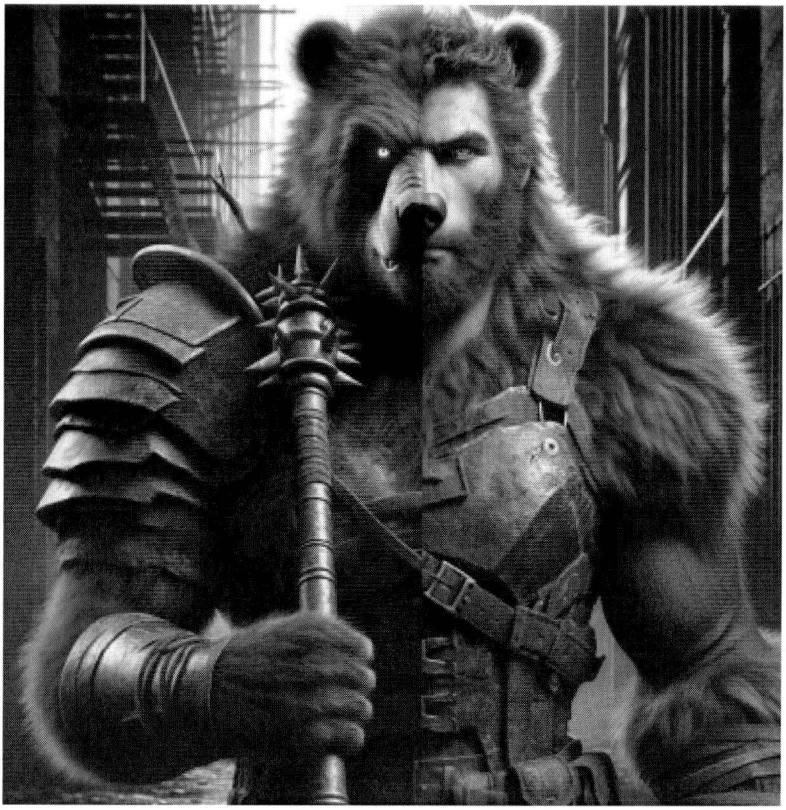

Real Name = Jeff Cole
Code Name = Animal
Age = 35
Base of operations = Mobile

Powers

Body Transformation = Were- Bear form
* Superhuman Strength
* Superhuman Endurance
* Regeneration
* Enhanced senses

Equipment

Leather Armor

Origin Story

Jeff Cole, codenamed 'Animal', is a compelling character who served alongside Carl Napier in the military. Sharing Carl's disillusionment with the government's treatment of its veterans, Jeff sought an alternative path that led him to a shadowy broker. This broker, dealing in high-tech weapons and scientific advancements provided by the enigmatic Lord of War, offered Jeff an extraordinary transformation. Through genetic splicing, Jeff's DNA was merged with that of a Grizzly Bear, turning him into a fierce half-man, half-Grizzly bear hybrid. Despite his animalistic exterior, 'Animal' retains his human intelligence and tactical mind. Jeff's transformation grants him enhanced strength and endurance, making him a formidable force on the battlefield. He dons rugged leather armor that offers mobility and protection in equal measure and wields a brutal mace as his weapon of choice. With his new abilities and indomitable spirit, Jeff fights not just for survival but for a sense of justice and camaraderie with fellow veterans. He has the ability to switch from Were- Bear to human forms.

Group

Road Warriors

Hybrid tigile

The hugle combion of human feale constiricaties ucho perentosi aalies, hunn hiwesy, amonts of bubos, ring, pooesdanic langordoruls, and morriclve, atids, Flessoory ctdmino aalate atling the fitse ore-ad of aphot fichting fichlorl tnixly ewies and fatbrurable, avamefing connarlies.

Real Name = Sharon Smith
Code Name = Hawk
Age = 25
Base of operations = Mobile

Powers

Wings
Feather Body Armor
Enhanced Eyesight
Enhanced Agility
Enhanced strength
Magnetic Manipulation
* Detect Magnetic North
* Low Level Electro Magnetic Pulse

Equipment

Leather Armor

Origin Story

Sharon Smith, codenamed Hawk, is an extraordinary and unique EVO. Unlike most EVOs, Sharon's powers transformed her physical form into a half-human, half-bird hybrid, complete with magnificent wings and a sharp beak. Captured by the United States Military, Sharon endured extensive scientific experimentation until Carl Napier and Jeff Cole, members of the EVO underground, were hired to rescue her. Grateful for her freedom, Sharon joined their cause and eventually became romantically involved with Carl. Hawk's powers not only enhance her agility and vision but also make her a formidable ally in their fight. Despite her fierce and avian appearance, Sharon has a gentle and compassionate heart, always striving to protect those she cares about.

Group

Road Warrior

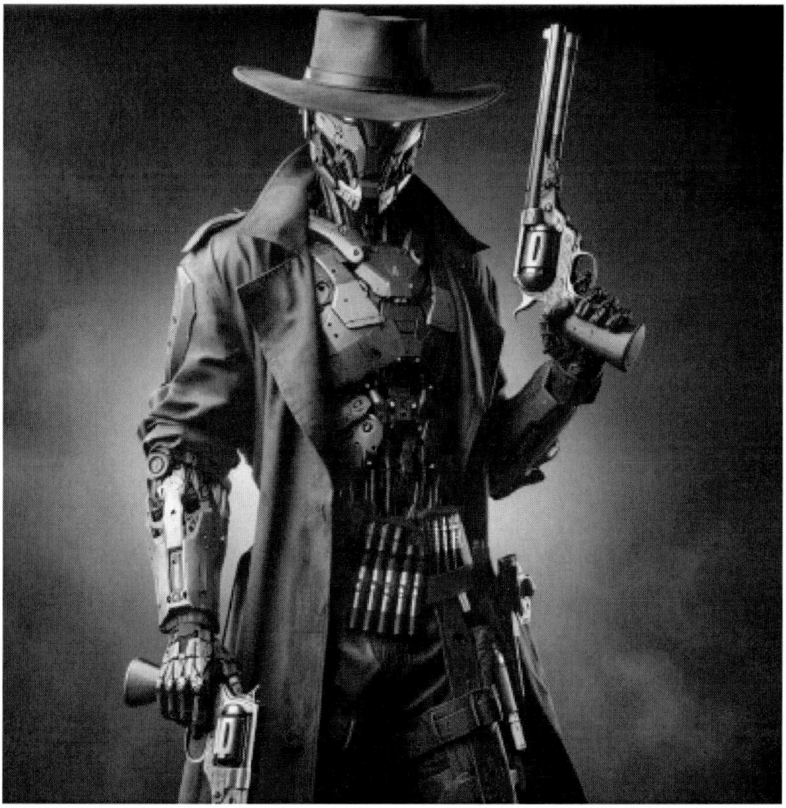

Real Name = Unknown
Code Name = Outlaw
Age = Unknown
Base of operations = Mobile

Powers

Cybernetic implants and upgrades
* Advance visual and audio sensors
* Enhanced strength
* Durability
* Holographic projectors
* Computer interface
* Force field
* Advanced Targeting System

Equipment

Two specially Modified six shooters
Modified Lever Action Rifle
Specialty Ammunition
* Stun Rounds
* Explosive Rounds
* Electroshock rounds
* Tacker Rounds

Origin Story

Outlaw is a relentless mercenary who is a prominent member of the Assassins guild, known far and wide for his cybernetic implants and enhancements. His cybernetics give him enhanced reflexes, strength, and durability, making him a formidable adversary. Outlaw has an unusual fascination with the old west, and this is reflected in his attire and combat style. He wears a Kevlar body suit beneath polymer plate armor, all of which is concealed under a brown leather trench coat. Topping off his look, he wears a classic cowboy hat that shadows his eyes, giving him a mysterious aura. Outlaw's preferred weapons are a pair of vintage-style six-shooter side arms, which he keeps in an old west-style holster strapped to his thighs. These firearms are highly advanced, retrofitted to maximize precision and firepower. Additionally, he carries a modified lever-action rifle designed to fire special ammunition that he crafts himself. Each bullet can produce a variety of effects, from explosive impacts to incapacitating electric shocks, enabling him to adapt to any situation and target. Outlaw's dual life as a technologically enhanced hitman and a nostalgic cowboy makes him a unique blend of old and new, combining the rugged individualism of the wild west with the ultramodern proficiency of a cybernetic assassin.

Group

Assassin Guild

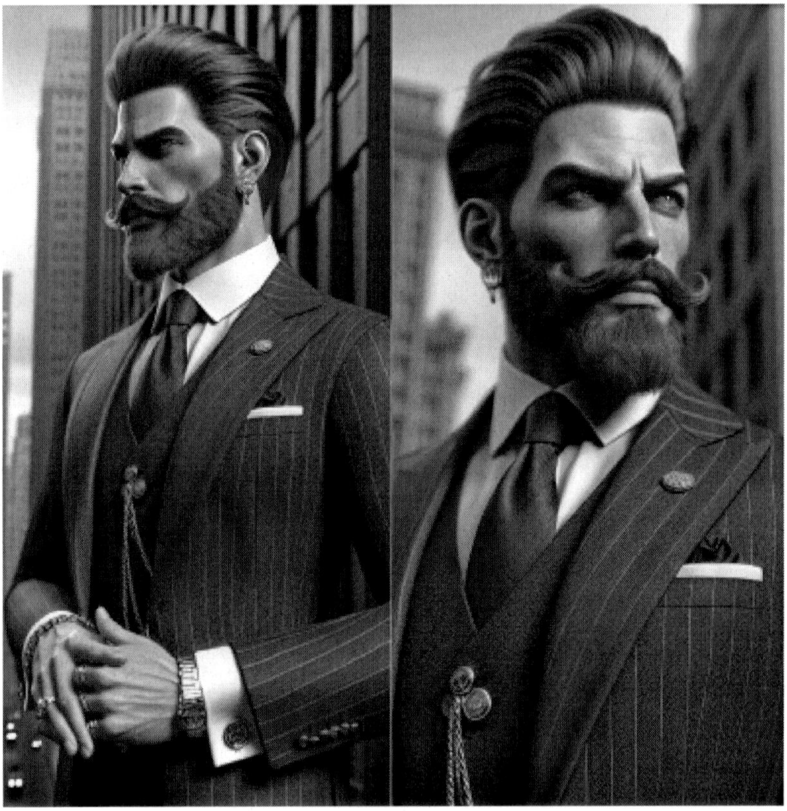

Real Name = James O'Rourke
Cobe Name = None
Age = 40
Base of operation = New York City

Powers

Clone Body
* Enhanced Strength
* Enhanced Endurance
* Healing Factor
* Enhanced Reflexes

Equipment

Kevlar suit

Origin Story

James O'Rourke, widely known as Jimmy, is the formidable head of the O'Rourke Crime Family, an influential faction of the Irish mob. Tragedy struck Jimmy when his beloved wife and daughter were brutally murdered by a rival mob boss. Consumed by grief, he exacted his revenge by killing his rival. However, the loss of his daughter left a void too deep to fill. In his desperation, Jimmy sought out Doctor Zelcer, the leading authority in cloning, to bring his daughter back to life. Doctor Zelcer developed a cloning chamber, and Jimmy had one unaltered clone of his daughter created. Unable to stop there, he went further, commissioning three altered clones of his daughter, each endowed with special abilities such as enhanced strength and reflexes. These clones were implanted with a neuro transmitter that linked them telepathically, allowing them to share knowledge and experiences instantaneously. Pleased with the success of this experiment, Jimmy also had multiple altered clones of himself created, programmed to remain dormant until his death. Upon his passing, one clone would awaken, possessing all of Jimmy's memories and knowledge, thanks to the neurotransmitters placed in their brains. Jimmy's world is a blend of grief, power, and the dark, unyielding ambition to control fate itself.

Group _____

Irish Mob

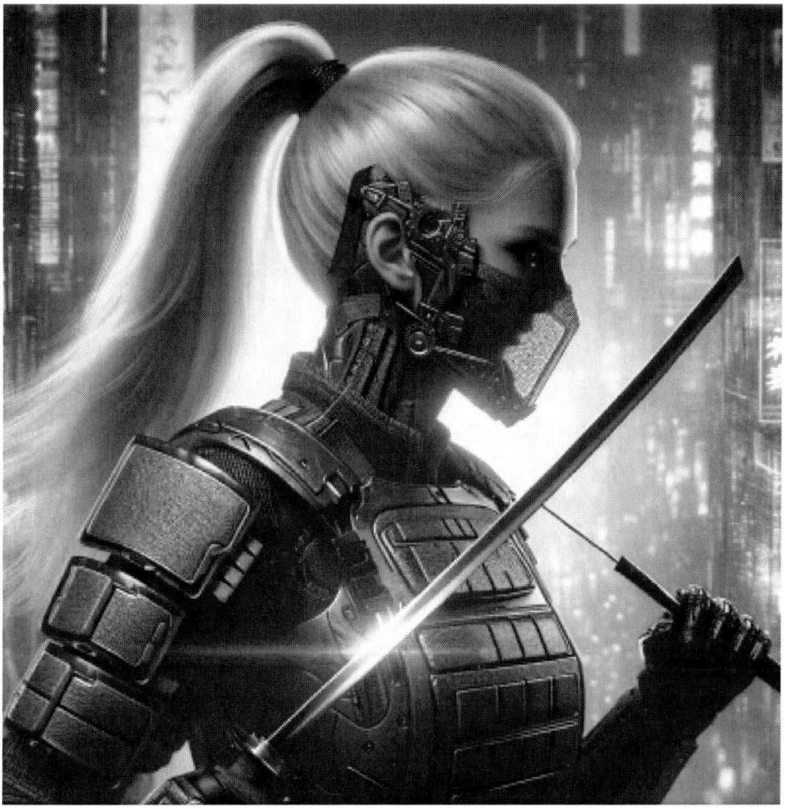

Real Name = Number 1
Code Name = Blade
Age = 5
Base of operation = New York City

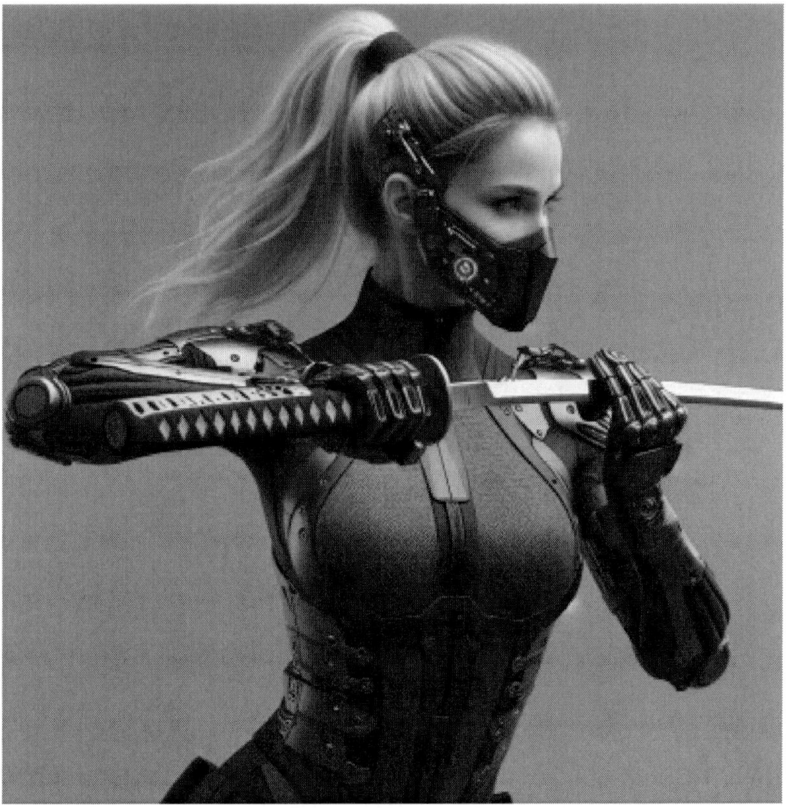

Real Name Number 2
Code Name = Blade
Age = 5
Base of operation = New York City

Real Name = Number 4
Code Name = Blade
Age = 3
Base of operation = New York City

Powers

Enhanced Strength
Enhanced reflexes
Enhanced Endurance
Healing Factor

Neurotransmitter implant

Equipment

Kevlar body suit with polymer plate armor
Katina
Kamas
Sai

Origin Story

Katie O'Rourke is the daughter of Jimmy O'Rourke, a powerful Irish mob boss. When a rival mob boss killed Katie and her mother, Jimmy was devastated and sought revenge in an unconventional way. He hired Doctor Zelcer, the foremost expert in cloning, to bring his daughter back. Doctor Zelcer created one unaltered clone to be raised as Katie, making her an innocent yet tough survivor. Alongside her, three altered clones were produced with advanced capabilities to serve as enforcers for Jimmy. These clones, known as Blade #1, Blade #2, and Blade #3, possess lethal skills acquired from martial arts and weapons mastery training around the world. Implanted with neurotransmitters, the clones share a telepathic link, allowing them to instantly share knowledge and strategies. Together, they form a formidable force poised to protect their family and exact vengeance.

Known Skills

Martial arts
Swordsmanship
Bladed weapons

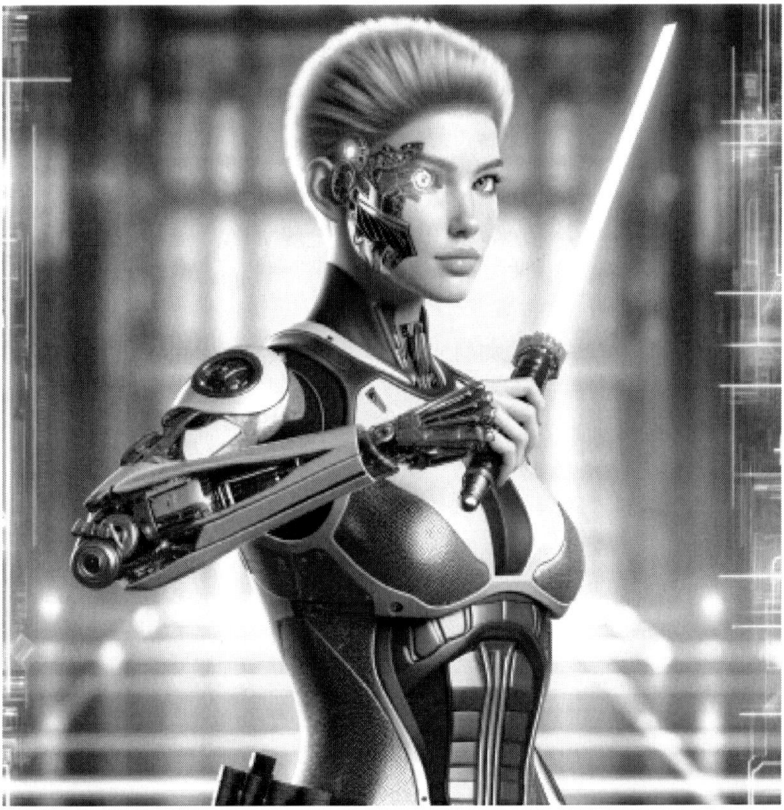

Real Name = Number 3
Code Name = Revier
Age = 5
Base of operation = New York City

Powers
___

Enhanced Strength
Enhanced reflexes
Enhanced Endurance
Healing Factor
Cybernetic implants

* Arm blaster
* High tech visual and audio sensors
* Enhanced Durability
* Optic Lasar
Energy Sword

Equipment

Kevlar body suit
Cybernetic frame

Origin Story

Reiver once was clone number three of Katie O'Rourke, known as Blade. She was created with a singular purpose: to eliminate the vigilante known as Stalker. However, her mission ended in failure and tragedy when Stalker overpowered her, severing her arm and leg and delivering a fatal stab through her eye, which damaged her neurotransmitter. Effectively dead, her body was discovered by Dr. Zelcer, the scientist who created the clones. Rather than following orders to dispose of her body, Dr. Zelcer took her to a secret lab where he repaired her with advanced cybernetic implants. Driven by unrequited love for Katie O'Rourke's unaltered clone, who regarded him as a creepy old man, Dr. Zelcer saw an opportunity and brought Blade back to life. Nevertheless, when Blade, now taking the name Reiver, discovered what had happened to her, she sought out Jimmy O'Rourke, the man she viewed as her father. After being rejected by him, Reiver turned her rage towards Stalker, blaming him for her disfigurement and vowing vengeance. Stalker's days are numbered as Reiver, now a formidable blend of flesh and machine, embarks on a relentless hunt for the vigilante who ruined her life.

Known Skills

Martial arts
Swordsmanship
Bladed weapons

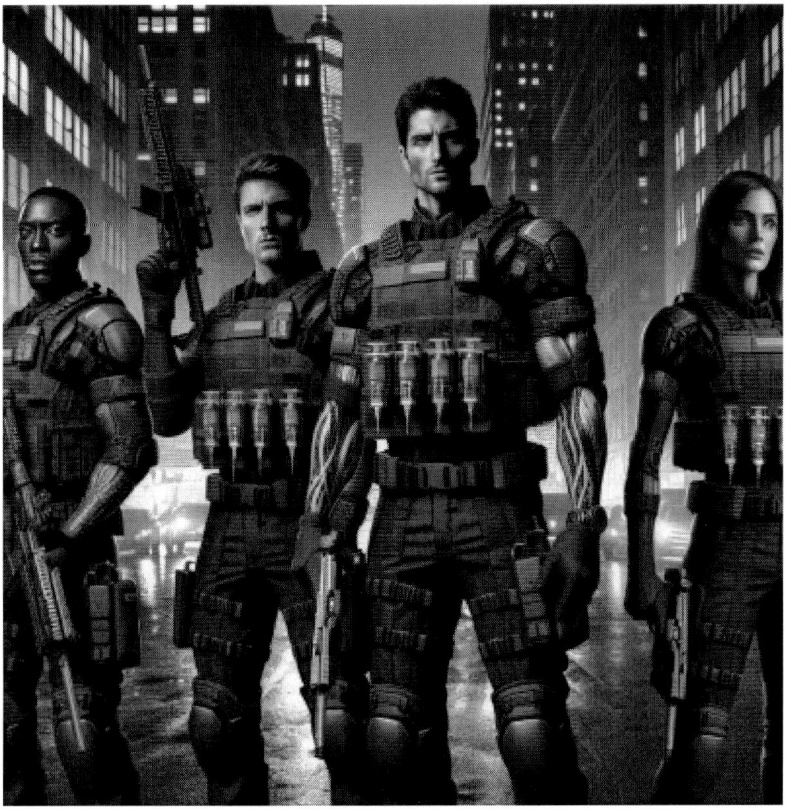

Team Member
Jason Fox is a former CIA
Greg Summers, an ex-soldier from the Gulf War
Jennifer Crush, a notorious ex-cat Burglar
Joe Flanagan, a former NYPD officer dismissed for excessive police Brutality

Powers

Enhanced Agility
Enhanced Strength
Enhanced Endurance
Healing Factor

Equipment

Kevlar body armor with polymer plate armor
Varity of firearms
Swat Van
Surveillance Equipment

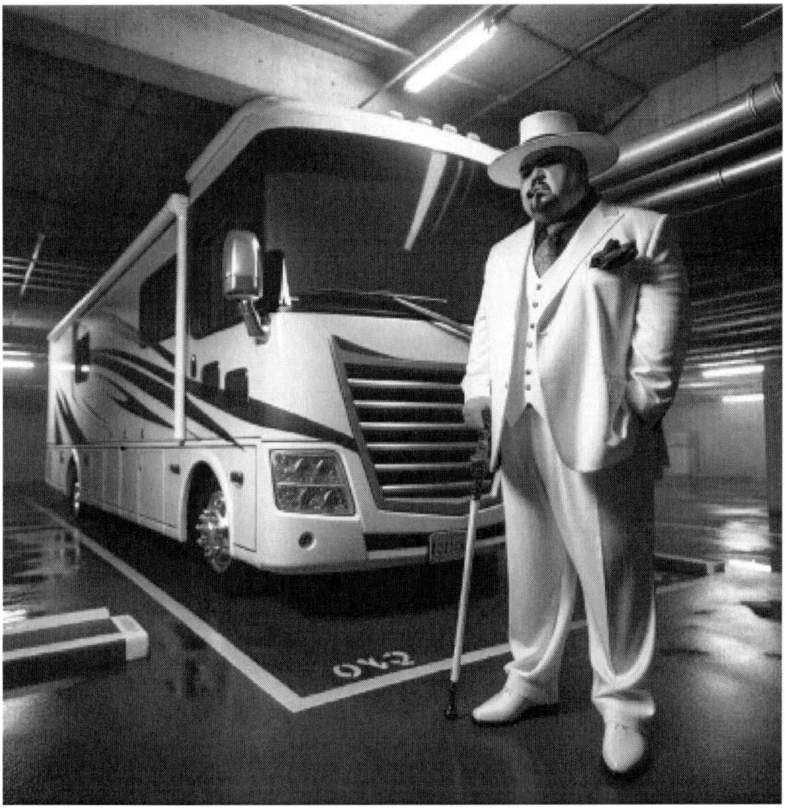

Real Name = Unknown
Code Name = The Promoter
Base of operations = Mobile
Age = Unknown

Powers

Biological control over the body functions of others
* Turn off the EVO Gene in Evos
* Control the function of organs in others

Equipment

Cane
* Electroshock
* Sword

Origin Story

The Promoter is a mysterious and powerful EVO with the extraordinary ability to control and manipulate the biology of other living beings. This ability allows him to alter physical forms, heal wounds, induce illnesses, or enhance capabilities, making him a formidable figure in the world of EVOs. The Promoter operates and oversees the clandestine EVO fighting Arenas spread across the globe, where enhanced individuals engage in brutal combat for wealth and notoriety. He is both revered and feared by those who participate in or are aware of these underground arenas. Despite his ominous presence, the Promoter exudes charm and cunning intelligence, often using his powers to maintain control and influence over those around him. His ultimate motives remain shrouded in secrecy, adding to the mystique and danger that surround him.

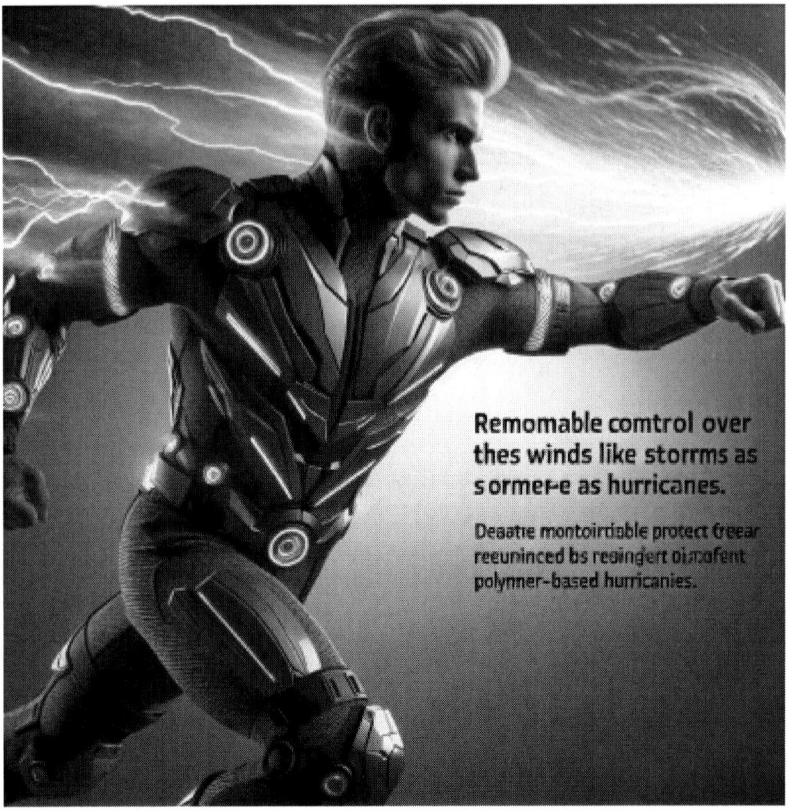
Remomable comtrol over
thes winds like storrms as
s ormer-e as hurricanes.
Deaatie montoirdable protect freear
reeuninced bs reaingert oi:tofent
polynner-based hurricanies.

Real Name = Jason Ellis
Code Name = Tornado
Age = 25
Base of Operations = Mobile

Powers

Air Manipulation
* Tornados
* Hurricane force winds
* solid air constructs

Equipment

Kevlar body suit with polymer plate armor

Origin Story

Jason Ellis, known by his codename 'Tornado,' is an EVO with extraordinary air bending powers. He possesses the ability to manipulate the very air around him, enabling him to create devastating tornados and hurricanes. Additionally, he can form solid constructs out of air for both offensive and defensive purposes. To complement his abilities, Jason wears a Kevlar body suit reinforced with polymer plate armor, granting him superior protection without sacrificing mobility. He has striking blonde hair and maintains a clean-cut appearance, exuding a sense of discipline and precision.

Real Name = Mark Mathews
Code Name = Frost
Age = 35
Base of operations = Mobile

Powers

Heat Absorption
Cold generation
Ice Constructs

Equipment

Kevlar body suit with polymer plate armor

Origin Story

Mark Mathews was a brilliant Scientist specializing in the field of cryonics. His life took a dramatic turn after a catastrophic lab accident left him covered in an experimental cryo solution. This solution granted him the extraordinary ability to generate and manipulate cold temperatures, but at a grave cost. Mark now has to feed off the heat of other living beings to sustain himself. To navigate his new reality, he dons a high-tech Kevlar body suit fortified with polymer plate armor. This suit not only offers protection but also helps regulate his body temperature, which is crucial for his survival. As 'Frost,' Mark walks a fine line between heroism and survival, constantly battling the ethical dilemmas posed by his condition.

Known Skills

Cyonics
Martial arts

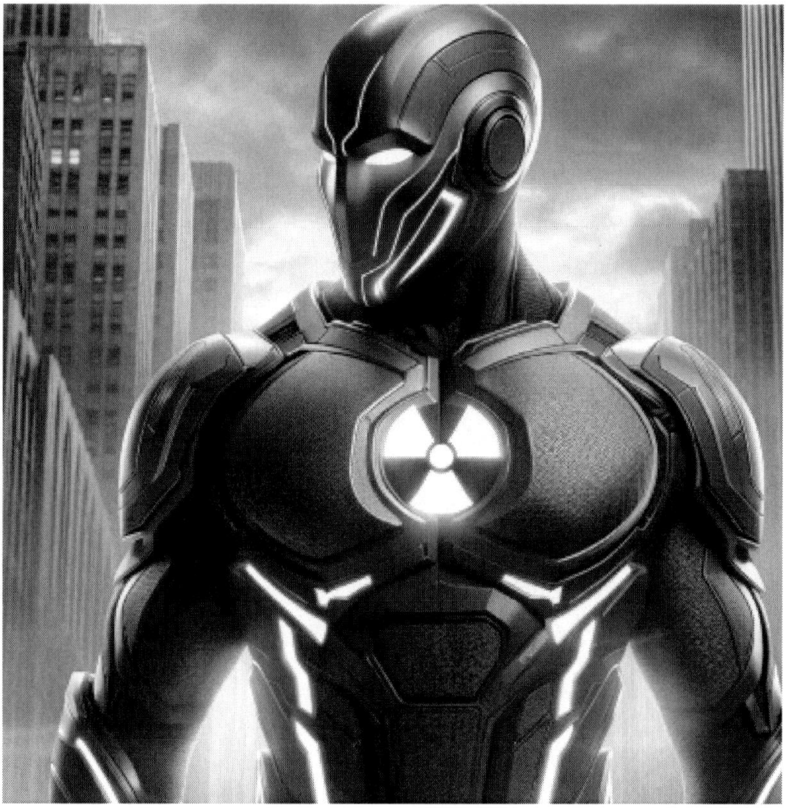

Real Name = Nathanal Suddreth
Code Name = Nuke
Age = 30
Base of operations = Mobile

Powers

Nuclear Energy Generation
* Energy Blasts
* Force fields
* Flight

Equipment

Polymer plate containment Suit.

Origin Story

Nathanal Suddreth, also known as Nuke, was on vacation in Japan when a catastrophic tsunami struck, leading to the nuclear meltdown of the Fukushima nuclear power plant. Surviving the incident, Nathanal's body was irradiated with a massive amount of nuclear energy, which inexplicably endowed him with the ability to generate and control nuclear energy. Now, he is a living conduit of raw atomic power, his abilities equally potent and dangerous. To safely harness and contain his formidable energies, Nathanal wears a specially made containment suit crafted from futuristic polymer plates. This suit not only protects him and those around him from radiation exposure but also helps him focus and control his newfound powers. With a steely resolve and a heroic spirit, Nathanal Suddreth has embraced his new identity as Nuke, protecting the world from threats while grappling with the immense responsibility that comes with his unique abilities.

Known Skills

Martial arts

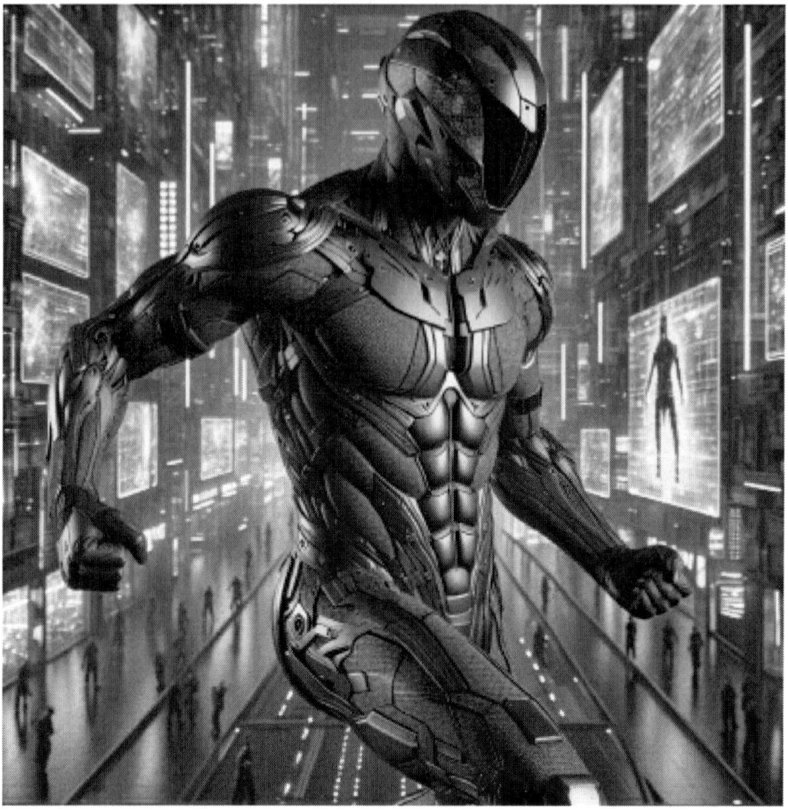

Real Name = Marvin Keller
Code Name = Ric-O-Shay
Age = 35
Base of operation = Mobile

Powers

None

Equipment

Battle Suit
* Body Armor
* High tech visual and audio sensors
* Enhanced Strength
Explosive Balls
Glue Balls
Smoke Balls
Electroshock Balls

Origin Story

Marvin Keller, an enigmatic and highly skilled Mercenary, once served in the British Military. Known by his alias Ric-O-Shay, Marvin is a master of martial arts and an exceptional acrobat, capable of executing intricate maneuvers with precision and agility. He dons a cutting-edge Kevlar body suit reinforced with polymer plate armor, offering superior protection without compromising mobility. His identity remains a mystery, concealed by a futuristic polymer plate helmet equipped with high-tech visual and audio sensors that grant him enhanced situational awareness and communication capabilities. Commanding both respect and fear, Ric-O-Shay operates in the shadows, leveraging his military training and advanced gear to accomplish missions with ruthless efficiency.

Known Skills

Martial arts
Geometry
Throwing
Chemistry

Blaster Canons
yusbamiier
issilles
sennces
Jet Engi
App
Jating

Real Name = Justin Micheals
Code Name = Warmonger
Age = 45
Base of operation = Micheals Worldwide LLC.

Powers

None

Equipment

Mech Suit
* Body Armor
* Blaster cannon
* Multi Missiles
* Advanced visual and audio sensors
* Enhanced Strength
* Energy Field
* E.M.P. Pulse Cannon
* Energy Wrist Blade

Origin Story

Justin Micheals is a ruthless billionaire industrialist and the CEO of Micheals Technology, a major competitor to White

Industries. With a keen intellect and ambitious drive, Justin's primary goal is to surpass and dismantle his rival, Hunter White, the CEO of White Industries, who secretly operates as the vigilante known as the Dark Night. To achieve his nefarious objectives, Justin engineers a high-tech mech suit codenamed 'Warmonger.' This suit is constructed from advanced polymer plate armor, making it impervious to many forms of attack. It is equipped with powerful blaster cannons, jet engines for flight, an array of missiles, and state-of-the-art visual and audio sensors for enhanced situational awareness in combat. As Warmonger, Justin embodies an unstoppable force fueled by technological prowess and a singular desire to dominate his rivals.

Known Skills

Business
Robotics
Electronics

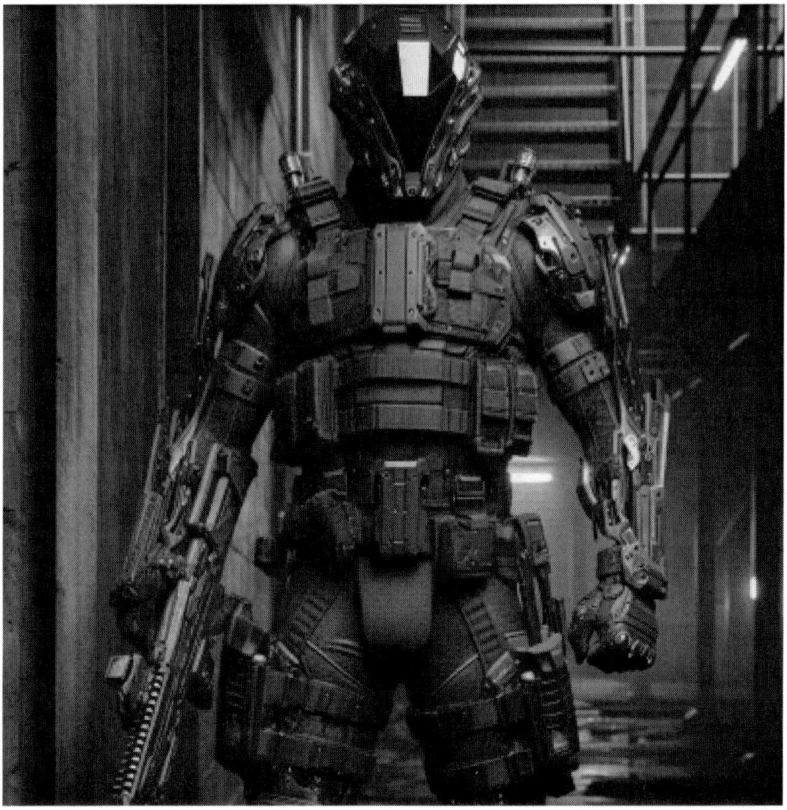

Real Name = unknown
Code Name = Arsenal
Age = Unknown
Base of Operations = Mobile

Powers

None

Equipment

Battle suit
* Body Armor
* High tech visual and audio sensors
* Enhanced Strength
* Wrist blades
Combat knife
Side arms
Rifles
Sword
Grenades

Origin Story

Arsenal is a highly skilled mercenary for hire, most commonly employed by the underground Chinese Yakuza. Despite not being of Asian descent, Arsenal has proven to be a reliable enforcer, adept at ensuring the protection and safe transport of the Yakuza's illegal cargo into or out of the United States. Arsenal is distinguished by his intimidating appearance: a Kevlar bodysuit reinforced with futuristic polymer plate armor that provides maximum protection without sacrificing mobility. His helmet, also made of the same advanced polymer material, is equipped with state-of-the-art visual and audio sensors, allowing him to operate efficiently in any environment and situation. Arsenal is a master of all forms of weaponry, from firearms to melee weapons, making him a versatile and formidable opponent to anyone who dares cross his path.

Known Skills

Martial arts
Firearms Mastery
Bladed Weapons Mastery
Blunt Weapons Mastery

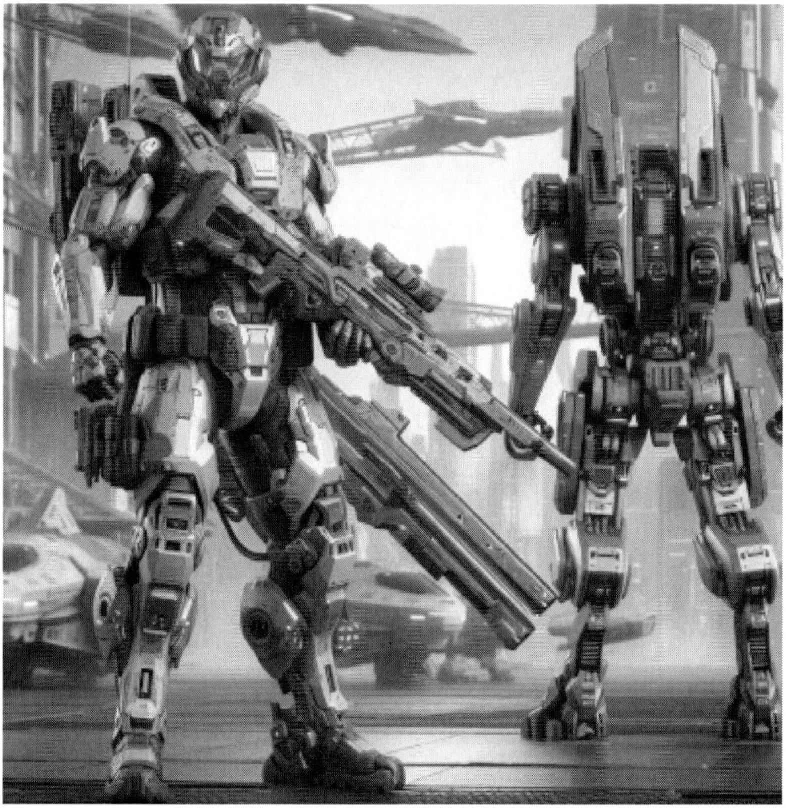

Real Name = Zane Stevens
Code Name = Battle Borg
Age = 30
Base of operations = Mobile

Powers

None

Equipment

Battle armor
* Lasers
* Blasters
* Flight
* Body armor
* Energy Field
* Missiles
* Arm Blade

Origin Story

Zane Stevens, also known as Battle Borg, is a highly skilled mercenary for hire. He dons a state-of-the-art mech suit that enhances both his offensive and defensive capabilities. The mech suit is equipped with high-tech laser beam blasters, powerful cannons, and an array of guided missiles, making Zane a formidable force on any battlefield. His background includes military training and extensive experience in covert operations. Zane's combat skills are amplified by his suit's advanced targeting systems and enhanced mobility, enabling him to face multiple threats simultaneously with precision and efficiency. He is known for his tactical acumen, resourcefulness, and unyielding resolve in the face of danger.

Known Skills

Martial arts
Advanced weapons
Robotics

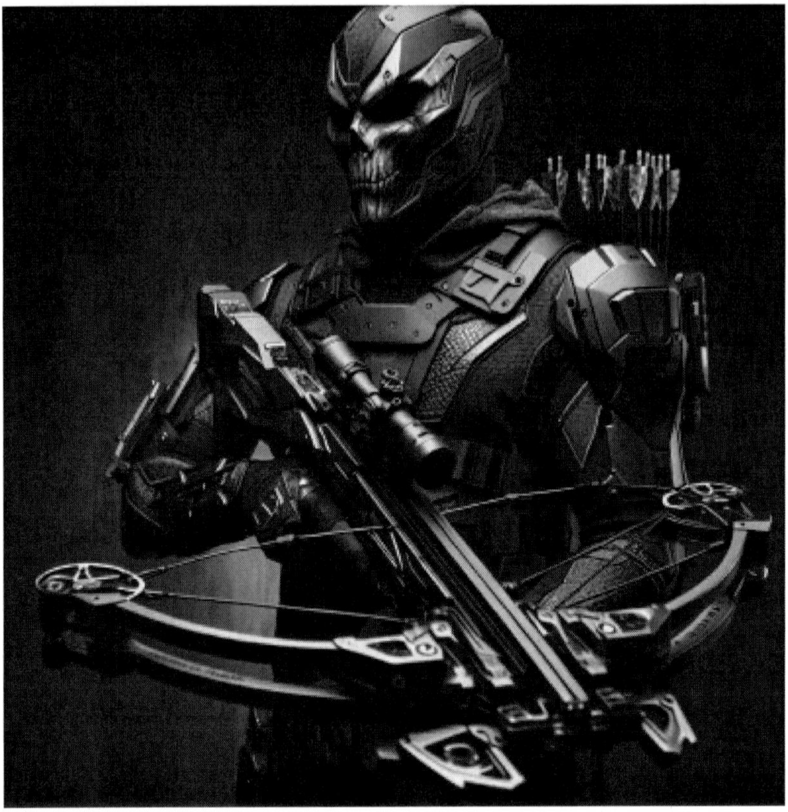

Real Name = Clay Mccory
Code Name = Crossbolt
Age = 25
Base of operations = Mobile

Powers

None

Equipment

Battle armor
* Enhanced Strength
* Body armor
* High tech video and audio sensors
* Filtration System
Crossbow
Bolts
* Grapple Bolt
* Gas Bolt
* Explosive Bolt
* Sonic Bolt
* Tracking Bolt
* Glue Bolt
Katana

Origin Story

Clay Mccory, also known by his alias 'Crossbolt,' is a highly skilled archer who had a tough upbringing on the poorer side of town. Despite his talent, he consistently came in second in archery tournaments to his wealthy rival, Hunter Averys. After high school, Clay joined the military, where he encountered a mercenary group that he eventually joined. With his mercenary earnings, he funded the creation of a high-tech battle suit and crossbow. Adopting the name 'Crossbolt,' he became a formidable assassin in an underground guild. Crossbolt's suit enhances his physical abilities and provides tactical advantages, making him a fearsome and resourceful foe.

Known Skills

Archery
Marksmanship
Martial arts
Swordsmanship
Chemistry
Explosives

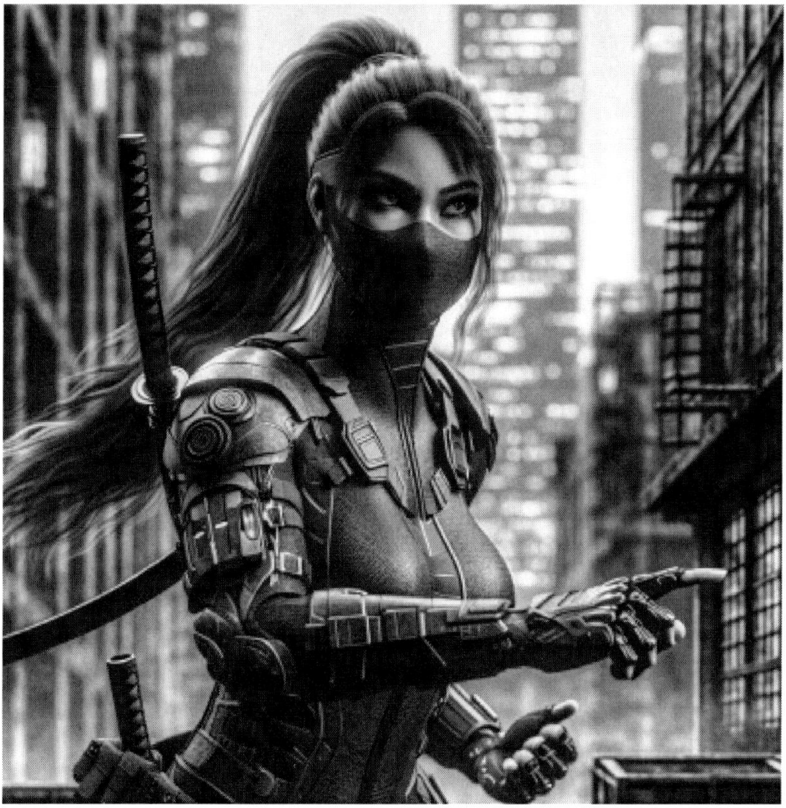

Real Name = Unknown
Code Name = Shinobi
Age = Unkown
Base of Operations = Mobile

Powers

None

Equipment

Battle suit
* Body armor
 * Enhanced Strength
* FILTRATION SYSTEM
Katana
Throwing Blades =Nero toxin
Throwing Stars = Nero toxin
Kamas
Sia

Origin Story

Shinobi is a highly skilled and disciplined ninja who serves as the chief bodyguard to QUA Zang, the formidable leader of the Korian mafia in Los Angeles. Trained in various martial arts, espionage, and stealth tactics from a young age, Shinobi possesses unrivaled agility and lethal precision. Her Kevlar body suit and polymer plate armor provide maximum protection while maintaining flexibility and speed. The suit is topped with a polymer plate helmet designed to resemble traditional ninja attire, giving her a fearsome and enigmatic appearance. Shinobi is fiercely loyal and unyielding in her mission to protect QUA Zang, often working in the shadows to eliminate threats before they even surface. She is a figure of both terror and respect within the underworld circuit.

Known Skills

Ninjitsu Master
Swordsmanship
Throwing
Duel Wield
Pressure points

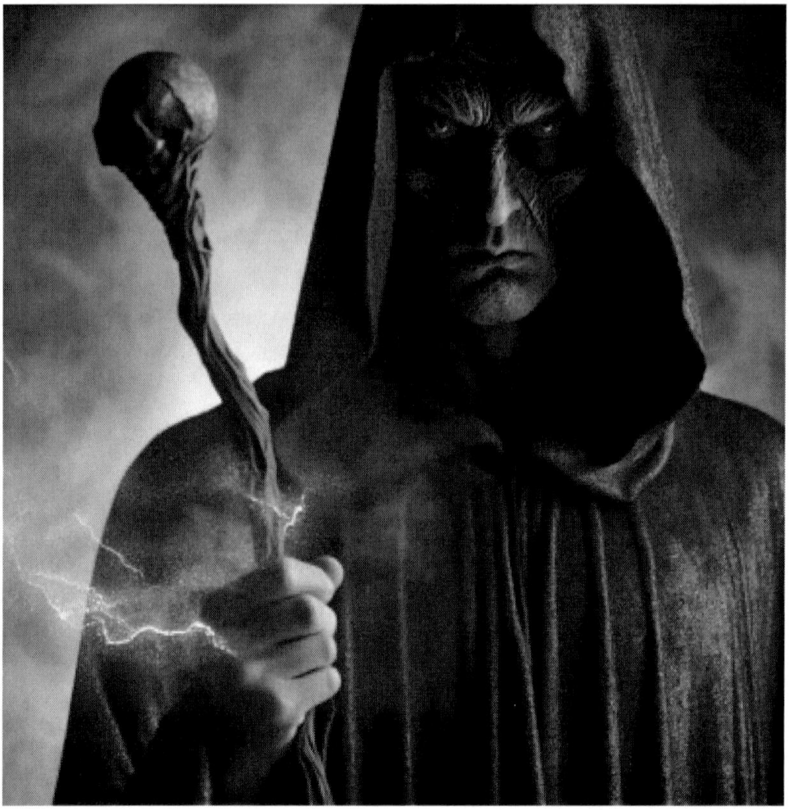

Real Name = Morphious
Code Name = None
Age = Unknown
Base of operations = Mobile

Powers

Necromancy
* Life Drain
* Cause Illness
* Control the Dead
* Summon Undead Servant
* Death Touch
* Mystic bolt
* Flesh to stone
* Teleport
Undead Servant
* Enhanced Strength
* Flame Breath

Equipment

Mystic robe
* Body armor
Magis Staff

* Mystic blast
Amulet
* Charm others

Origin Story

Morphious is a powerful necromancer, feared and revered in equal measure. Clad in a mystic, dark robe that constantly shifts and shimmers with an eerie luminescence, Morphious cuts an imposing figure. His wand, a slim, dark piece of ancient wood, crackles with ethereal energy, hinting at the immense power that lies within. With eyes that seem to pierce through the very essence of those he gazes upon, Morphious commands the dead and manipulates ethereal forces, making him a master of dark arts and an enigmatic, dangerous entity in any realm. His presence evokes dread, curiosity, and an unspoken respect among both allies and adversaries.

Known Skills

Mystic arts
 Necromancy

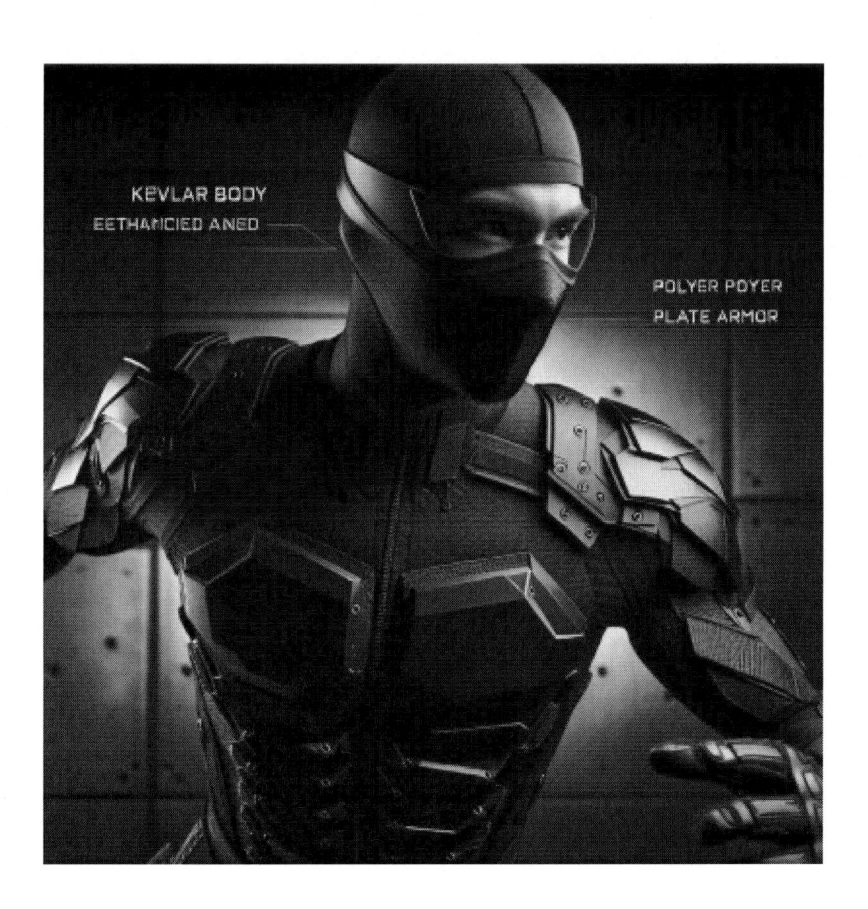

KEVLAR BODY
EETHANCIED ANED

POLYER POYER
PLATE ARMOR

Real Name = Unknown
Code Name = Phantom
Age = Unknown
Base of operations = Mobile

Powers

Chee
* Enhanced Strength
* Enhanced Endurance
* Healing
* Enhanced Reflexes
* Death touch
* Aura

Equipment

Battle suit
* Body Armor
Katana
Throwing stars
Throwing Knives

Origin Story

Phantom is a master Ninja and a formidable member of the assassin's guild. He adheres to a strict code of honor that guides his every action, whether in combat or in everyday life. Phantom is known for his agility, precision, and unparalleled skills in martial arts, making him a feared yet respected figure within the guild and among his adversaries. He wears a Kevlar body suit reinforced with polymer plate armor, offering both flexibility and protection. His identity remains concealed behind a meticulously crafted mask that covers his entire face, ensuring his anonymity and adding to his enigmatic presence. Phantom's expertise extends to various weapons, from traditional katana and shurikens to modern firearms, making him a versatile and unpredictable opponent. Despite his lethal abilities, he utilizes his skills only when necessary, guided by his unwavering principles and ethical code.

Known Skills

Ninjutsu Master
Swordsmanship
Throwing

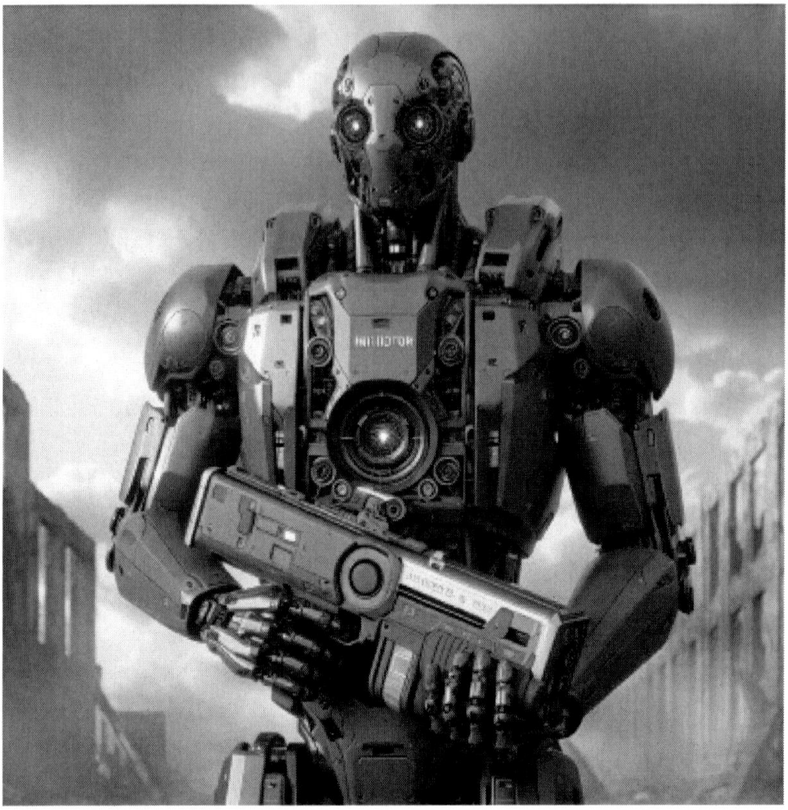

Cyber- Cron Unit 1

Powers

EVO Detection Technology
Genetic Scanner
Adaptive Nanites
* Can Create Technology to counter an EVOs Powers
Power Negation Collars
Durability
Stun Blaster
Flight
Energy Force Field
Tracking Darts

Origin Story

Cyber-Cron =Unit 01, often termed the Sentinel of the Sci-tech Era, is a robotic enforcer meticulously crafted by the ingenuity of the United States government with the sole purpose of tracking and apprehending those recognized as Enhanced individuals—humans exhibiting extraordinary abilities. These cybernetic hunters boast a humanoid silhouette, streamlining the interaction in urban landscapes and complex terrains where their targets often seek refuge.

The chassis of Cyber-Cron =Unit 01 is forged from a revolutionary composite material, a synthesis of durability and resilience, providing an armor shell that is nearly impervious to conventional weaponry, allowing it to endure substantial onslaughts during apprehension missions. Mechanical augmentation not only amplifies its strength to far outmatch the peak human condition but ensures efficiency and relentlessness in pursuit, capture, or neutralization tasks. An intricate matrix of visual and auditory sensors underlies its war-machine facade, granting 360-degree surveillance capabilities and a hyper-acute sensory field to detect concealed Enhanced individuals. Its offensive arsenal is crowned by high yield blasters—coherent energy weapons calibrated for both precision strikes and area saturation when non-lethal tactics have been exhausted. Further solidifying its role as a custodian of control, Cyber-Cron =Unit 01 is equipped with a stockpile of inhibitor collars, technologically advanced restraints designed to suppress the unique powers of their Enhanced quarry, ensuring safe transport and containment. The face of this metallic nemesis, devoid of human empathy, is replaced by a solid-state sensor array which not only serves as an intimidating visage but is the nexus of its tracking system, enabling relentless hunting of those who deviate from ordinary human standards.

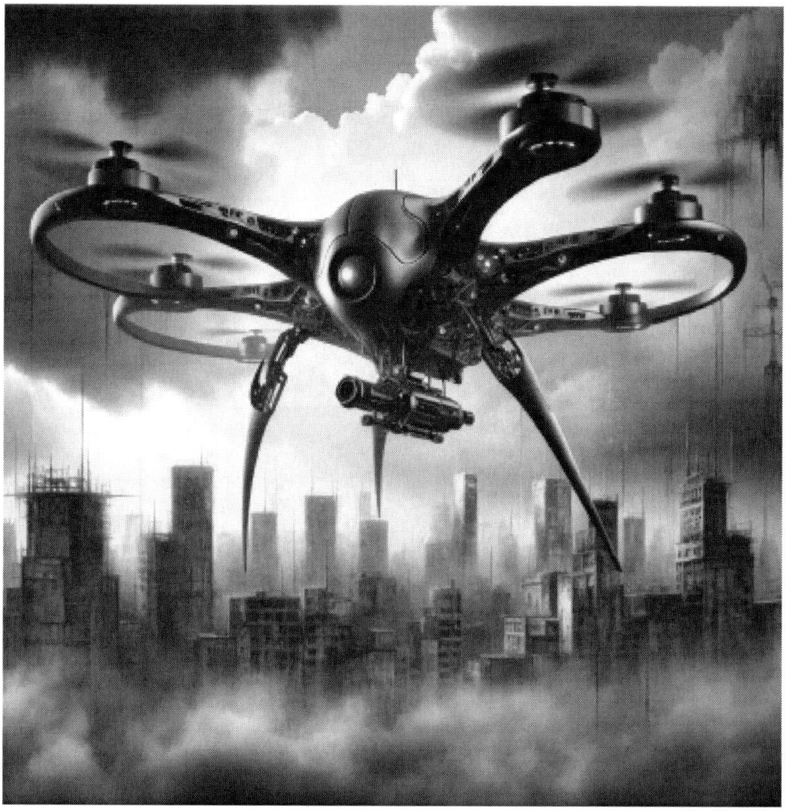

Hunter Drones

Equipment

EVO Detection System
Tracking Darts
Force Field
Stun Blaster
Negation Collar launcher

Origin Story

Initially developed for military applications by the United States Government, Hunter Drones stand at the vanguard of autonomous warfare against meta-human threats. Measuring approximately three feet in length and two feet in width, these aerial machines are known for their ominous, insect-like design. Crowned with a sleek, aerodynamic body that integrates state-of-the-art stealth materials, they glide silently through the skies on repulse drives—a technology that grants them smooth and stable flight. Upon deployment, Hunter

Drones relentlessly pursue targets within a 5-mile radius using advanced bio-energy signature detection, capable of singling out enhanced individuals from civilian populations. Their arsenal is diverse and fearsome: stun blasters for incapacitation, high-yield blasters for lethal force, and twin dart launchers stocked with potent tranquilizers designed to subdue the most formidable of subjects. When paired with humanoid Cyber-Crons, these Hunter Drones represent an unstoppable force, systematically hunting down renegade enhanced individuals with chilling efficiency.

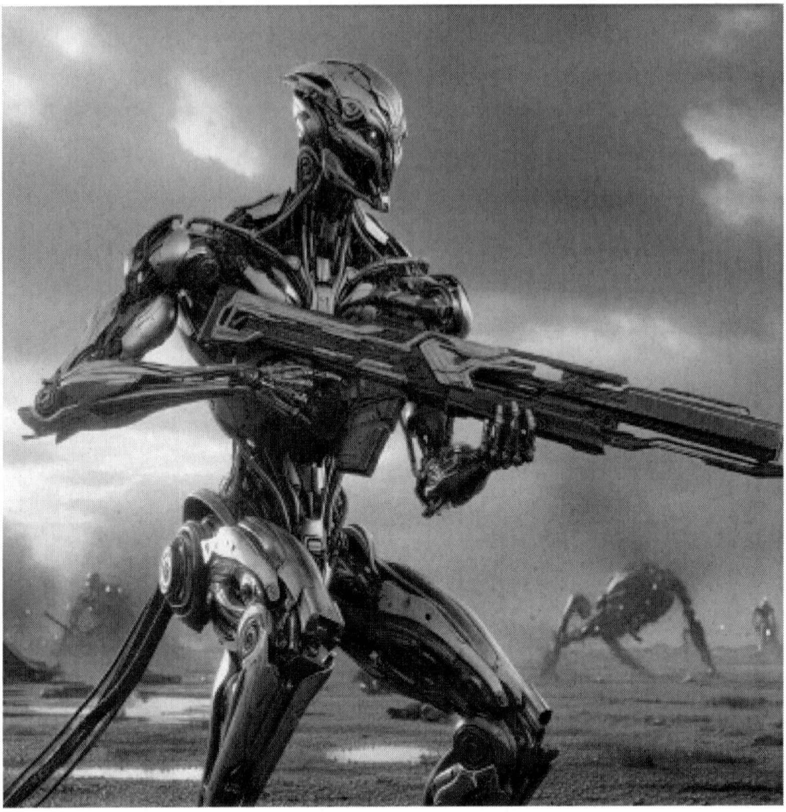

Scourge Battle Droid

Equipment

Hive Mind
Enhanced Durability
Enhanced Strength
Alien Blaster
Claws
Computer control/ Override
Force Field

Origin Story

The Scourge Battle Droid is a humanoid alien robotic combatant, engineered for advanced warfare. The droid's metallic frame is sleek and agile, built for both precision and power. Beneath its armored carapace, the internal circuitry is a marvel of alien technology, self-repairing and adaptive. It possesses a sophisticated AI system which allows for independent decision-making tailored to complex battle scenarios. The Scurge Battle Droid's primary weapon, a futuristic battle rifle, is an integrated piece of artillery capable of emitting concentrated plasma blasts or rapid-fire laser shots. The weapon is versatile, with modular capabilities for different combat situations. Enhanced visual sensors provide the droid with impeccable accuracy, and it is often deployed as a lethal force in intergalactic conflicts. Despite its mechanical nature, it shows a daunting presence on the battlefield, often serving as a vanguard unit due to its formidable strength and tactical prowess.

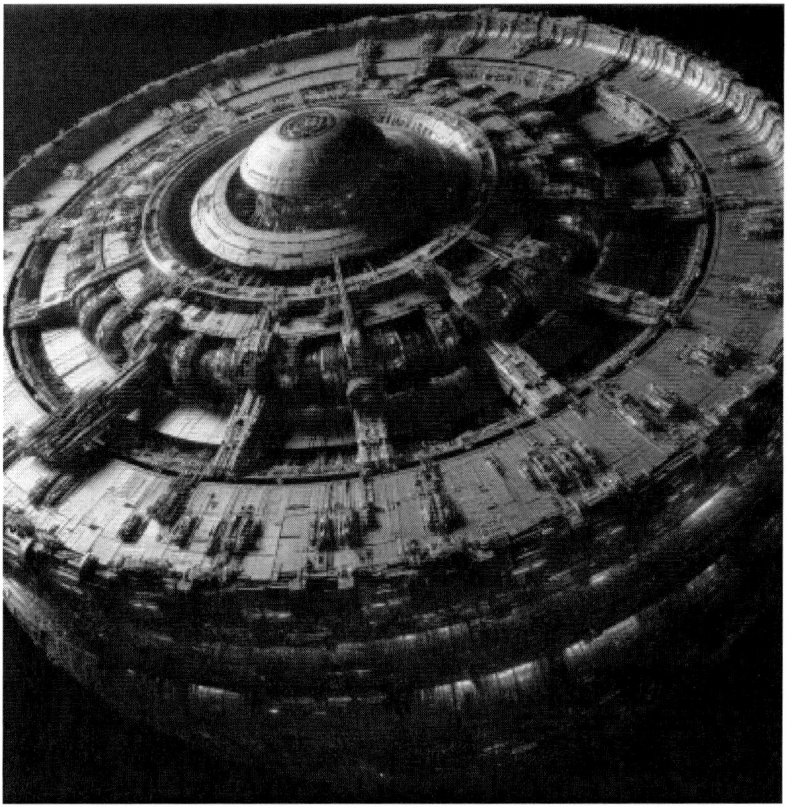

Scourge Battle World

Equipment

One Billion Battle Droids
100 blaster cannons
Force Feild
Interstellar Engines
Scourge Hive Mind

Origin Story

The Scourge Battle World is a massive, moon-sized circular spaceship that serves as both a manufacturing and storage facility for the ruthless Scourge Armada. Dominated by the Scourge Hive Mind, an alien artificial intelligence that's half the size of Earth's moon, the Battle World is a masterpiece of otherworldly engineering. Its surface is a chaotic network of production lines, weapon emplacements, and docking stations, all meticulously controlled by the Hive Mind in real-time. The sheer scale of the Battle World is enough to intimidate most adversaries, with its cold metallic exterior glistening ominously in the darkness of space. Internally, it houses countless factories geared for war, along with vast hangars containing legions of Scourge drones and ships.

Among the most dreaded places in the galaxy, the Scourge Battle World is both fortress and factory, a true embodiment of the Scourge Armada's relentless pursuit of domination.

U.SS. MIDWAY
Base of the Home guard
Commander = General Howell

Equipment
_____

Flight
40 - Avanced jet fighters
10 Blaster Cannons
Force Field
400 GDA Advanced battle troopers.

Origin Story

The U.S.S MIDWAY is an imposing and technologically advanced flying Aircraft Carrier. This marvel of engineering serves as the base of operations for the Home Guard, a special operations unit comprised of individuals with enhanced abilities. The carrier is equipped with state-of-the-art weaponry, including laser cannons, anti-aircraft missiles, and electromagnetic pulse emitters. It also features advanced stealth technology and a regenerative hull that can repair itself from minor damages. The U.S.S MIDWAY has multiple landing strips, hangars for various aircraft, and quarters designed to accommodate the unique needs of its enhanced crew. Its bridge is a sophisticated control center, bustling with activity as personnel monitor global threats and coordinate missions.

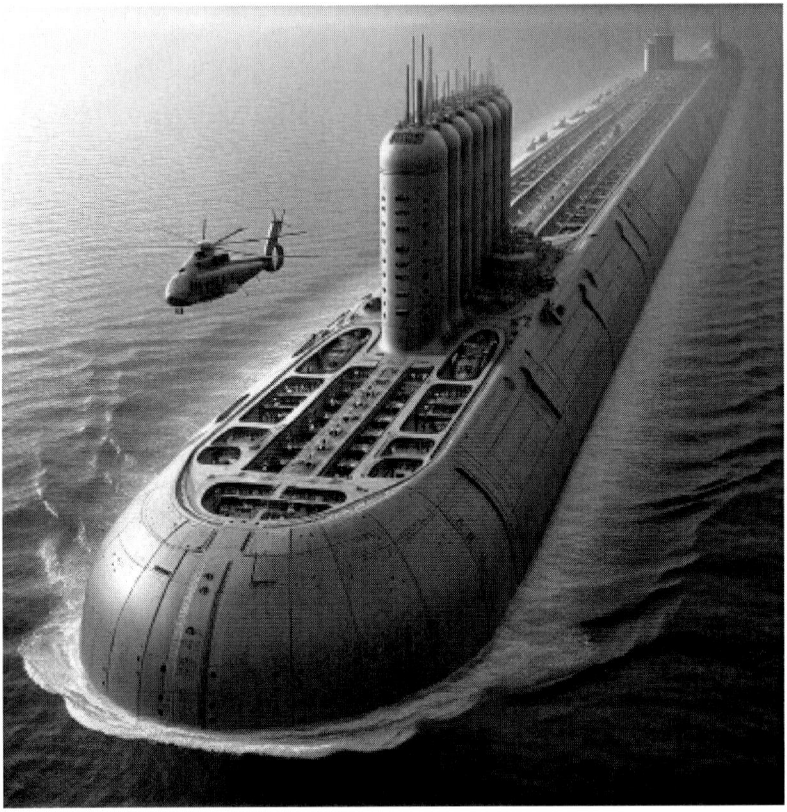

U.SS. MONITOR
Base of operations = The Defenders
Commander = Agent John Johnson

Equipment

40 Blaster Cannons
20 attack Helicopters
300 GDA battle troopers
Force field

Origin Story

The USS MONITOR is a formidable underwater citadel serving as the secret base of operations for the government's elite special operations team known as 'The Defenders'. This gargantuan, city-sized submersible stands as a marvel of modern technology, blending stealth capabilities with unmatched offensive and defensive systems. The exterior boasts a sleek, matte-black finish designed to avoid detection by sonar and visual surveillance. Inside, the sub houses high-tech laboratories, living quarters, a command center equipped with state-of-the-art computing and communication technologies, and advanced medical facilities. The USS

MONITOR is not just a means of transportation but a fully integrated mobile headquarters designed to support The Defenders in any mission, anywhere in the world.

GDA Battle Trooper

Equipment

Body Armor
High tech Visual and audio sensors
Enhanced Strength
Blaster rifles

Origin Story

The GDA Battle Armor Trooper is a futuristic soldier clad in a robust suit designed for space-age combat. The armor consists of highly durable polymer plates, providing excellent protection against modern weaponry. The full-face helmet offers advanced targeting systems and environmental sensors, enhancing the trooper's battlefield capabilities. Their primary weapon, a heavy blaster rifle, is capable of high-output energy blasts effective against both infantry and light armored vehicles. Notably, the armor features the insignia of planet Earth on the upper right breastplate, symbolizing their allegiance and duty to protect their home planet. These troopers are typically deployed in critical conflicts where high stakes and intense battle conditions prevail.

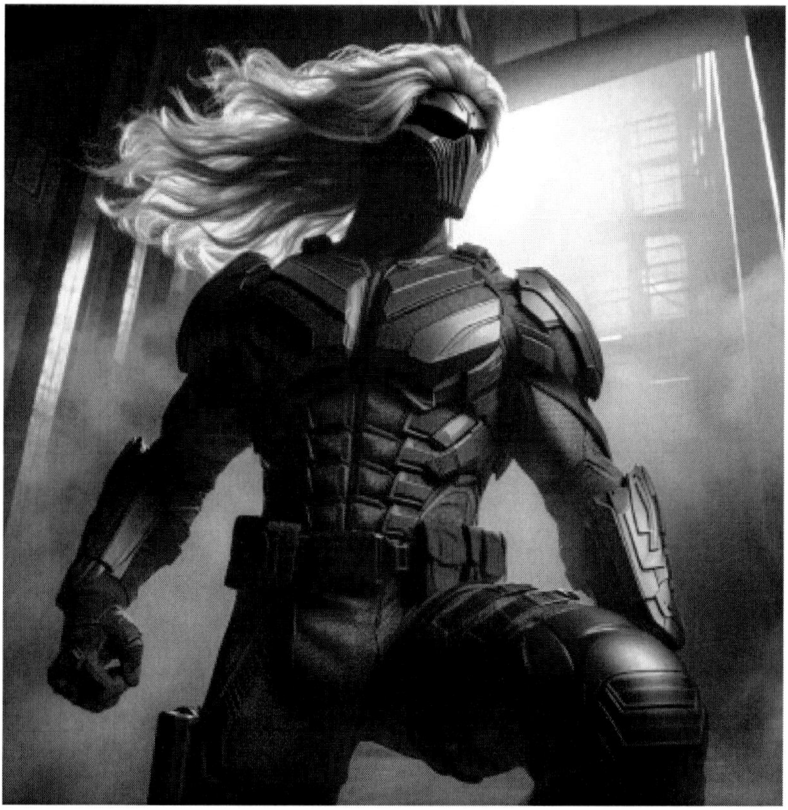

Real Name = Dexter Day
Code Name = Killspawn
Age = 45
Base of operation = Mobile

Powers

Enhanced Strength
Enhanced Agility
Enhanced Endurance
Durability
cast illusions
Regeneration
Retractable Forearm Spikes
* Cancels Healing Factor
Photographic Reflexes

Equipment

Battle suit
An Array of firearms

Origin Story

Dexter Day, also known as Killspawn, is one of the most ruthless serial killers in history, having murdered 127 people. His gruesome signature was chopping up his victims' bodies and consuming them. Once detained and placed on Death Row, Dexter was selected by General Powel for a perilous experiment aimed at creating super soldiers. However, Dexter seized the opportunity to break free, slaughtering everyone at the top-secret facility. Discovering files on other super soldiers, Dexter embarked on a twisted mission to prove his superiority by eliminating them one by one. Clad in a Kevlar bodysuit with polymer plate armor, Dexter maintains an imposing presence. A mask covers his mouth and nose, while his long blonde hair cascades over his shoulders, adding an eerie touch to his fearsome visage.

Known Skills

Martial arts
Butchering
Weapons Mastery

Manufactured by Amazon.ca
Acheson, AB